ONE FOR THE MASTER,
TWO FOR THE FOOL

ONE FOR THE
MASTER
TWO FOR THE FOOL

A Bruce MacLeod Mystery

by Larry Townsend

■ ■ ■

Boston ♦ Alyson Publications, Inc.

Typeset and printed in the United States of America.

This is a paperback original from Alyson Publications, Inc.,
40 Plympton St., Boston, Mass. 02118.
Distributed in England by GMP Publishers,
P.O. Box 247, London N17 9QR, England.

This book is printed on acid-free, recycled paper.

First edition, first printing: November 1992

5 4 3 2 1

ISBN 1-55583-209-1

PROLOGUE

He stepped sharply on the accelerator, causing the red pickup to leap forward — a jackrabbit start as the light turned green and the car ahead of him bolted across the intersection. He was following a small sports car — also red, driven by a young man he'd met in the alley behind an all-night bookstore in West Hollywood. The guy had seemed almost desperate that Jeff accompany him; only now his frenetic driving was making it nearly impossible for the follower to keep up. But he was high. Jeff had noted it in their first exchange of words. They had been standing in the shadows near the end of the alley, under the overhang of an enormous bougainvillea. The guy was dressed all in leather, even wearing tight-fitting gloves. As he had hinted at the exotic exchange he contemplated for them, his leather-covered hands had been stroking the firm contours of Jeff's chest and midsection.

Now Jeff was trying to keep up with this potential ... what? Master? He wasn't sure. It was an entirely new experience for him: his first night in the city, his first encounter with an experienced leather guy, the expectation, the unknown, the excitement ... the fear. He wanted it, whatever "it" might turn out to be. His fantasies and limited exposure to an occasional piece of SM fiction were his only guideposts — that and the few less-than-fulfilling exchanges he'd had with a couple of kids back home.

The little red car made an abrupt turn into a dark side street, lined with old houses dating back to the twenties, surrounded by massive trees and bushes that nearly obliter-

5

ated the streetlights. Another turn, another darkened street, and the sports car pulled into a driveway. Its lights went out, and it all but disappeared into the shadows. Jeff pulled to the curb in front of the house, the combination of fear and desire forming a strangely paired set of sensations within his viscera. The great decaying mansion reminded him of something from a Charles Addams cartoon. Yet, in reality, it lacked any humorous implication.

"Come on," his companion urged, leading the way up the stairs to the front door. The whole area was silent, and seemed deserted despite the relatively early hour, not much past ten; but there was a threatening aura about the place, an almost malevolent feeling that clutched at Jeff's awareness like a chill winter wind trying to penetrate his layers of protective clothing.

"It's okay," whispered the other. He took Jeff's hand and led him inside the murky entry hall. "We're by ourselves. No one's going to bother us." The guy forced a nervous chuckle — evidence of his own uncertainty, except that Jeff was too intimidated to notice. "I use this for a workshop," his host continued. "The playroom's downstairs." Again he led the way, through a room that contained some furniture, or machinery, all draped in dustcovers — then down a flight of creaking stairs into a musty-smelling basement.

There had been a dull, bluish night-light midway on the stairs, but the illumination faded at the bottom. The young man still had hold of Jeff's hand. He squeezed it, now, then let go. "Hang on just a second," he whispered, moving off into the darkness. "I'll get the light."

A moment later, an amber glow began to emanate from several recesses around the periphery of the room. This increased in brilliance, until a number of forms began to take shape before Jeff's awe-stricken gaze. He shuddered, fear suddenly threatening to dominate all of his other emotions, momentarily suppressing even his raging lust. The room seemed crowded with men, all strangely silent, as if each figure were holding its breath. He felt trapped, betrayed by the man who'd brought him here, who'd told him they'd be alone. But they *were* alone, he suddenly realized, and the pounding rush of blood through his temples receded. The room was filled with mannequins, dummies covered with material to resemble skin, some outfitted in leather harnesses or hoods, all posed as if frozen in some act of submission.

Then, somehow, the truth was more frightening than his original perception ... the simulated life more threatening than an assemblage of living men. And more overtly sexual — oversized genitals bound with ropes and strips of rawhide, all erect, all seeming to pulse with life in the dim, reddish glow of the dungeon.

And his host was growing perceptibly more strange by the moment. He had originally appeared as no more than a handsome, somewhat dissipated young guy in leather jeans and jacket. Now inside the house he was becoming different; his whole affect had changed from the seeming innocence of their initial encounter to a spooky, mysterious manner. He had started to whisper as soon as they entered the basement room, making vague references to an esoteric world of sexual mysteries that seemed far beyond anything Jeff had ever imagined. He spoke as if an SM exchange connoted some ritualistic properties, with an incomprehensible depth of meaning. Previously, Jeff had only imagined the fetish games — those that came most naturally to mind — tying a guy up in some deserted locale, a barn or abandoned shed, whipping him and making him crawl ... most often submitting himself to be the victim, mentally experiencing the pain which became pleasure. The longing, somehow, had been for a chance to test his ability, as if his endurance under punishment would serve as proof of his own manhood. But this guy was something else — weird ... yet nonetheless fascinating with his aura of degenerate sophistication. But most of all he was real!

Jeff forced his fears to recede. They were illogical, and this was a situation more wondrous than anything he had ever been able to imagine. He was in a genuine dungeon, with a good-looking partner who was obviously willing to engage in the very games Jeff had been dreaming about since before the hair began to sprout on his balls. They were in this wonderful fantasy room with the door locked behind them, some eerie semiclassical music drifting in from a complex of speakers. The guy had produced a packet of coke and he talked Jeff into trying it. For the second time, Jeff almost bolted; instead he decided to go along, feeling that to do otherwise would mark him as even more of a hick than his ignorance had already made him out to be. In truth, he had never done more than share a few joints with his friends back in Iowa. This stuff was heavy-duty, even more so because he had no idea how it was going to affect him, how much he could safely absorb.

Finally, when it came to the action, the guy persuaded Jeff to be Top, to use all of this equipment on him — half of which the kid had no idea how to operate. Feeling disappointed, he tried, did the best he could. But now the guy was so ripped it was impossible to tell if he was enjoying it or not. And Jeff was in even worse shape, stumbling about, bumping into the mannequins, at times seeming to perceive some life in them. He was unreasonably fearful, anxious that he might not be doing things correctly, definitely unnerved through it all, yet sexually aroused and unable to stop until he finally reached his own climax — a long, protracted orgasm that may or may not have been shared by his companion. He couldn't be sure, couldn't get his eyes to focus in the dim, uneven illumination. Later, he only knew for certain that he had left just as dawn was breaking. The guy had seen him to the door, shoved some folded bills into his hand, and muttered something about seeing him again.

He could not remember driving back to the motel, although he obviously had, because he awakened in his own bed in bright daylight. He tried to force some mental image of the return trip, smiling to himself at the possible problems he could have encountered in his drugged-out condition. Earlier on that same day, he had gotten lost several times when he'd tried to move about the city. Had the guy given him directions? He grasped the sides of his head, trying to force the memory to solidify, but it was no use. Somehow he'd gotten back to his dingy little room. Again he couldn't be sure, but he seemed to remember snuggling up to Alfie on the other side of the bed when he returned — feeling a resurgence of desire as his cock grew and pressed against the solid warmth of his friend. But he must have fallen asleep before anything could come of it. Now he was alone ... almost ten o'clock. A strange night, his first outing in the big city. An experience to remember — weird, real weird.

8

ONE

D r. Bruce MacLeod was not a man easily ruffled. A qualified psychiatrist, M.D., Ph.D., successful counselor with plenty of experience behind him, he had learned to control his emotional displays, and to mask any anger or dismay hc might feel toward a client. However, as he stood on the front steps of his Beverly Hills home watching a taxi carry his visitor away, he could not suppress a less-than-professional comment to his remaining guest.

"Alice," he said, turning to the attractive woman standing beside him, "your brother is a twenty-four-carat asshole!"

"He *can* be abrasive, can't he?" she replied with a throaty laugh. "But seriously, Bruce," she continued, "I didn't know what else to do, or who else to turn to. You do all that volunteer work at the Center, so you know a lot of the ... whatever you call them — the street kids. I thought you might be able to help him."

Bruce put his arm about her, and guided her back into the house. Alice's husband, Abe Javits, was a close friend, and also Bruce's fiscal mentor through his highly successful financial advisory business. More than this, the two men were even more closely identified because of their respective roles *vis à vis* the police department. Bruce was on retainer as a consultant in criminal profiling. Abe was a police commissioner — which fact had given Bruce pause when Alice first called about her brother, Daniel Donovan. The man was in town from the Midwest, because his nineteen-year-old son had left home, and apparently headed for Hollywood. At first glimmer, a police commissioner might seem better equipped to find a lost soul in the big city than a shrink. But as Dan's tale had unfolded, Bruce had begun to appreciate Alice's logic in asking for his help.

The whole problem had started back in Iowa, when Donovan had used his son's pickup truck one day while his own was laid up for repair. He had found a very distressing collection of sketches in the toolbox. The kid, being a naturally gifted artist, had done a series of drawings, depicting handsome young men in a variety of SM bondage situations. Without stopping to consider the potential consequences of his actions, Donovan had confronted his son in anger, and the next day the kid was gone. One of the young man's friends, Alfred Stimson, had apparently accompanied him; and because Alfie had sent a postcard to his parents, Dan knew that the boys were in the Los Angeles area.

Bruce seated Alice in one of the large leather chairs in the room overlooking his heavily foliated backyard. It was mid-April, so the pool was still hidden beneath its dark green cover, surrounded by tropical ferns and well-groomed shrubbery. "It won't be long before you can start using that again," she noted, thinking to herself that Bruce's household probably made more use of their pool than anyone else she knew.

"Soon," Bruce agreed, "soon."

"Well, again, I'm sorry, Bruce, but Dan caught me off guard, and I just dragged him up here. I had no idea he'd be so antagonistic. Taking off in a cab, for God's sake, instead of waiting for me to run him back!"

"I expect he'll hire a car tomorrow. I told him to stop by once he had some pictures printed up that I could show around, ask if anyone's seen them."

"That was very nice of you, under the circumstances," Alice returned. "Frankly, I'm surprised you didn't punch him in the nose."

Bruce's handsome features contorted into a grin, his hazel eyes seeming to twinkle in gold-flecked splendor. "I wouldn't punch out your brother," he assured her. "Besides, I might want to take up the violin." He laughed again, holding up his hands and flexing the long, thick fingers. Alice could feel herself loosening up, shedding the anxiety her brother had heaped upon her.

10

"Where's the rest of the household?" she asked, as Bruce poured them each a goblet of Chardonnay. *Change the pace, change the subject,* she thought.

"Frank's still in New Orleans," he replied, "but they should finish shooting in another week or ten days. I hope, anyway."

"You really miss him, don't you?" Alice commiserated. "I know how it is if Abe's away overnight. You get so used to having someone snuzzling up on the other side of the bed."

"Or tied up beside it," Bruce suggested as he handed her the glass.

"Oh, you're too much," she chided him. But she had to return his smile. Despite her diminutive size and almost Victorian bearing, Alice was a very accomplished dominatrix, a fact which had probably formed the basis for her original relationship with Abe. Knowing Bruce as she did, she assumed he acted in a similar role with Frank. "What about the rest of the family?" she asked.

"Well, Rudy's in school," he told her, referring to their black Labrador retriever. "Somebody convinced Frank that with a little training the big lummox would protect us all from whatever's apt to show up to get us. Today is graduation day, and Dennie's gone to pick him up." Dennie Delong was Bruce's longtime friend and now live-in "man Friday," running not only the household, but Bruce's in-home office as well.

"You just might be happy to have some extra protection," Alice reminded him. "I saw all that commotion when we drove up the hill. It *is* the Orsini place over there, isn't it?"

Bruce confirmed that it was.

"It was really a terrible thing," she continued, "and so close to your house. Although, you know, I didn't realize they were only a couple of blocks away."

"Oh, it's a bit more than that. They live — lived — in the old Lola Burke mansion. You zip right by their street on the way up here, but if you walk it — as we do occasionally with Rudy — it's a good half or maybe three-quarters of a mile. And it's over the city line. We're in Beverly Hills; they're in Bel Air."

"Well, it's still too close for comfort," she insisted. "Two people getting murdered like that, right in their own home — with that ten-foot wall around it, and all. Do they have any idea, yet, who did it?"

"I don't think so, but I'm really not sure," Bruce admitted. "They haven't come around questioning the neighbors, as far as I know. It's just happened, of course — too late to have been on the evening news last night. I should think Abe would have a better handle on it than anyone."

"Oh, he never tells me anything."

"Unless you beat it out of him."

"If it was official, I couldn't get it out of him with a cattle prod," she assured him. "But seriously, I don't think anyone's told him anything, yet. We just heard it on the morning news at breakfast."

"So did we," Bruce replied. "They said the two of them — Felix and Ruth — had been found strangled, their bodies discovered by the older son when he came home after midnight with one of Felix Orsini's South American managers. Man had something to do with a film distribution company that belonged to the Orsinis. Beyond that, I really don't know much about them. I only met them that once, when they showed up for an AIDS fund-raiser a couple of years ago. Remember? The black-tie affair at the Century Plaza?"

"I remember it," Alice agreed. "That's the only time I ever met *him*, but I was on a philharmonic host committee with Ruth Orsini for about six months last year. She was really very nice, and *very* devoted to her sons. But I think Felix was driving her crazy," Alice added in a conspiratorial tone. "He had all these people around all the time, because he insisted on doing business out of their house. I know she wanted him to take an office suite someplace, but he wouldn't do it. He had two secretaries working there as full-time employees, plus an assortment of South Americans — managers, or something," Alice explained. "Ruth told me all about it when we had lunch with a couple of other women one day. After two good stiff margaritas, she got pretty vocal about the whole thing."

"Well, as I said, I really didn't know either one of them, but I think Dennie talked to Felix a couple of times when he was out walking Rudy. And Frank had some kind of discussion — or Rufus, his agent, did. Some TV pilot that never came off, but I don't know if Frank ever actually sat down with him."

"Did they have a dog, too?" Alice asked, wondering what else would occasion an evening stroll in a neighborhood where no one ever seemed to be on foot.

"No, I don't think so. Felix apparently liked to walk. In fact, I used to see him four or five years ago — right after I first moved in. He'd be out with both boys, teenagers back then. They'd walk a fair distance on a nice summer evening, I guess. But not recently, not with the kids, anyway. I remember Dennie saying something about talking to him a couple of months ago. Mentioned their conversation because he wanted me to ask Abe about that distribution company. They were thinking of going public, and Dennie was curious about the stock in case they did. I don't think it ever happened, though."

"It's funny that the news report seemed to concentrate on the distribution company. I mean, calling them 'international film distributors' when they were much better known as producers," Alice remarked.

"That's how the reporters were describing them on the radio this morning," Bruce agreed, "but I don't know what they actually produced. Were they into movies as well as TV?"

"Oh, *mostly* movies, I think. They did a number of those teenage exploitation films: adolescent vampires, and surfer beach things. And they made a *lot* of money. See, you're getting old," she added. "You just aren't 'with it' any more."

"Guess not," Bruce agreed, "not if I have to watch teenage vampires getting it on in the surf. Of course, I'm over thirty-five, now; as I start to get a little more senile, those surfer chicken types may become more appealing."

"I doubt that! But, anyway, I think you might be very happy to have Rudy trained as a guard dog," Alice insisted.

"I don't know. I can't image the Orsinis were done in by some roving maniac. It looks much more like a well-choreographed, in-house affair, complete with business associates, family, servants, friends, and enemies — all the ingredients for a good premeditated murder that's done to benefit the murderer — or murderers."

"Bruce, you can be so cynical sometimes! I just hope you don't get careless and leave a door or window unlocked at night. At least until they catch whoever did this. Remember back to

13

the Manson murders. They thought those were drug-related killings, too; and it took them forever to realize it had been done by a bunch of loonies, who could just as well have come back into the area and hacked up some of the other neighbors."

"We'll be careful," Bruce assured her. "But I think my biggest problem is going to be your brother and his missing kid. The Orsini murders are well outside our life space."

■ ■ ■

"So, it looks like Alice's dropped a real hot potato in your lap," said Dennie as he trundled two bulging shopping bags into the kitchen. Rudy, obviously much relieved to be home and free from the restraints of his obedience class, was prancing around at the big man's feet. "Get out of the way," Dennie grumbled. "Damn dog's favorite trick is to get right in front of me, then stop so I trip over him."

Bruce had accompanied Dennie into the kitchen, and now leaned back against the counter as his friend began to unpack the groceries. "You might be able to help," he suggested, "if you ask around in your various nefarious haunts. They're apparently a pair of real beauties. Somebody's bound to see them, and should remember them if they do."

Dennie paused in his motions, thoughtfully stroking his well-trimmed beard. "And you think they might be into SM?"

"According to Dan Donovan, the kid's drawings would seem to suggest it."

"I'll ask around tomorrow," Dennie assured him. "Maybe one of my contacts in the publishing business will get a line on them, if this ... what's his name ... Jeff?" At a nod of agreement from Bruce he continued, "...if Jeff comes around looking for a job as illustrator. But, if they're underage, they may have some problems getting any kind of work — other than you-know-what."

"I think that's what Daddy's really afraid of—" Bruce broke off his discourse and looked up with a flash of irritation as a loud crash resounded through the otherwise quiet neighborhood. "Goddamn builders!" he grumbled. "They're putting up a house on every square foot of land they can find."

"That guy called again yesterday," Dennie said, "the one who wants to buy your lot up above the pool. You were in a session, so I just told him to get lost. Sorry, I forgot to tell you."

"It wouldn't matter. He'd get the same answer from me. The reason I bought the damned lot was to keep anyone from being able to look down into the pool area. We don't need an audience when we want to go skinny-dipping."

"Which is practically every day, all summer long," Dennie laughed. "When's the grand opening, by the way? The pool guy wanted to know so he can gussy it all up for us."

"What do you think? Another couple of weeks? It's starting to warm up, but there's still a little chill in the air. Would you go in, in weather like this?"

"Maybe not," Dennie admitted. "But Frank's only off on location for another couple of weeks — empty bed for you," he added with a pseudo-pained expression. "Why not have it set up for him when he gets back? Then you can celebrate two grand openings at once."

"Asshole," Bruce laughed, then frowned again as another rumble of heavy equipment shook the house. "These builders are going to shake us right down the hill," he muttered, heading toward the front door. "Our next-door neighbors have taken off for their condo on Maui to avoid this racket. I wanta see what they've dumped on the street; last week they half blocked the driveway with a big load of lumber."

Dennie shook his head, laughing to himself as he heard Bruce's voice fading into the distance. Neither one of them appreciated the builders' noise, dust, and lack of consideration for the neighborhood, but Bruce was getting more irritable about it every day.

He misses Frank, Dennie mused. *Makes him impatient with everyone. Of course, Frank still has his house in Encino, on the other side of the hills. Spends nearly every night with Bruce when he's in town, but still decided to keep the other place as his official residence — afraid of the Hollywood gossipmongers. Once this new picture he's working on gets released, he's going to be even more in the spotlight. His agent knows the score, of course, and he was adamant that Frank not make this his legal residence. House just sitting vacant over there — wonder if someone might discover that, suspect something. Be rough on Bruce if Frank had to stay away.*

15

∎ ∎ ∎

A cool breeze riffled through the upper branches of eucalyptus trees along the street in front of Bruce's property. He had come out with Dennie as his friend took Rudy for his final walk before bedtime. Happy to be out of his earlier confines, the big Labrador cavorted at the end of his leash, poking his nose into each clump of vegetation along the gutter. At the appropriate corner they turned left, toward the old Lola Burke mansion — each making the choice automatically and without comment.

Bruce laughed. "Well, that's a unanimous choice for the sensational."

"Yeah," Dennie agreed. "I think there's still a police guard on the gate. Anyway, it's a lot quieter than last night."

"Walking one's dog *is* a good excuse to be a nosy neighbor."

They were still some distance from the old landmark — a great mausoleum of a house, set well back from the road and surrounded by ten-foot, vine-covered walls. Although it had been owned for several years by Felix and Ruth Orsini, prominent in their own right as film producers and directors, everyone still referred to the place as "the Lola Burke mansion." Built in the mid-twenties by one of Hollywood's most flamboyant stars, it stood as a monument to the excesses of that golden era of filmdom. In the early thirties, when talkies had proven that they were here to stay, Lola's nasal whine had disqualified her for the big screen. She had retired behind the walls of her fortified home until despair and alcohol had done their work, and she quietly expired one afternoon beside the pool. That had been during the middle of World War II.

The house had remained vacant for a number of years, and had almost been torn down to make room for half a dozen newer, less pretentious homes. However, one of the local historical preservation societies had stalled off the wrecker's ball until the Orsinis came along with the bucks to buy the place, and the will to renovate it without destroying its basic character. Thus the old house had regained some of the verve it had originally known in years past, as the socially active couple and their two teenaged sons took up residence. Unfortunately, that overtly happy period had come to an abrupt

16

and tragic end on the evening before Bruce and Dennie took Rudy for his evening constitutional along the edge of the property.

"According to the news, tonight," Dennie said, "the parents were strangled with garrotes while the two kids were out. The cops're talking about gang involvement."

"Gangs? Up here in the hills of Beverly?" Bruce looked questioningly at Dennie, as a sudden lunge by Rudy pulled the bigger man momentarily off balance.

"No, gangs like in Mafia."

"That's more properly called 'the Mob,'" said Bruce casually. "But we can't make light of this. Some madman killed two of our neighbors, and apparently nobody has the answer. The radio this afternoon said the cops were questioning the kids."

"Doesn't seem logical to me that a pair of society brats are going to throttle their folks with silken braids."

"Stranger things have happened," Bruce replied.

They had reached the nearest gate, where a black-and-white police car stood just outside the wrought-iron barrier, the whole front side of the property wrapped with a strand of yellow "crime scene" ribbon. The two young officers in the car watched the pair of strollers, but made no move to interfere with them. The two men reached the end of the cul-de-sac a few moments later and started back up the slight incline.

"Anyway," Dennie remarked, "you've got more immediate problems. What are you going to do about the Donovan kid?"

"There isn't very much I can do, really. The old man's going to bring some pictures by tomorrow, and I'll show them around the Center — maybe put up a reward notice on the bulletin board. I'm still hoping you might come up with something through some of your friends, particularly anyone who's running employment ads. The kids might just happen to answer one of those."

"You'd have a better chance cruising Santa Monica Boulevard," Dennie replied dryly. "New kids in town ... it's a likely place for them till they get their bearings and zero in on something better."

Bruce sighed. "Whatever. If they are out on the street, I hope someone gave them a course in safe sex."

■ ■ ■

A red pickup with Iowa plates moved slowly through the dark, nearly deserted streets in the Echo Park section of Los Angeles. It was gang territory, an area where decent people were in their homes with doors and windows closed once the sun had set. Only a few cars roved the streets, and an occasional pedestrian hurried home from the bus stop.

But Jeff was not especially aware of driving through a no-man's-land; nor did his mind register any sense of the fear which relegated the local citizenry to their seclusion. He was hunting for the house where he had spent the previous evening, not precisely sure what he might do if he found it, merely determined to retrace his steps — or more accurately, his tire treads — while the memory was fresh in his mind. The experience had been unique, and the recall was making his cock swell hard — almost painfully hard — in his crotch.

He turned onto a street that seemed familiar, feeling the flush of excitement as he recognized a landmark brick tower halfway down the block ... then the house, *the* house! He slowed almost to a stop, gliding past the aged wooden facade at a crawl. No lights showed in any window, nor was there a car parked in the driveway or at any adjacent curb. He made mental note of the house number, and looked at the street marker when he reached the next corner.

He made a U-turn in the intersection and took another slow pass along the street in front of the house. *Silly,* he told himself. *No one's there, and if he was home he'd probably have someone else with him. Don't think he lives there, anyway. Some kind of workshop, he told me, place where he makes his dummies. Weird guy, but hot. Sure's got the equipment. First time for this hick from the sticks. First time, only time.*

As the pickup gradually accelerated and finally passed out of sight around the corner, a somewhat haggard young man emerged from the shadows beside the detached garage. He waited a few moments, apprehensive lest the red pickup return for another look. Then he shrugged and hurried to his own car, parked several doors down the street. *Wonder who that was?* he mused. *Probably some creep my brother dragged in off the street. Fuckin' queer asshole!* Rupert Orsini slid into the driver's

18

seat of his rented sedan, making sure all the doors were locked before he ventured forth into the potentially hostile night. *Fuckin' cops, questioning the two of us, as if we'd ever do anything together.* He tromped on the gas, tires screeching through the stillness of the neighborhood.

T W O

His eyes burned as if from lack of sleep. For the second morning in a row, he lay on the bed staring at the peeling paint on the ceiling, aware of continued sounds of life outside the window. The motel was next to a truck terminal, with a freeway interchange less than two blocks away. It was noisy, and the room was uncomfortably warm despite his having left the window open. But none of this would have prevented his dozing off. He was famous for his ability to sleep under any circumstances, something his parents, friends, and teachers had remarked upon with varying degrees of levity or displeasure.

An hour or so before, he had managed to drift off, but had come awake with a sudden, wrenching start. His body, naked atop the sweat-soaked sheet, had been drawn up tightly into a protective, fetal position. The voices he had heard in his dream were coming now from outside, although the real words were unintelligible, partly in Spanish, partly in heavily accented English — all obviously from nearby human sources who knew nothing of his presence, cared nothing about him. In his dream the sounds had been twisted by his depleted senses into something very different, sinister. He had been in the dungeon again, surrounded by the mannequins, with Paul hanging naked against the X-frame behind him — gagged, hooded, silent, as he had been two nights before. It had been the dummies who had spoken to him, moving away from their assigned positions, standing or crawling toward him, threatening him until he had cried out in choking terror and bolted awake — only to find himself fully aroused, balls fairly bursting with lust while the rest of his body lagged in the aftermath of the drug consumption which had accompanied the more immediate experiences of the previous night.

He went to the window and looked out into the parking area. His pickup was missing, but he vaguely remembered Alfie telling him about an ad he'd seen for a job. His friend must have taken the truck and gone into town. He went back to his pile of clothes and rummaged through them to find his watch — almost noon. He dropped back on the bed and lay there for another hour, wishing he could fall asleep again, knowing he couldn't. He felt grimy, sticky with sweat, but lacked the energy to drag himself into the shower. He was hungry, too, and thirsty, but could not muster the strength to pull on a pair of jeans and go down the hall to the vending machines. He was only mildly uncomfortable, he told himself. He'd survive it.

He stretched, arching his body upward from the sagging mattress, feeling strong muscles flex along the length of his being. He shifted to the side, moving away from the clinging moisture that had formed beneath him ... onto Alfie's side of the bed. He ran one large, blunt-fingered hand down his belly, across the solid flesh of his hard-worked abdominals, into the tangle of his pubes. His cock was resting across the depression where his left leg joined the lower extension of his torso — half-risen, the ruby crown poking its Cyclops eye outward from the darker folds of foreskin. His scrotum was plastered against the downward curve of thigh. He moved his feet, widening the space between his legs, allowing his balls to slide lower.

He reached down and took hold of himself, wrapping his hand around the base of his genitals, squeezing gently to force the big globes into gleaming relief against the sac. His cock responded immediately, soft tumescence beginning to swell and stiffen, answering his subconscious command. He started to stroke himself, feeling skin slide along hardening core, reddish brown hood alternately puckering to conceal the crown, then slipping away to expose the shiny bulb with its vertical slit, already oozing a trace of translucent fluid. He clamped his legs together, imprisoning his nuts, trapping them between the hard walls of flesh, crushing them until the pain traveled up his side. The discomfort served only to excite him further, and the motion of his hand increased. He loved the sensation, the awareness of his youth and his beauty, big cock and balls, hard body with the definition of a high school gymnast. He closed his eyes and tried to picture his own physical perfection strapped into one of the devices his host of night-before-last had commanded be used on himself. If only Alfie could have been there, he thought, applying the bondage to hold his naked body in one of those replicas. Like being in a real dungeon, helpless, unable to stop whatever use his Master might wish to make of him. His cock had come to full arousal, now, straining upward, lust causing his balls to rise against the solid base. Spasms of desire made him flex, every muscle and sinew tense, outlining their perfection against sweat-moistened skin.

The sound of a key grating in the lock arrested his motion. Slowly, his hands dropped to his sides as the door swung inward and his friend stood in the opening. Alfie was a bit taller than Jeff, and a few pounds heavier — medium brown hair, not much darker than the other's dusky blond ... same even features, so close a resemblance that many people took them for brothers, or more — mistook one for the other. Now, coming in from the heat of the California sun, Alfie seemed disheveled, indifferently handsome. His mirrored sunglasses accented the swarthy tan of his face, emphasizing the smooth skin, the high cheekbones. He wore his hair in a long crew cut, an imitation of Jeff's, just short enough to require minimum attention.

"I see you're awake," he said, grinning. "Looks like you missed me." His gaze had focused on the other's groin, where the evidence of Jeff's arousal remained manifest.

"I woke up and you were gone," Jeff replied defensively. He allowed his hand to touch his cock again, pleased that Alfie seemed unable to tear his gaze away from it, pleased that his own physical perfection was capable of arousing this response. Whereas he might play the slave in his mental sex games, he knew that in reality he held his friend in a bond of devotion, of passion that the other was powerless to sever. In that sense Jeff was Master, although he had no desire to assert his ascendancy beyond this one, single element of power. *If only Alfie could reciprocate this desire to be bound and abused, use me the way I fantasize my body being used...*

"I was asleep when you came in last night — or this morning — and I had to leave before you woke up. Shit, you were so out of it you didn't even move when the alarm went off." Alfie moved to the bed and sat next to the naked, sweat-moistened form of his friend. He leaned over him, white t-shirt across the other's midsection, one hand stroking the chest, teasing a nipple, the other reaching down the length of warm, expectant flesh, groping unseen until his fingers closed about the swollen tube. "And what did *he* get into last night?" he asked, squeezing gently as he felt the shaft continue to harden within his grasp.

Jeff watched the other's features, amused, knowing the power he continued to exert. Alfie would never admit it in so many words, but he was anxious, fearful that his friend might expose himself to the virus, thus endangering them both. He was asking, now, without actually saying it: *Did you do anything that wasn't safe, last night? Can we go on together as we have been, knowing that we're both negative?*

"He got sucked on," said Jeff, "and jacked off. That's all. Except he got paid for it again — not two hundred like the job night before last, but..." He motioned vaguely toward his rumpled clothes on the floor, across the width of bed. "Guy swung on me. Gave me forty bucks."

"What'd this one look like? A young guy like last time?" Jeff could sense the anxiety in his friend's tone, enjoyed his ability to create the concern.

"Nah, he was a little older, more'n thirty, anyways; but not bad-looking. He stuck the money in my pocket when I was leaving. I didn't expect it, you know, hadn't hustled him; but if it's that easy, maybe we don't need to worry about regular jobs right off. You could pick up the bucks as quick as me. Sure beats shoveling fries at Wendy's for minimum pennies."

"Making money on sex is too dangerous," Alfie told him. "The customers are apt to give you a disease, and the cops'll be out to bust you."

"And you think peddling dope is going to be safer?" asked Jeff. He lay back watching his friend's even, innocent features, felt the cloying grasp about his penis begin to assume a more rhythmical motion.

"It worked easy enough back home," Alfie assured him, "and the guys who supplied Chuck, my supplier, they're out here

23

and I know how to get in touch with them. Why not? As long as we don't use the crap ourselves." He continued to stare into his friend's eyes, unaware of the naivete his youthful features radiated, but knowing that Jeff had been given some unknown drug during his session the night before last, and hoping he wasn't going to pursue the guy for a repeat performance. That was one of the basic tenets of their relationship: they had agreed that each was free to do as he pleased as long as the sex he played was safe. The drug issue was another story — neither boy had been using anything stronger than grass, and until now neither had wanted to.

Jeff seemed to read his partner's thoughts. "I only used the stuff because the guy gave it to me," he protested. "I don't even know what it was. I couldn't look for a repeat if I wanted to."

"I'm not accusing you of anything, man," Alfie whispered, burying his face against the sweaty surface of his friend's chest. "You know I came with you 'cause I wanted us to be together. Using drugs could fuck us up."

"Maybe," Jeff replied. "But you were ready to cut out anyway, remember? Even before my old man came down on me. You thought you might be being followed when you went into town, and ... shit, you knew your way around back there. Who you gonna sell the stuff to if you *do* score it out here?"

"I'll worry about it later," said Alfie. He lifted free of his friend's body and quickly shifted his own position to lie fully clothed atop the naked form, forcing his arms around the slender shoulders, driving his lips hard upon the other's. He thought he sensed a momentary lack of response; then reciprocation, as Jeff's arms moved to return the embrace and his mouth opened to complete the exchange.

Despite his apparently casual entrance, Alfie had been genuinely relieved to find his friend awake and unharmed. He had hurried to the interview he had arranged by phone, only to find that it was a phony — an old guy who had advertised for a houseman, when all he really wanted was sex. On the way home he had risked several speeding tickets in his anxiety to get back and check on Jeff, who — he was certain — had been doing drugs for a second night in a row, and had definitely been under the influence of something when Alfie left. He had allowed his imagination to conjure up all sorts of dire scenarios involving bad dope, coma, hallucinations, even cardiac arrest. The fears had been totally unrealistic, but nonetheless real in Alfie's mind. Now, with his own body pressing down on Jeff's, he allowed his anxiety to translate itself into a more physical expression.

He kept himself fully atop his friend, felt the other's cock swell and press upward between his thighs. As he twisted his upper body to permit their lips to touch again, he could feel Jeff's fingers tugging at his t-shirt, pulling it up until Alfie lifted his chest enough to permit it to slide off over his head. Then he braced himself with his arms supporting his upper body so that Jeff's fingers could unfasten his wide leather belt and shove his jeans down over his narrow hips. Once his own cock had sprung free of its enclosure, he dropped back into full contact, sliding his arms under Jeff's sweat-slick shoulders. He held tightly, allowing his previous unfounded fears to drain away with the continued warm contact of his own flesh against his friend's hard, moist being. Their mouths were locked again in a frantic exchange, and once more Alfie felt the desperate yearnings deep within him.

He was so in love with Jeff, it had become an emotion beyond his ability to express. Trying to put his feelings into words made him sound foolish and awkward, far too soft and sentimental for the cynical world in which they lived. Neither could he bring himself to deliver the physical abuse that he knew Jeff craved. The act of binding his friend's wrists behind his back was as far as he had been able to go. Just the idea of causing Jeff pain was an impossible concept. He simply could not do it, although he knew his friend desperately desired it. Even now, with his own passions enflamed, he could only express his love in the more conventional way. He felt his cock slide in rigid demand against Jeff's.

He lifted free of the other's body, knelt between the wide-spread thighs, and held the two dicks together, slowing gliding his fingers along the combined girths, tantalizing himself as well as his companion. Then he wriggled back a few inches and brought the two cocks tip-to-tip. Gently, he pulled Jeff's fore-skin down until it covered both cockheads, and held it in place within the grasp of his palm, forcing the other's shaft to strain for release as it was pressed downward toward the mattress.

His gaze locked with Jeff's as the springy tension suggested a modicum of the bodily torment the other really desired. The blue eyes were glazed with pleasure, barely able to focus on the strongly muscled form that manipulated him. "Tie my hands," he whispered. His eyes were closed now, and the desperate hardness of his cock had increased until he was experiencing a heightened sensation from having it forced into an unnatural position.

With a sigh, Alfie released his grip and seized Jeff's upper arms, rolling him onto his belly. He now straddled the hard rounds of ass as he drew his friend's wrists together against the small of his back. Reaching behind him, he grasped his belt and pulled it free of his jeans, which were still gathered about his ankles. As he looped the leather around the other's wrists, he could hear the groan of contentment, felt the stronger pulse beneath his fingers. He knew how desperately this object of his passions would respond if he could only administer the punishment he craved; but it was impossible. Even the act of binding the wrists was difficult for him. As he did it now, in response to Jeff's whispered demand, he felt a surge of guilt, and also a sense of fear that his reticence was going to cost him the very thing he wished so desperately to possess and to protect.

■ ■ ■

Bruce MacLeod hung up the phone in his office, really shaken after the conversation with his lover. Frank had called from New Orleans, saying that he might be delayed an extra few days and graphically expressing how much he missed being with Bruce — describing in some detail the activities he wished to experience upon his return. But he had continued beyond this, expressing an almost desperate dismay over the activities of the press.

"There's this one shithead in particular," Frank had told him. "The son of a bitch is an up-front gay, writing for both the straight press and otherwise, actually full-time for one of the supermarket scandal sheets. And he's just hell-bent to 'out' me."

"Have you discussed this with Rufus?" Rufus was Frank's corpulent, crafty agent. "He might have a line on the guy, and be able to shut him up."

"I've got a call in for him now. I'll let you know what he says. But if the bastard puts it in print, nothing's going to help."

"I wish I could be there with you."

"Yeah, me too," Frank replied. "But if you were, this ass-hole'd probably find some way to videotape us. At least, for the moment, I don't think he suspects any SM angle. That would make it even juicier for him."

"I'd be careful what I said over the phone."

"I'm calling from my trailer ... you know, dressing room. I don't go through a switchboard."

"I'd still be careful," Bruce had added.

Now, thinking back on the conversation, the psychiatrist was caught in a classic dilemma. In a way, he agreed with the idea of outing — forcing prominent persons to admit they were gay — but only under certain restrictive circumstances. A politician who was unresponsive to the Community certainly deserved to be exposed, and various "role model" types, in professions where the exposure could do them little or no harm, were clearly fair game — more so if they drew any appreciable portion of their income or popularity from the Community. Rock stars and TV producers were good examples. But sports figures, as well as actors on TV and in films, could be seriously damaged by such revelations — especially early in their careers. In these situations it should be up to the individual, Bruce felt, to admit his sexual orientation when and if he felt comfortable doing it. After all, a role model who is forced from the occupation that made him famous — and hence the vaunted example — not only loses his job, but the loss of career also destroys his image.

"We can't let this happen to Frank," he muttered, as the phone rang again. "Mr. Donovan is here," Dennie told him.

"Send him in," said Bruce, reluctantly. Suddenly confronted with a serious and more personal problem, he would have loved to sidestep the situation with Dan Donovan. But he knew he couldn't, and was on his feet, hand extended as the heavyset, older man came in.

"I appreciate your making time for me," said Donovan. "I'll try not to impose, but I've had a few other thoughts; and I've also got the pictures," he added, passing Bruce the envelope he had been carrying in his left hand. Although he made no attempt at a direct apology for his hostility of the previous afternoon, his entire manner communicated a sense of remorse.

As his guest settled onto the sofa, Bruce stood by his desk, looking at the stack of photos. There were only two pictures, each reproduced twenty-five times. "This other kid has to be Alfie?" he asked absently, responding with an involuntary hint of lust as he stared at the handsome, brown-haired youth standing next to Jeff. Both boys were stripped to the waist, posing with picks and shovels, grinning for the camera. In this setting they looked very much alike, Bruce thought, Alfie only slightly bigger and a hair darker than Jeff. Each was strikingly attractive enough to pose for high-fashion clothing ads.

"Yeah, the one picture's of Jeff by himself; the other's of the two of 'em together. They came out to one of my projects one day with a couple of other kids, and took a bunch of pictures. I don't know what it was all about, 'cause none of 'em — including Jeff — ever did a hard day's work in their lives."

"Just needed the props, I'd guess," said Bruce, wondering to himself if they had come back at night or some other time when no one was around. *Now, those would be pictures I'd like to see,* he thought. "Want some coffee?" he added aloud. "I think Dennie just made a fresh pot."

A few minutes later Bruce was sitting in a leather chair, across the coffee table from Dan Donovan. They could hear the printer start up just outside the door as Dennie ran out some notes from Bruce's computer. "Must be nice, working out of your house," Donovan remarked, taking a sip from his cup. "Cuts down on all the commuter hassles."

"It's a lot easier all around," Bruce agreed. "Now, what ideas did you come up with?"

"Well, actually it was Betty ... my wife, you know. When she called last night she got me thinking: there must be places where kids stay in this town, when they don't have anyone to help them out. If I could get someone to show me around — you know — the back streets of Hollywood."

"Dan, I know you're really uptight about all this, and I can understand the various ramifications of your feelings. I'll put you on to someone who can show you around if you want, but don't you think Jeff's going to get in touch with you on his own, if you just give him some time? If not you, at least his mother?"

It took the other man a moment to respond, and in that brief interim Bruce seemed to read ... something. He couldn't be sure, but his instinct told him that Dan Donovan had a second agenda.

"I suppose he might," replied his guest at length, "but if he gets into something really bad in the meanwhile ... hurt, or killed, even. You ... you hear about things like this all the time, especially for a kid who's attracted to the weird things Jeff seems to be after. If that happened, I don't think I could live with myself. I know Betty would never forgive me, and — Well, Jeff's our only kid. And we sure as hell aren't going to have any more."

Bruce nodded in understanding and agreement, but his previous feeling became even stronger as the two men continued their discourse. Whatever had prompted Dan Donovan to come looking for his son, it was more involved than he was willing to admit. Of course, Bruce was antsy, anxious really for Dan to leave. His conversation with Frank had upset him more than he would have liked to admit, and he wanted a few minutes by himself to think about it before his next patient arrived.

In the end, the situation resolved itself. He took the photos from Donovan, assuring him that he would show them around that evening when he went to the Center for his regularly scheduled group session. And at that point a tremendous crash shook the house, causing both men — along with Dennie — to rush to the front door. Across the street, a gang of workmen was off-loading a flatbed truck full of timber.

"They should be using a crane," said Donovan.

"They should be working in the next county," Bruce responded dryly. But the commotion had drawn them all outside, and Dan took this as his cue to depart. "I'll be at Abe and Alice's tonight," he said as he turned toward his Avis Mustang, "in case you need to reach me."

"That guy's going to be a pain in the ass," remarked Dennie as they watched Dan drive off.

"Well, he's Alice's brother," Bruce replied. "Actually I feel sorry for him, and I'll do what I can to help. But right now I'm more concerned about Frank." And he went on to relate his earlier phone conversation with his lover.

"Did he tell you the name of the reporter?"

"Yeah, kind of an unusual name." He paused a moment in thought. "Haven Monroe; that's it. Ever hear of him?"

"Sure. You know him, too, Bruce. Remember the fund-raiser they held at that disco last year — The Back Lot? He did all the press conference stuff for them."

"Right. He wanted to interview me, but we managed to turn him on to that big stud from the bank. I think throbbing testicles overcame his professional dedication."

"Whatever it was, he left you alone," Dennie agreed. "But he *is* a real prick. He got on that UCLA defensive back, last fall. Remember? Outed the guy in his senior year, fucked up his chances for a pro contract. Then he got caught a few months later going through the garbage behind some councilman's house. That's when Channel 6 canned him. I don't know who he's working for now."

"Some supermarket rag, from what Frank told me. He apparently left L.A. and went back east — New York, or maybe D.C. At the moment he's in New Orleans, sniffing around Frank."

As the two men remained by the front door, a white Toyota convertible pulled into the circular drive, top down — slender, middle-aged man behind the wheel. "Hi, Doc," he called. "Business so bad you have to stand out on the street and pull 'em in?"

The newcomer parked behind Dennie's Buick and jumped out onto the dark surface of the drive. "I've never been so royally received," he added. "Really makes a guy feel wanted."

"I thought you were treating him for repressed ego," said Dennie, laughing — knowing that the client's problem had to do with something very different.

"That's right, but now I'm ready for my close-up, Mr. Delong," said the man, returning Dennie's banter.

"I've created a monster," Bruce said. "Come on; let's go in and get to work."

■ ■ ■

Henry van Porter was a tall, slender black man with handsome, almost pretty features. Although getting close to thirty, he looked younger. He was also far more intelligent than his clowning behavior allowed most people to perceive, because Henry — in addition to being an aspiring comedian — was in every sense a flaming queen. The kids at the Center called him Henrietta, which he enjoyed — mostly because the appellation implied a degree of acceptance, even friendship on the part of these other people. He was generous and kind to those who seemed to need his help or understanding, and on those occasions when he thought it more effective to be otherwise, he was capable of shedding these gaudy behavioral masks. He could thus be quite sane ... "professional" when the situation called for it.

Henry had always been drawn to Bruce, ever since the psychiatrist had first begun to donate his time at the Center, where Henry worked as receptionist. And, strangely, Bruce had developed a genuine fondness for Henry. More than that, he trusted him — both his honesty and his judgment. So it was into Henry's hands that Bruce entrusted the Donovan pictures.

"My, my, ah'd sho' like ta get a little'a that white stuff!" Henry bubbled.

Bruce shook his head at the beaming features. "You know, that Stepin Fetchit act is going to get you clobbered one of these days," he cautioned. "Remember all those things we talked about," the psychiatrist added. He referred to the several counseling sessions he had given Henry to ward off a mild bout of depression.

"'Tain't so," Henry told him, defensively. "Besides, that wasn't Stepin Fetchit. That was Rochester," he said with a pout.

"Whatever," Bruce countered. "You're enough to make a bigot blanch and a liberal faint dead away."

"That's me, a memorable Hollywood character," Henry replied, momentarily slipping out of his accent, then immediately assuming another persona. "But ah'll try'n find yo' boys fo' ya, Boss. Jes' leave it ta ol' Henry." He remained at his desk in the shabby foyer and watched Bruce striding down the hall to his session. *That's sure a nice man,* he thought. *Someday I'm gonna do something really good for him. Meanwhile, I'll find these dippy kids, if I can.*

But Henry never even came close to finding the two boys, and when it did come time to help Bruce it was in a way the lanky young man could never have imagined.

31

THREE

Hugo Fitzpatrick liked to think of himself as mean — nasty mean, with no real sense of humor, although he'd appear to laugh willingly enough when he was in a group, and everyone else laughed ... even if they laughed at him, as was often the case. He was awkward in company, never knew the correct response, and had never been able to defend himself in the exchanges of verbal fencing the kids used to enjoy in school. In truth, he had grown to hate them — to hate every damned stinking one of them, especially the girls. He hated them the most, because he knew he was even more helpless with them than he was with the boys. After all, you couldn't hit a girl.

He came off as anything but bright, and the other kids considered him stupid. He would never have made it into high school, much less up to his senior year, if it hadn't been for the new liberality that promised a high school diploma to any student who wanted it, and who was willing to sit through the requisite number of classes to get it. They didn't have to read; they didn't have to add two plus two. If they came to school, caused no serious trouble, and appeared to be doing the best they could, they received the coveted reward. Of course, Hugo had more going for him than many. Where the Good Lord had crossed some wires in his brain pan, He had been more than generous with the rest of the body. Topping six feet in his senior year, Hugo spent every hour he could in the school gym, lifting weights or working out on the parallel bars and rings. He weighed just over two hundred pounds, packed solidly on a lithe, powerful frame. His hair was full and dark, almost black. His eyes were a silvery, bird-of-prey gray; his features were sharp and even, like a classic Roman hero. He was, in fact, such a magnificent physical specimen that many kids were initially drawn to him — boys and girls alike. Thus Hugo's isolation and friendlessness resulted purely from his own evil temper and hostile disposition, although the school do-gooders sought to blame his asocial attitudes on his "family of orientation."

His father had been long gone before Hugo was old enough to realize that two parents were the norm in the households of most schoolmates. When he did come to recognize the difference in his own circumstances, he experienced the first surge of the bitterness that would eventually become the central core of his existence. Only his mother served to keep him emotionally afloat, recognizing his mental deficiencies and doing her best to shield him from the reality of his disability. But she had neither the resources nor the skills to cope adequately with the negatives of society.

Her one great contribution to Hugo's developing psyche was to instill in his youthful mind a great many fantasies. She began reading to him when he was barely old enough to understand the words, and she continued doing this long after he should have been able to read the books himself. She was particularly drawn to stories of King Arthur and his knights, of Robin Hood and Ivanhoe. She later expanded her repertoire into the works of Rafael Sabatini — stories of pirate heroes and savage adventure — and the books of Edgar Rice Burroughs — the Tarzan epics, with their peculiarly learned meanderings. Through all of this, she instilled in Hugo's developing brain the basis of a strangely convoluted morality, along with a futile craving for an intellectual existence that would always be beyond him.

On his own, as a teenager, Hugo discovered that many of the stories he cherished from his earliest days had been reproduced in comic books — with pictures and simple dialogue that he was able to read. He became an avid collector of these publications, and he soon began to work a few hours after school at the used book and magazine shop where so many of these treasures were to be found. The owner, an old man who also ran a small locksmith business out of his storefront, developed a fatherly interest in Hugo, especially when he discovered that the otherwise limited mentality had a decided affinity for the mechanics of locks and keys. Little did the old fellow realize that he was training his own nemesis, for Hugo soon utilized his new skills to enter the shop at night, and pilfer the comics he could not afford to buy.

It was prior to Hugo's high school experience that his mother finally found her niche. After floundering about for years trying unsuccessfully to earn a living as an office worker, and later as a waitress, Emma Fitzpatrick eventually settled into a degree of complacency — if not true contentment — by hiring herself out as a domestic. Over a period of time she refined her client list until she worked for only two households, and eventually just one. By this time Hugo was in his junior year, and occasionally accompanied his mother on Saturdays or during summer vacation, picking up a few extra dollars doing yard work or some of the heavier cleaning tasks inside the great house.

The place was a large Beverly Hills mansion, which had been built for a latter-day silent-movie star. It now belonged to Felix and Ruth Orsini, the well-known Hollywood producers. The couple lived in the palatial home with their two sons Rupert and Paul, Rupert being the elder — in his third year at college when Hugo first accompanied his mother to the house. Paul, the second son, was only a year older than Hugo — just out of high school, but not yet in college when the two boys achieved a friendship, of sorts — at least, a relationship.

Although not as aggressive as his brother, Paul was the more interesting of the two. While Rupert was marginally bright, he was also somewhat of a nerd, very wrapped up in computers and math courses at the university — most of which were really beyond him. He was emotionally disabled outside of the schoolroom, because he was almost totally lacking in social skills — certainly lacking in any sense of morality. In spite of this, or perhaps because of it, Rupert was decidedly his father's favorite, and the older brother did his best to play the part his dad seemed to wish for him.

Paul's interests ran the gamut from pop art and music to contemporary literature, and to some surprisingly sophisticated forms of fantasized sexual expression. He had tried his hand at improvisation in several areas of these creative fields, but he had been just astute enough to realize that his limited talents would never win any laurels in the arts. Yet, in two areas he perceived in himself more than a glimmer of ability. He had a reasonable feel for sculpture, and had made a number of mannequins that had been purchased by a local department store — in truth the first notable success in his life. Proud of their son's achievement, the Orsini parents had turned over a large outbuilding to him, this located at the very rear of the property. The resultant privacy permitted the youngster to experiment within a far wider ranging set of interests than his parents could have possibly imagined.

It was here that Paul began trying to animate some of the sexual fantasies which had filled his mind since puberty — and this soon proved to be his second-greatest talent. With his mannequins as silent witnesses, he experimented with various bondage techniques. He tied himself up with rope and with chain, and later with more exotic materials as his fertile mind cast about for ever more wondrous adventure. But he lacked a partner, and badly as he wanted someone to play these games with him, he was afraid to solicit any of his limited number of sexual contacts to go beyond the usual vanilla, safe-sex formulae. He found a soul mate, finally, in Hugo, who had aroused his interest from the first — a year or so before, when he had first seen the strikingly handsome youth working in the house with his mother. As with the others, however, Paul had been afraid to make an advance.

On a providential Friday afternoon the powerful, darkly tanned youth was working in Mrs. Orsini's flower garden — the one where she grew blossoms to be cut and used in the house. Stripped to the waist, Hugo was making a fabulous display of gymnastic musculature. Every curve and plane of his body gleamed with sweat, and dark fur was plastered down under the arms and across his dirt-smeared chest. His long black hair fell like a stallion's forelock across his brow, and his eyes seemed to glow with a silvery translucence beneath the bright California sun.

From the window of his workshop, Paul watched in awe as this beautiful young man displayed himself to such incredible advantage. But this wasn't any kind of pose; the kid had no way to know anyone was watching him. Nor could he be expected to know that never, in all Paul's short, pampered life had he ever wanted anything so desperately! It was sexual desire, combined with the lust of a collector who saw an object he knew he had to possess. His own throat was parched from excitement as he opened the door and offered Hugo something to drink.

There was a momentary flash of suspicion in the silvery eyes, as the youthful laborer stopped and drew himself erect. His flat, striated midriff pulled in upon itself as Hugo stretched and gazed at the other young man. Despite his beautiful exterior, the dark, clogged recesses of Hugo's mind were slowly turning, laboriously sifting the possibilities. The guy seemed friendly enough, about his own age, reasonably good-looking: blond, shorter, far lighter in build than Hugo. And rich. *Asshole probably never did a hard day's work in his life.* The resentment was there, the hatred ready to spring fully formed into the forward part of his mind.

But somehow Paul seemed to sense all of this, to respond to it before Hugo had a chance to completely organize his own responses. "You looked so great out there, I hated to interrupt you," he added honestly, "but you must be ready for a rest and something to drink," he continued. Then, as Hugo seemed momentarily at a loss, he went on: "Besides, I get lonely down here with no one to talk to, and no one I can show my stuff off to."

Paul's tone had contained exactly the right degree of admiration — of friendliness and humility, plus the added element of mystery — arousing curiosity as Hugo took the first tentative step toward him, shrugging, asking, "What kind of stuff?"

"Men," said Paul, grinning as he saw the shadow of doubt manifest itself again on Hugo's face. "Artificial men," he added, backing inside, where the contrast of the darker interior made him fade into a blur for several seconds until Hugo had joined him and his eyes had adjusted to the lesser illumination. "Wild," he whispered, obviously awed by the collection. Paul had drawn the draperies to partially darken the room, and to give it as much of an eerie atmosphere as was possible in the middle of a bright California day.

"Really wild, man," repeated Hugo, as Paul closed the door, carefully watching his visitor. In the few moments before inviting Hugo inside, he had rearranged a couple of his figures — binding the wrists together behind one mannequin's back, placing another on his knees in front of a third. Although none of the dummies was "anatomically correct," the homoerotic implications were immediately obvious, even to Hugo.

At this point in his life, Hugo was only halfway streetwise. He had never hustled, although he knew it went on. Being a high school student in Hollywood, he had ample opportunity to watch the action taking place all around him, and he'd been aroused by it — stimulated in a way he didn't understand. He had been tempted to try, but fear held him back ... fear of the unknown, fear of rejection, fear of the police entrapments he had heard discussed by some of his fellows who had played the game. So, up to this summer between his junior and senior years, he had never had sex with anyone, female or male. Yet his body was responding to the impending experience, and although there had been no overt sexual invitation, he knew.

The partially darkened room, the strangely lifelike figures in their suggestive poses, all struck a receptive chord. It was such an unexpected encounter, he was off guard and manipulated before he knew it was happening. Paul had thrust a cold can of beer into his hand and invited him to sit down. The coolness from the air conditioner sent waves of pleasure up his back, like the stroking of soft fingers along the ridges of his spine. He was outwardly — physically — relaxed; but a degree of tension, of fear, really, lay just beneath the surface. If Paul had approached as an aggressor, this factor might have come to the fore. Instead, the older boy was all gracious host and enthusiastic admirer.

"You're really doing a number on Mom's garden!" Paul told him. "Ever since you did whatever it was you did to it last month, the flowers have been growing like crazy." He sat on a wooden chair a couple of feet in front of Hugo, leaning his head back to take a deep swig from his beer. In so doing, he stretched his slender torso beneath the white calypso shirt, exposing his own deeply tanned skin when the unbuttoned fabric parted all the way to his waist. None of this was lost on Hugo, who also noted the two open buttons on the jeans, and the blondish tangle beneath. He felt an urge to plunge a finger into the

37

inviting cavity, to explore the warm flesh that lurked just perceptibly along the edge of denim.

But Paul continued talking, asking about Hugo's school, his tone almost reverential — an expression of admiration for anyone who could handle himself in the environment of a public high school. He leaned forward once, left hand resting on the stylish tear above his kneecap, fingers sliding off to graze Hugo's thigh as Paul lifted both arms in a gesture to accompany his discourse. All the variables were working as Paul had planned. Hugo was not much of a drinker, and coming in hot and sweaty from the outside, his head was starting to spin ever so slightly from the alcohol. There was an intimacy and sexual suggestiveness to the shadowy darkness, the mannequins, Paul's obviously available body. The young high-schooler wasn't sure exactly what to do, but knew he should do *something*, because he was, after all, the man, the leader. At an almost imperceptible gesture from Paul, Hugo responded. He glided slowly to his feet, and in the ensuing few seconds Paul was on his knees in front of him, gazing up in adoration along the hard, muscular midriff. Nor did the larger boy protest as he felt the waist come loose on his jeans, the sweat-softened denim slide down his thighs.

When Paul took Hugo's hooded crown between his lips, and slid along the length until the entire shaft was buried in the hot moisture of his mouth and throat, it was all Hugo could do to keep from falling. He had never experienced such debilitating euphoria. His legs were shaky, trembling; and his alcohol-induced dizziness became more intense. He fastened his enormous hands securely on either side of Paul's head, and pressed himself hard against the kneeling figure as he sought to steady his balance.

The hard grasp only served to emphasize Paul's submissive posture, and Hugo became dully aware of the dominant role being forced upon him. He suddenly found himself standing in a position of command over another guy — a guy who was older, richer, and obviously much smarter. All the factors added up to a total combination that was exactly right. Hugo was feeling a physical pleasure he had never known before, and he was experiencing all of this as the unchallenged aggressor ... the boss. It took very little further manipulation from Paul to develop this concept from the familiar "boss" to the newly experienced status of "Master."

Within a matter of days, Paul had worked his wiles until Hugo was totally enslaved — albeit in the role of Top. But in doing this, Paul had also involved himself in the same trap. Despite his superior intelligence, his sexual exploits had been limited and had not given him the experience to fully understand the implications of the situation he was creating. His fertile imagination had sustained the action through the first session with no problem. The exchange had been simple, the only kinky aspect being when he suggested that Hugo might like to "tie my hands behind my back." The bigger boy had complied, a bit uncertain until Paul had verbally guided him through the action.

They had both been very aware of time, knowing that either Mrs. Orsini or Hugo's mother could come out at any moment to check on the gardening, or assign some additional task. It was therefore into the second and third sessions — when Paul had gone to pick Hugo up, and secretly brought him back in the evening — that they began to develop the patterns of behavior that would indelibly characterize their relative roles. While both boys were naive and inexperienced — in any form of sex, let alone SM activities — each was captivated by the mystique. Paul had thought about it and fantasized, for years. Hugo, with a slower wit, had never imagined the wild scenes that had intrigued his partner — at least not in a sexual setting. But he *had* visualized himself in the role of Master, albeit in the very different context of a medieval lord, or as a powerfully muscled humanoid dominating the lesser species of the rain forests.

In fact, had Paul realized the depths of Hugo's fantasies, he might not have been quite so willing to submit himself to the bigger boy's control. But their relationship, in its early stages, was based on strangely convoluted roles. Hugo, the Top, did exactly as his bound and supposedly submissive slave suggested he should. This led them into situations that Hugo could never have contemplated on his own — very exciting, lust-fulfilling encounters. These in turn made him more aware than ever of his companion's mental superiority; and despite his own ascendancy in their sexual relationships, he acquiesced to the other's supremacy, painfully aware not only of his mentor's greater intellect, but also awed by the fact of the other's being rich. And to Hugo, being rich was a condition that carried with it all the ramifications of power and privilege. Thus, even in his slow and sometimes unresponsive mind, the big bruiser was able to perceive the limits — both spoken and otherwise — which formed the parameters of his role.

If the affair had come into being between men of greater maturity, it would probably have followed a more reasonable course, with serious thought given to the other aspects of their lives. However, the abrupt discovery of such an extraordinarily enticing relationship blinded even Paul to the potential for problems — the most poignant being the possibility of their activities being discovered, or even suspected. In these first few days the behavior of each was determined far more decisively by the demands of their adolescent gonads than by their higher senses.

The parents, of course, were oblivious to their sons' activities, as parents so often are. But Paul's brother Rupert soon noted the sudden heightening of his sibling's dedication to a heavy time schedule in his private domain — the little house at the foot of their mother's garden. He was particularly intrigued, because Paul always left in his car as soon as he could get away after dinner, then later made a point of slipping back onto the property and directly into his workshop. The older brother finally decided it was time to satisfy his curiosity.

Rupert had already reconnoitered the site on the previous night, while Paul was away, but his younger sibling had drawn the blinds and locked all the doors and windows. And besides, Rupert had something else planned for that evening, so he'd had to depart before Paul's return. The next night, however, he had plenty of time and was determined to discover his little brother's secret. He expected that it would most likely involve some new artsy-fartsy project, probably with some equally dippy accomplice. Whatever he might discover, he was sure it would afford him an opportunity to once again belittle his kid brother in front of their father.

Concealed in the shadow of the oleander that grew thickly against one side of Paul's little house, Rupert watched in surprise when the small red sports car came to a halt beside the door to disgorge both his brother and the very big, very handsome kid whom he had seen coming to the house with their cook. In the first moments he was puzzled, but uncertainty quickly gave way to shock as he watched the two young men walk toward the door, pause in the darkness of the overhang, and abruptly grasp each other in a very heated embrace, kissing with a passion that bespoke something very far afield from an art project. He had been so surprised — so shaken, in fact, that he failed to respond before the two lovers had gone inside and locked the door behind them.

After a few moments he moved toward the entrance, hoping to glean some idea of what transpired inside. But Paul had started his stereo, and all Rupert could hear was a thumping disco rhythm. He stood there a few more minutes before it occurred to him that there had to be a duplicate key among the collection hanging on the back of a door in his mother's dressing room. The folks were out for the evening — no problem.

He was gone for less than fifteen minutes, returning with a ring of keys. He listened again at the door, but could not hear anything except the music. With a shrug, he began trying to find the proper key, presuming — correctly — that the disco would drown out the sounds of his experimentation. When the lock finally turned under his careful ministrations, he eased the door open against the sudden blare of sound, no longer muted by the door panel. He had not been in the outbuilding since his brother had taken it over a couple of years before, and for a moment he again found himself dumbfounded. The front room was bathed in a bluish glow, but the tranquil color was regularly diluted by the periodic white blast of a strobe coming from the other room.

There seemed little reason for stealth, and Rupert moved quickly across the cluttered space. He felt vaguely intimidated by the jumble of mannequins, some whole, some merely disembodied parts. At the door to the back room he stopped in stark disbelief. His brother was naked, bent over what appeared to be a sawhorse, his wrists and ankles bound to the wooden legs. Equally nude, except for a wide leather harness across his back and chest, Hugo stood over the prostrate figure. He was wielding a heavy black strop, that fell with regular,

41

precise strokes across the upturned buttocks of the captive. Although the anterior portions of Paul's body were blocked from his brother's view by his bound position, Rupert could clearly see every part of Hugo. There was decidedly no question of the powerful youth's sexual arousal as he brought the wide heavy leather down smartly across Paul's naked, upturned ass.

Although Rupert had never been especially inclined toward male-to-male sex, and certainly not anything to do with SM, being so suddenly and unexpectedly confronted by the bizarre display could not help but have a profound effect. All his previously sublimated sex drives, controlled and channeled toward academic achievement in mathematics and computer sciences, now seemed to gather unbidden in his loins. He was helpless for several minutes, unable to do more than stand in the doorway and watch as his brother received a solid thrashing from the other, with both participants seeming to enjoy the exchange. The flashing strobe caused the action to appear frozen in a series of weird tableaus — like bright, still pictures dropped into an ongoing film run.

The older brother had been watching for perhaps ten minutes when Hugo shifted position and saw him. For a fleeting moment, the youth's eyes blinked, uncertain whether he was looking at a real person or one of Paul's dummies. Then Rupert, raising hackles of fear on Hugo's back, took one slow step in the direction of the two naked young men. As the slow functioning of Hugo's mind still refused to believe that the approaching figure could be real, he cried out in absolute, total terror. This, in turn, caused Paul to twist his head around and glimpse his brother — a seemingly upside-down apparition as viewed from his humiliating position.

Seeing the devastating effect his presence had produced, Rupert knew he was master of the situation. He could easily walk away and hold the threat of his knowledge as a constant tool to control and bully his brother — but he pretty well dominated him, anyway. He certainly held the superior position in his parents' eyes, and was clearly the choice to succeed to the family business. Thus, he rejected any thought of leaving this strangely appealing scene. In fact, his own sexual lust was pressing hard upon his consciousness, much as his swollen penis was demanding release inside his jeans.

Almost lost within the overpowering blast of sound from the speakers, was Paul's desperate cry for Hugo to release him. But the young giant remained frozen in shock as the living apparition moved slowly toward him. Ignoring the plaintive cries of his brother, Rupert bore down on the handsome pseudo-aggressor. "On your knees!" he shouted against the avalanche of sound. When the other remained rooted in place, he shouted again, "Get down on your knees, shithead, or I'll tell your old lady what I've seen you doing!"

He stepped up to Hugo, placed his hands on either shoulder, and pushed the bigger boy down. Terrified, now, on a different level, the muscular kid allowed himself to be directed. He went slowly onto his knees, watching in fascinated horror as Rupert unbuttoned his Levi's and wrestled his cock free of the briefs which had twisted around its swollen length. When the older boy presented his rigid cock, obviously expecting Hugo to service it, there was a moment of clashing wills. Hugo had never even taken Paul's penis in his mouth, although there had been moments when he had been tempted to do so. But Rupert was another story. He simply did not wish to touch him, in fact found him sexually repulsive. But he was terrified lest the older brother fulfill his threat, and in the end Hugo submitted.

He nuzzled the swollen crown with his lips, finally ran his tongue around the fleshy bulb, and after several minutes of avoiding the inevitable, he opened his mouth and accepted the other's tool. Through all of this, Paul had continued to plead for release; but he now lapsed into silence as he realized no one was paying him any mind. He was also immobilized by his brother's sudden assault, and he experienced a peculiar surge of sexual reawakening as he watched Hugo submit in a way he had never considered possible.

From his upside-down position, he watched in disbelief as his brother plunged his cock repeatedly into the unresisting mouth. He saw the globs of phlegm collect in a foamy mass about the lips, then cascade down in slimy strands. He was amazed, not only by the vehemence of his brother's assault, but even more by the very fact of his committing an act that had previously seemed so totally foreign to his personality.

For his part, the sensations which now seemed to explode within Rupert's body were unlike anything he had ever known before. Their intensity far exceeded the bland, passionless release he knew from his occasional secret, sweaty encounters with a Sunset Boulevard hooker. And it certainly transcended any masturbatory responses he had been able to wring from his own body. Now, he was responding with a wild abandon, with a lust that had hitherto been unknown — unsuspected. With hardly a thought of what he was doing, as if his arms and hands were moving of their own volition, he quickly stripped to the waist. Then, grasping Hugo's head for support, he stepped out of his loafers. He unfastened his belt and shoved his jeans down his thighs, stepping out of them as well.

When he stood naked as the others, his whole body began to tremble with excitement. He was suddenly a savage in some jungle rite, using sex to expunge his body of all other human emotions, of fear, of civilized inhibitions. As he felt the ultimate pressures gathering in his balls and knew he was on the verge of climax, he abruptly yanked free of Hugo's lips. Without a word, or even much thought, he turned toward his brother's upturned ass, still strapped in helpless exposure. He slapped a hand against one cheek, then the other. Then he grabbed at the collar on Hugo's harness and forced the submissive giant to kneel behind the bound and helpless figure. He shoved the handsome face against the twin mounds and commanded him to lubricate the passage.

Hugo might have resisted, now, but he had thus far succumbed to the other's threats, and he had debased himself as he had never thought he would — had committed the act which, when Paul had done it to him, had given Hugo his greatest sense of power. At this stage he was depleted, however, like a rape victim who has reached the end of any possible resistance, who has given up and surrendered. He felt defeated, overwhelmed, and he obeyed. His tongue snaked outward and plied its way in between the twin mounds of muscle, probing for the hole. Then he was inside, almost oblivious to the raunchy taste, the fecal odors which assailed his nostrils.

Above him, Rupert's slender, naked torso pressed forward. The cock, still wet and slimy from Hugo's ministrations, was playing about the side of the giant's face as he drove his tongue ever deeper into the captive's anus. And beneath them, Paul could only stay in the position his bonds forced upon him, feeling his body invaded by the one, and knowing he was soon to be penetrated by the other ... by his own sibling. And that, in itself, aroused a new and different sensation. The brothers had never been particularly close, forever being pitted against each other by the competitive demands of their parents. But now, knowing Rupert was going to fuck him, Paul was gripped by a tremendous anticipation. It was the expectation of an almost ultimate humiliation, as if he were on the verge of becoming even more totally and decisively abused.

Then Hugo had been pushed aside, and Rupert's long, slender cock was sliding into him. The physical pain was minimal. Certainly, the flesh was far less substantial than Hugo's huge shaft, and Paul had endured that many times during the last few weeks. But strangely fulfilling was the sense of total domination, of his body being possessed, being conquered by an enemy who wanted only to humiliate and forcibly possess him, and over whom he exerted no control.

■ ■ ■

After this night, the relationship between the two brothers was irreparably altered. Despite his own indulgence, Rupert maintained a hammerlock on his sibling's sensibilities. He was unquestionably in command, and in almost every instance Paul felt compelled to submit to him. Occasionally, Rupert made sexual demands, and Paul always gave in. However, the younger brother was not without his own resources, and he eventually began to seek another location for his activities. This led to his establishing a workshop in the old house in Echo Park, which he did in secret several months later. It would be quite a while before Rupert discovered the location, although in truth he might easily have done so far sooner if he had been interested enough to try.

Rather, he enjoyed the power he wielded over his brother in all their interactions within the household. He was more than ever the prime contender for his father's favor, the more so as the elder Orsini became increasingly aware of his second son's tendency to accede to Rupert's every demand.

For Paul's part, he was deriving just enough perverse satisfaction from this sudden domination by his brother, that he was initially content to allow the situation to remain unchanged — or at least unchallenged. As long as Rupert maintained his silence, Paul was able to continue his association with Hugo, who now seemed more dependent than before. It was almost as if the larger boy were looking to Paul as his teacher, his guru. The two began taking long walks in the warmth of the summer evenings, exploring several areas in the neighborhood, and enjoying the opportunity to play at stalking people who were enjoying the supposed privacy of their homes. These walks served the secondary purpose of delaying the start of their sexual rites until Rupert had either gone to bed, or taken off for some other activity.

Still, the older brother would sometimes enter into their scenes, and in doing so he further solidified the respective roles he and Paul were to assume in the future. Rupert was the unquestioned leader, and despite some overt resentment on Paul's part, the younger brother's basic masochism permitted him to accept his subservient position, secretly to relish and enjoy it.

Hugo, however, came to detest the older brother even more intensely. He endured him because he feared him, and because he knew it was what Paul wanted him to do. But Rupert's body did not excite him. He was repelled by the clammy skin, and the faintly musty odor he always sensed on the other's being. One day, he told himself, he'd get even.

FOUR

rank slid his lower body into the pool, balanced another moment on the edge, then let the rest of his slender, naked form slip into the water. "It feels colder than last year," he called over his shoulder before striking out for the far side. The backyard was dark. The underwater floods were off in the pool, so that only the city sky glow cast a tenuous suggestion of light.

"The heater's only been on since this afternoon," said Bruce. He stood in the doorway, watching this man he had come to love, reveling in the certain knowledge that the small, handsome being was *his*, that they belonged to each other. In a sense he was like a collector gloating over his hoard, except that Frank comprised the entire set — dark, almost black hair, sparkling green eyes, body like a renaissance sculpture, very Latin handsomeness. But more, for under all that external beauty Bruce had discovered a reciprocal mind, an entity that had smitten him even when Frank had been a patient. Now, more than a year into their relationship, that initial attraction had matured into something much stronger.

Laughing, Frank emerged from the shallow end of the pool, massaging his genitals as he watched Bruce mischievously from a sideways stance. "That temperature's not conducive to a good display," he quipped. "How can I be expected to seduce you, looking like Princess Tiny Meat?"

Bruce returned his laughter. "Where did you learn that?" he asked. "I haven't heard talk about P.T.M.s since I was a kid."

"That long ago, huh?" Frank teased. "No, it was in one of those pocketbooks Dennie loaned me to read on the trip. He said it was to further my education."

"It apparently worked." Bruce approached his lover, holding out a large white towel, which he wrapped around the naked form, holding the smaller body tight against his own. Bruce was wearing only a pair of faded cutoffs, and he could feel Frank's fingers working at the buttons until the single covering slid down his legs, and his friend's warm palms were tracing the full length of his back and buttocks.

"I really missed you," Frank whispered, as he felt himself being turned, so that his ass was pressed against Bruce's crotch.

"With all those young hunks running around the sets?" Bruce had now stepped free of his cutoffs, and pressed his risen sex into the damp terrycloth, sculpting a trough between Frank's tight little buns.

"Listen," Frank replied seriously, "even if I'd been so inclined, I wouldn't have dared even look at them, not with that Monroe asshole watching my every move."

"What's happened with him?" Bruce asked as they moved inside, leaving their cast-off clothing beside the pool. Frank's return had been delayed, then delayed again. It was almost the middle of June, almost summer; but Southern California was undergoing a sudden chill.

"I'm not sure," Frank replied. "He's working out of D.C., I think, so I'm not sure if they'll spring for his coming out here. I can't imagine I'd be important enough to them to justify the effort."

"If this new production goes over as big as Rufus thinks it will, you might be." They had reached the door to Bruce's bedroom, now — both naked, both aroused, ready for a renewed exchange.

"Fuck that son of a bitch," Frank returned hoarsely. "I'll worry about him and his yellow rag later. More important things to do right now."

They moved into the special space between Bruce's bedroom and the master bath. The house had originally been built with two large dressing areas, complete with walk-in closet, one on each of the dual approaches that separated the two rooms.

48

Bruce had retained the "Mister" portion intact. The slightly larger lady's dressing room had been converted into a dungeon. The walls were black leather, over heavy foam-rubber padding. The floor was covered with several layers of black vinyl sheeting. A variety of chains and leather harnesses were suspended from heavy metal eyelets in the cork-padded ceiling. An extensive collection of whips, paddles, and other toys hung from racks built onto the backs of the two doors that opened into the room: from the bedroom and from the bath. The wall between the wide passageway and the enormous closet had been removed, resulting in an L-shaped space, with ample room for any kind of vertical or sling suspension. The built-in shelves, originally designed for m'lady's accessories, now contained neat rows of leather ball stretchers, tit clamps, small weights, and various other SM appliances.

A subdued, amber glow emanated from several concealed fixtures at floor level, and just below the ceiling. It created an even, almost shadowless aura within the entire space. Muted strains of Richard Strauss's *Symphonia Domestica* whispered from the multi-speaker system, as Bruce touched a button to start the CD changer. He had gone to some pains to assure that all was exactly as it had been the first time he and Frank had used his special room: sound, lighting, placement of the larger, more obvious items. Nor was he disappointed in the resulting effect on his partner.

Frank stood in naked anticipation in the center of the space, waiting silently for Bruce to initiate the action. The velvety perfection of his skin, the handsomely chiseled features, the glow of light against the hard-muscled body ... all combined to establish the mood for Bruce, much as his efforts had done for Frank. When the host moved to place his first restraints on the smaller man, he did it from the front, pressing his own solid form against the other, allowing their lips to lock in clinging demand as his arms went around the narrow waist and his fingers deftly fitted a pair of Pearson handcuffs onto his lover's wrists. Deliberately, Bruce inhaled just as the manacles clicked into place, pulling the air from Frank's lungs, emphasizing his total domination. He tightened his grip on the smaller form, holding their bodies pressed firmly together, trapping both his own and his captive's cock between the solid walls of their lower bodies.

When he stepped away at last, he left Frank standing almost unsteadily in the center of the room. His head was canted forward, the dark forelock falling in disarray across his brow. His eyes were focused on the floor in front of his feet. Although his entire body was in a posture of total submission, his cock projected at an upward angle from his groin, as if proclaiming its independent demand for attention.

Bruce moved up with a full leather hood, complete with blindfold and gag. Tipping Frank's head back with one hand, he slid the appliance over the other's pate, then moved behind to tighten the lacings. As Frank felt his lover's body against his backside, his fingers snaked out to toy with the cock which moved with tantalizing, almost teasing contact across his ass and lower back. Bruce allowed the contact for the time it took him to complete his adjustments on the hood. He then seized the captive hands and lifted them until they were positioned well above the prisoner's tight little buns. He took a heavy chain dog collar from the collection on the bedroom door and locked it onto the handcuffs after passing it once around Frank's neck, securing it so that the captive had no choice but to keep his arms elevated, with his hands against the small of his back.

For Frank, it was a moment of such long-awaited bliss, he could already feel the eager rush gathering in his balls. His sudden deprivation of two primary senses — sight, and to some extent sound — were easily as significant acts of surrender as permitting his wrists to be secured behind his back. He could feel Bruce moving about, but could never be sure exactly where he was, or what he was doing. He felt the touch of fingers deftly fastening a leather appliance around his nuts, causing him a brief spike of pain as the orbs were pulled downward, secured by the leather wrapping. Bruce had selected a lace-up device, with an extra length of rawhide. This permitted him to wrap the ends securely about the base of both the cock and balls, creating a fresh sense of imprisonment that almost brought Frank to climax.

Bruce paused, then, allowing his subject a few moments to regain his equilibrium. There was always the temptation to move too quickly, to rush the moment instead of savoring each delicious moment of the exchange. As he stepped back, he could see a fine strand of fluid stretching down from Frank's cock, excitement oozing from his balls to form a stringy display that finally broke loose and puddled on the black latex before the captive's feet. Without warning, he reached out and took hold of both nipples, applying a gentle pressure that gradually increased, as Frank's initial sharp intake of breath devolved into a series of deep-throated groans. But the discomfort was producing a fresh discharge of preseminal fluid, as the smaller man responded fully to his Master's touch. Finally, Bruce relaxed his grip, but stepped closer to permit their cocks to touch in grazing contact, further tantalizing the captive's senses.

He then ran his hands along the sides of Frank's body, over the firm curves of his lats, onto the hips and back to grasp the tight little buns — "honey buns" he called them as he whispered against the leather hood, asking his prisoner how he might enjoy the feel of a leather strap across his back and ass. Frank could only groan into his gag, but his entire body was so enflamed, any contact from the other's hands was akin to a sexual possession. He wanted whatever was going to happen, feeling his body as if it were only vaguely real. He could see nothing but darkness, and hear just those sounds which Bruce contrived for him to hear. Otherwise, his sole bridge to the real, physical world were the bonds that his Master had placed upon him.

Minutes later, Bruce selected a wide, heavy loop of leather and began to play this across the naked backside, against the other's firmly rounded cheeks. Then gently, he began to stroke the helpless posterior — very slowly, very gradually increasing the strength of his blows until Frank's responses accelerated in kind, acknowledging by the subtle movements of his body that he was experiencing the pain, but willing that it possess him. Finally he did attempt to pull away, groaning, eventually twisting in a futile effort to avoid the contact. But his cock never lost a modicum of its rigid projection, and despite his obvious response to the more acute pain, his mind was just as obviously translating it into a deeply and long-awaited pleasure.

The scene continued, then, for better than two more hours. Bruce kept both of them on the verge of climax, usually without the need of genital contact. For each it was the fulfillment of several months' anticipation, an expression of desperately restrained lust layered upon the deeper feelings that formed the core of their relationship. Exciting as the exchange might have been under any circumstances, the love which each felt for the other could serve only to make every contact, each sensation, more profound.

In the end, Bruce shifted Frank's wrists to either side of a steel collar, locking them in place so that his entire body was more accessible, without the arms obstructing his sides. The hood was removed and the small, solid body directed back into the bedroom, where Bruce had thrown a black leather cover across the king-sized mattress. He pressed the captive figure onto the cool, slick surface, each of them almost painfully aware of the leathery feel, of the subtle aroma that rose up about them from the hide.

Bruce held him tightly, kissing him deeply, aware of the residual taste left by the leather gag. He could feel Frank trembling — whether with lust or emotion he could not be sure. But Bruce could sense the desperate craving in the other's body, perhaps in his spirit as well. He knew that Frank fully reciprocated this exchange on every level. Almost as a reflexive motion, he reached for the drawer in the nightstand, but paused when he felt Frank's body tense beneath him. "Over a year, remember?"

Bruce looked down, barely able to see Frank's features in the dim illumination. He was astride the other's thighs as he leaned forward, grasping the smaller man's biceps and pushing him down more firmly against the bed. "You swear you've been honest with me?" he demanded.

"Yes, sir," Frank whispered hoarsely.

Bruce sat back, teasing his cock as he continued to stare into the shadow of his lover's face. "And you want to feel this big cock up your ass without a rubber?"

"Yes, sir!" Again the whispered response. "Please! I want your cum inside my body."

Bruce hesitated only another few seconds before reaching for the plastic container of lubricant. Since the beginning of their relationship, over thirteen months before, they had engaged in only safe sex. But they had also agreed to a one-year cutoff. Now was the moment for their greatest display of mutual belief, a symbolic act of faith and in effect a further declaration of their love. Bruce slipped a pillow under Frank's butt, shot a touch of gel into his asshole, and maneuvered himself into position. His arms were looped around the other's legs, forcing the captive body to curl backward, the thighs to separate until he was able to push his cock downward and have it graze the hidden recess. Frank responded to the cloying contact with a sigh, and an almost subconscious twitch to place himself closer to the rigid cock that was poised to invade him.

Another few heartbeats, and Bruce was sliding into him — advancing gently, then backing off, pushing in again, and retreating for half the distance. Frank felt the desperate hardness of his own cock attempting to increase, even beyond the almost painful swelling it had already achieved. A puddle of pre-cum was gathering in his navel, as he felt the hard pressure sliding ever deeper. Bruce's grip increased against his upper arms as his lover fought back the urge to climax when he penetrated the final modicum, and his pubes came to rest against the upturned cheeks. Frank's head was turning from side to side. His whole body seemed to be gathering for the final peak of sensation. He, too, was struggling to hold back the frantic rush that tugged at the base of his balls, threatening to erupt and end the tantalizing expectation.

For several protracted moments, each man held still, allowing his body to circumvent the moment of no return, forcing his physical being to follow the dictates of his mind — to prolong this glorious sensation, with its emotions as strongly felt as the tactile exchange. Slowly, Bruce began to slide in and out of him, and Frank twisted in uncontrolled abandon. If his hands had been free, he would have been unable to keep them from stroking himself to climax. Even so, he could feel the rush building up again in his balls, which were now fighting the constraint of the leather stretcher as they tried to pull tight against the base of his shaft. Then he couldn't help himself. He was beyond control or restraint. With a cry of desperate relief, he felt the tide rising tightly through his nuts, and sensed Bruce stiffening against him. Both of them were held in suspended motion as the ultimate sensation swelled and took possession of them.

Then Bruce was lying on top of him, both of them gasping for breath, neither willing to break the contact. Frank felt the gradual softening within him, and moved his lower legs to lock them around Bruce's thighs, to keep him in place for those few extra seconds as his lover's cock lost its heightened rigidity, and the final drops of fluid seeped into him.

■ ■ ■

Frank and Bruce were still in bed, not quite asleep, but unwilling to get up — arms and legs entwined, hard bodies pressed together, cocks alert and demanding. It was about nine-thirty, but Bruce had purposely left his morning free, this first day after Frank's long-awaited return. They heard the doorbell, followed a few moments later by Dennie's heavy tread. Curiosity made both of them concentrate on trying to hear the conversation, but they could make out only the murmur of voices. Then the door closed and Dennie's footsteps retreated to the far end of the house.

"Whoever it was, Dennie didn't let him in," Frank whispered. He snuggled back into the warm enclosure, letting his regenerating arousal find its place between Bruce's thighs. He could smell a trace of the oil Bruce used to keep his leather appliances supple, felt the dried residue on his skin from the night's activities, and his mental imagery drove him to seek a reciprocation of Bruce's final possession.

Later, when they were dressed and in the breakfast nook, Dennie came to join them. "Christ, I've been afraid to move out of my room for fear I'd bust up the mating ritual," he remarked.

"You came out to answer the door," Bruce reminded him. "Who was it?"

"I was afraid it might be Dan Donovan, but it turned out to be some kid looking for work," replied the big man. "I'd have sloughed him off, except he was such a beauty — great big guy, with hands the size'a meat hooks. I told him to come back when the boss was here."

"I thought you only liked little guys," Frank said teasingly, "like our little houseboy — who seems to be missing, by the way."

"Listen, when they're as gorgeous as this dude, I like 'em around just for decoration," Dennie assured him. "And as for that little asshole of a houseboy, I canned him when he started slipping out at night and dragging back street hustlers."

"Yeah, I told him to put a stop to that in a hurry," Bruce added. "And, by the way, you don't need to worry about Dan. Alice says he finally gave up the search and went home. But as for this kid who came to the door, if you think he'd be any good — at gardening, I mean — we can use him. José told me last week that he was looking to retire, and both his boys are going to school full-time. He promised to find me somebody, but ... well, if you like the kid, Dennie, you hire him," he concluded with a playful pinch of the big man's cheek, just above the close-trimmed beard.

"Jesus, you guys are slaphappy this morning! Somebody musta gotten a good stiff shot in the ass!"

"You know it!" Frank assured him. "I'd been storing up for that session since right after Mardi Gras. Lived with a hard-on almost every waking hour. In fact, it's a good thing I didn't have any nude scenes to do for those last few weeks."

"You're not running around nekked in that New Orleans thriller, are you?" asked Dennie.

Surprisingly, Frank blushed as he replied, "Well, just a quickie — back shot, as I climb out of bed with Lila. But it's okay, Bruce," he added, laughing at his friend's momentarily distressed expression. "She likes girls, so it was big giggle for both of us."

"I hope you're being careful, opening up to people," Bruce said seriously. "Someone's always out to make a fast buck, exposing the other guy."

"Oh, I never said anything," Frank replied, "but everyone seems to know about her. I don't think she cares, and, well, even though nothing was ever said, she just seemed to assume. You know. One day when we were rehearsing the bedroom scene she groped me under the covers, and mumbled something about 'Who's the lucky guy?' I told her it was Charley. That's the horse in the scene where I get shot riding in a hansom."

"Shit, this sounds like a wild flick!" said Dennie. "When's it going to be out?"

"Six to eight months, I'd guess," Frank told him. "You can both be my dates to the premiere, unless Rufus makes me go with a girl," he added, laughing. Then, more seriously: "And who's this Dan character, and what's he looking for?"

"I guess I forgot to tell you, with all the other problems you were having," Bruce replied. "Dan Donovan is Alice Javits's brother. He got into an argument with his nineteen-year-old son, back in Iowa, and it seems the kid came out here. Donovan came out, trying to find him, but after nearly two months of futile effort, he finally gave up."

"Do you think the kid's really in the area?" Frank asked.

Bruce shrugged. "I'm beginning to think the boys — that's Donovan's son, Jeff, and his friend — I think they must have gone on to some other city — San Francisco, maybe — although Dan's been there, as well as San Diego, and didn't have any luck."

"It's a shame, too," Dennie muttered. "They're real beauties."

"Shame on you!" Frank said, laughing. "It's time you found yourself a real man, instead of lusting after those little twinkies." He placed an arm around Bruce's neck, and pulled his lover tight against his side. "But it sounds like Alice's brother gave it his best shot. I'd bet the kids just didn't want to be found."

"If they're both still alive," Bruce mused.

"If they weren't, someone woulda found a body." Dennie got up to clear the table. "Besides, I like twinkies," he added suddenly, harkening back to Frank's teasing remark. "'Course, I like 'em young, but I also like 'em butch. And, they don't always have to be *real* young. Let's just say I have very catholic tastes."

"Oh, bless you, Big Daddy," Frank laughed. "May you live to sin another day!"

■ ■ ■

At the sound of a car engine, Jeff jumped to his feet and crossed to the window. He lifted one of the slats in the venetian blind, then dropped it in disappointment. No reason to expect Alfie back in a car, anyway, not unless he got some trick to drive him home. The two young men had moved into a dingy apartment in an old brick building just off Vermont Avenue, on the edge of Hollywood. They had made contact with a guy named Howard — no last name — who rented a big house up above Los Feliz. Howard gave parties, and ran a modeling agency–escort service — "generous older men" getting together with younger, attractive guys. "Madam Howard," as the kids called him, was well organized and reasonably ethical. At least he saw to it that the johns never mistreated their "boys" — unless a kid *wanted* to be mistreated. But they always got their money, and they never got hurt, and everything was done quietly, so the cops had never been a problem. "Madam" owned the building they lived in, and deducted the modest rent from the young men's earnings, thus saving them the problem of having to deal with regular landlords: first and last and security. The place was comfortable, if not elegant, and living here had afforded them both a sense of having a home.

Only now, Alfie had been gone for three days — not on a call arranged by Howard. Jeff had checked on that. He'd simply gone out on his own after a minor argument with Jeff, and never came back. He hadn't taken the pickup. That was still parked in its assigned place, behind the building. Strange, because Alfie had made a point of picking up the keys on his way out the door.

Jeff was nearly frantic. The two boys had agreed not to hustle the streets. There was no need for that, because Howard kept them amply supplied with johns. Thus money wasn't really a problem. The little apartment was their only expense, and they were actually putting a fair amount of cash aside for the time when they decided to move into a decent place on their own. For the moment, though, they had thought it best to stay where they were, where no one asked questions. Because of their connection with the service, there had been no need to contact any of the social-service agencies or other do-gooders. And since they hadn't been plying the streets, they hadn't made contact with any of the guys who hung out at the Center. So far it had seemed to be working well for them. Until now. Now, Jeff was beside himself and he had no one he could even talk to ... except Howard, who was less than helpful. In fact, he seemed a little suspicious — though exactly of what, Jeff wasn't sure. He only knew that he would not get any support from "Madam," and would probably be well advised not to discuss his fears with him.

For the first time since leaving home, he felt an urge to call his mom, and even regretted not being able to speak with his dad. *Iron-assed bastard. I always knew he wouldn't under-*

stand, but if he'd kept his nose out of my private storage place,
he'd never have seen all those drawings. Figured I might
someday tell him I was gay; he might have finally come around
to that. The rest ... the SM bit, no reason he'd ever have to know
about that ... no more than one man knows what another does
when he goes to bed with his own wife. Nobody's business,
anyway. Shit! Why did he have to look in that shell? Why didn't
I think about it, and hide the fucking key? The same questions
he'd asked himself at least a hundred times before.

Well, I can't stay cooped up here like a caged bear. I gotta
do something. Haven't even got a joint left. Alfie never did make
contact with his source — least he said he didn't. Wouldn't
have told me, anyways. Never liked me using it ... just grass.
Still didn't like for me to do it. You'd think I was snorting coke,
the way he carried on about it. Wonder if I oughta call home,
or...? Really wish I knew what to do. God, I really love Alfie,
even if he doesn't dig the things I really want him to do. But,
Christ! If something's happened to him, I don't know what I'm
going to do.

■ ■ ■

Bruce was just winding up a session with an old client when
Dennie buzzed him — a definite no-no except in a dire emer-
gency. He excused himself and picked up the phone. "It's Alice,"
Dennie told him, "and she's in a real panic. Won't tell me why."

"Have her wait just a second. Pat and I are about finished."
He pressed the HOLD button, put the receiver down, and
calmly concluded his session — taking less than a minute, but
leaving his patient with the impression that he had deferred to
him in a moment of crisis. The man left with a sense of
fulfillment, and Bruce clicked Alice onto the line.

"What's up?" he asked.

"Jesus, Bruce, it's finally happened. I put Dan on the plane
back to Des Moines day before yesterday, and this afternoon
Jeff called me!"

"That'll be a big relief for your brother — strange timing,
though. Almost as if the kid knew. I assume you told him his
dad's been out here."

"Of course I told him, but the first thing he made me do was
to promise not to tell Dan that he'd called me. Well, the long

and the short of it is that he's coming to dinner tonight. Bruce, do you think you could ... you and Frank, of course ... could you maybe join us? I'm sure you'll know best how to handle him. He's very stressed out 'cause Alfie's apparently disappeared. At least he's been missing for several days, and I'm sure that's what got Jeff upset enough that he called me."

"Sweetheart, you don't need to ask again. Just tell Maria to make one of her famous tamale pies, and I'll follow you anywhere." He paused, as if testing the waters, hoping his suggestion of lightness would have the right effect. Apparently it did.

"Eight o'clock, then," she said. The note of panic was less strident in her tone. "And thanks, Bruce. Anyone who can think of his stomach at a time like this has to have it together." She forced a ripple of nervous laughter, and hung up.

Bruce sat for several moments in puzzled thought. In truth, his stomach had not responded with the lust for tamale pie that he had pretended. A heavy lump had suddenly settled in the center of his gut, and despite his never having met Alfie he felt a strong sense of foreboding. The carnivorous streets of Hollywood had devoured many youngsters who had thought themselves omnipotent. At least Jeff had taken a step in the right direction — had enough sense to look for help when he seemed on the verge of being overwhelmed.

Dennie tapped on the door and came in. "What was that all about?" he asked.

"Jeff finally called Alice. Frank and I are supposed to be there for dinner to meet the kid and try to do what we can to help him."

"I don't envy you that job. Where's the punk been all this time?"

Bruce shrugged. "I didn't think to ask," he admitted. "At this point I don't think it makes much difference. Jeff called because his friend Alfie has disappeared."

"Where he's been might make a lot of difference, if something's happened to this Alfie character, and the cops involve the kid. No idea where he might have gone, huh?"

"Apparently not. I guess we'll find out as much as we can from Jeff, tonight. Oh, and by the way ... just in case Donovan calls, don't say anything to him. Alice promised Jeff she wouldn't tell his dad that the kid had called her."

"'Oh, what a tangled web we weave...'"

"Yeah, I know. I'm glad I don't have another patient scheduled this afternoon. I want to give all of this some thought, maybe make a few phone calls. Hollywood's really not that big. Someone has to know where those kids have been, what they've been doing — give us something to go on." He leaned back in his leather swivel chair and propped his feet up on the desk. He was turned halfway toward the sliding glass door, and absently watched the new gardener — "Huey" was the name he'd given Dennie — plodding about the backyard.

The big dark-haired youth was stripped down to just a pair of tattered cutoffs, squatting at the edge of lawn, cultivating the Hawaiian ferns. As he had done a number of times before, Bruce wondered what this guy's story really was. He arrived three times a week, apparently on foot. At least he didn't appear to arrive in a vehicle, unless someone was dropping him off at the corner. But every evening he simply left, and never seemed to be watching for anyone to come for him.

Well, that's the least of my worries right now, Bruce thought. *I wish I knew what the situation was with Jeff Donovan and his friend. Wonder if the kids were lovers. The old man wouldn't have known, wouldn't have wanted to know, probably. Regardless, they have to have been close, like brothers if not otherwise. Funny, though, their being here all this time, probably in Hollywood, and none of my guys ever got a clue as to where they were or what they were doing. Two good-looking kids like that, they'd have to attract attention if they were out and around unless ... Well, I'll probably get the answers tonight.*

■ ■ ■

Hugo had seen Bruce watching him through the window and felt a surge of pride, assuming the psychiatrist had been admiring his physical perfection. The man had not paid him a great deal of attention, he had to admit, but he was nevertheless convinced that his body was the object of everyone's admiration. After all, he was easily the most handsome man on the premises, except maybe for Frank. But Frank was small compared to Hugo — whom they all called "Huey," because he'd convinced them he was someone else — not the fugitive witness, wanted for questioning in the Orsini murders.

60

He preened inwardly, proud of his successful subterfuge, fooling all these bright, successful men. Not one of them suspected his true identity. His mind drifted again to Frank. The guy was no threat to him, in the sense of being stronger or more desirable, except that Hugo was passionately attracted to the smaller man. He realized that Frank and Bruce were lovers, and for that reason the little guy had never given him a tumble. He couldn't find it in his thoughts to hate Bruce, as he had so many others. But the man did stand in his way, in that Frank refused even to look in his direction while so hung up on the shrink.

Still, it had been Frank who had invited Hugo to "take a dip" when the rest of them enjoyed the pool before dinner. That had given Hugo a chance to display his powerful genitals, to strut this additional element of physical perfection before the others. Granted, he didn't have much on either Frank or Dennie, but then he'd never seen either of them hard. He wondered if he could best them, would really have liked to try. He'd especially like to play naughty-naughty with Frank, if only there were some way to get rid of Bruce long enough to do it. But Hugo couldn't think of any way to make this happen.

At the moment, he was enjoying Bruce's attention. He deliberately shifted his weight from one knee to the other, turning more so that his kneeling form was directly in the psychiatrist's line of sight. He felt his nuts slide past the fringed edge of denim, hanging free and in clear sight. He glanced up slyly, hoping to catch the other man's gaze on his crotch, but Bruce had turned partly away from him and was punching a number into the phone. With a shrug of annoyance, Hugo shoved his balls back inside his shorts, and the first real glimmer of hostility toward Bruce began to form in his mind.

■ ■ ■

"That shit, Haven Monroe's in town!" Frank said angrily. They were in Bruce's Mercedes, driving along Sunset Boulevard toward the Coast Highway and the Javitses' Malibu condo.

Bruce briefly glanced at his lover, then back at the traffic that was gradually thinning out as they started down the incline beyond Brentwood. "Are you sure? He hasn't been nosing around the house, I don't think. At least Dennie hasn't said anything about strangers, other than those goddamn builders!"

"No, he's supposed to be out here to cover the Orsini murders for that scandal sheet he works for — going to do some 'sensational lies,' as Rufus calls them. He's the one who tipped me off. So, with the Orsini house so close to yours, he has the perfect excuse to nose around the neighborhood. In fact, Rufus says he thinks the fucker's been here for a couple of weeks. I knew he'd left New Orleans before I did, but I just assumed he went back to his rat hole in D.C. Only, Rufus says he's already got one story in print on the Orsinis — headlined in his supermarket yellow pages." Frank's angry tirade trailed off as the Mercedes passed through the Palisades and they were able to see the setting sun through the screen of eucalyptus, reflecting brightly off the ocean.

"He probably doesn't know you're coming to the house," Bruce reminded him. "That isn't exactly common knowledge. And if he did find out, there are lots of reasons other than the real one. You could easily be a client, or just a friend stopping by to visit. He can't see into the bedroom, after all."

"He knows," Frank replied glumly. "At least, I'm pretty sure he does. My fault. I think he followed me home from Rufus's office tonight. I wasn't watching, and didn't spot him until I'd pulled in the driveway and was waiting for the garage door to go up. I happened to glance down the way, and there he was, turning around at the end of the cul-de-sac. Least, I think it was him. Looked like a rental car, but it had tinted glass and I couldn't be sure. But if it was, he not only saw me pull in, but knows I've got the electronic gismo to open your garage."

"I wondered why you were so upset when you came in." Bruce placed his hand reassuringly on Frank's thigh. "Why didn't you tell me sooner?"

Frank covered his friend's hand with his own. "Oh, you were busy winding up the paperwork with Dennie. Besides, I didn't want him to fly off the handle and go after the fucker."

"Well, I don't think he'd do that. We'll have to talk it over with him when we get home ... make sure he knows the guy's apt to show up on the front doorstep. Huey, too, for that matter. We don't want the kid inviting him in for a beer."

"Yeah, you're right," Frank sighed. "There's nothing I can do except try to stay out of Monroe's way, and hope he gets distracted enough with the Orsini case to forget about me."

"If he does show up, I'd love to sic Huey on him," Bruce laughed. "I think the kid's got a crush on you. He'd probably make mincemeat out of Monroe."

"Why do you think that — the kid having a crush, I mean?" Frank was grinning in spite of himself.

"Oh, just the way he watches you," Bruce told him. "Every time you come into view, he has to adjust his crotch. I think he'd like a little." With that, he gave his lover a forcible squeeze, then put both hands on the wheel as he turned off the highway, onto the street leading to Abe and Alice's.

Frank sat back in the leather bucket seat, saying nothing, but secretly pleased to think he had provoked such a heavy response from the handsome giant. He also indulged in a brief fantasy of the powerful youth doing some of the things he would enjoy having happen to the sleazy reporter.

FIVE

"**N**o, that's not quite the way it was, Jeff." Bruce stood facing the youngster, each of them leaning one arm against the bar in Abe and Alice's Malibu townhouse. "Because your father was so upset over the way he treated you, he came out here to try finding you and setting things straight between you. The fact that I tried to help him find you doesn't mean that I'm 'on his side.'" But even as he said it, Bruce again had the feeling that Dan Donovan had not told him the complete story, the full reason for his prolonged trip to Los Angeles.

"He's telling the truth," added Alice from her place beside Frank on the long white sofa. "Bruce wouldn't even agree to help Dan until your dad promised not to try forcing you to do anything you didn't want to do."

"But, why'd he go to a shrink, anyway, when your husband's a police commissioner?" Jeff demanded. "Seems to me, it would've been a lot easier for Uncle Abe to find me than it would've been for him," he added, inclining his head toward Bruce.

"You hadn't done anything that would make the police interested in finding you," said Bruce. "Even a missing-persons report wouldn't mean much when a nineteen-year-old man decides to leave home and go out on his own. Your father hoped — erroneously, as it turned out — that I might have had the contacts to find you. I know a lot of people who are into the gay underground, so to speak, and..."

Jeff's handsome features blushed a bright scarlet, and he looked as if he were about to bolt from the room. "I really didn't want to get into all that! The big hassle — it was just Dad's idea, because he didn't understand where I was coming from," he blustered. "I mean, why did he have to assume all those things about me, without even asking me if it was true?"

"But it is true," said Bruce evenly, gesturing with his hand to stop Jeff's imminent denial. "Look, Abe and your Aunt Alice are my best friends, and they know I'm gay. Frank and I..."

"Oh, shit, I don't believe this!" Jeff's color was gradually returning to normal, but his level of anxiety was clearly rising. "You guys just trapped me into this! I wondered why Aunt Alice invited an extra couple of people. What are you trying to do to me?" The bright blue eyes seemed to flash, as if somehow reflecting the handsome young man's anger.

"We're only trying to help you, son," said Abe. He was seated on a bar stool that he had pulled out from the counter until it was almost opposite the spot where Bruce was standing. No taller than Jeff, Abe was about forty, had a wiry build, with salt-and-pepper hair and rather handsome, sharp features. "You're upset because your friend's disappeared. We'll try to help you find him. You've also been surviving in this town without friends and without much money, and believe me, I know how tough that is. If you want any other kind of help that we're able to give you, we'll do that, too. Whether you want to see your father or not, that's up to you. But Alice invited Bruce and Frank here tonight, because she thought they would be the people most likely to be able to give you the kind of assistance, or advice, whatever—" He broke off as he saw that Jeff was swallowing hard, and that his eyes had started to glisten.

"No one, *no one's* given me anything, unless he got something from me — not since I left home," Jeff said, groping for the words, yet still saying more than he had probably intended.

It was almost as if he had projected the thought into a group of telepathic receptives. *The kid's telling us he's been working the streets. What else did he have to give but his body?* And in about the same moment, Jeff realized the implication of his words, and once again his face turned a bright red.

"It doesn't matter," said Bruce. "We all do what we have to do to survive. Later, we may look back on it as a bad period in our lives, but we also know that our behavior *then* has made

65

it possible for us to be here *now*. In the long run, that's all that matters; at least it's all that's important, assuming we haven't hurt other people along the way."

"You mean my folks?"

"I wasn't thinking so much about them," Bruce admitted, "although they would certainly have to be considered. But no, I was really thinking in more general terms, not about anyone in particular. Of course, it's only natural you'd be concerned about your folks, and Alfie."

"You don't think I did anything to him?" asked Jeff, his tone and expression so obviously stricken, it was impossible to doubt him.

"Unfortunately, that could become a problem if the police get into this," Abe explained. "Most line officers aren't very understanding when it comes to dealing with homosexual men. It's something we've been trying to change, but there's still a basic Neanderthal mentality on the part of many cops. They're going to question your relationship — which I assume was sexual in addition to whatever else it might have been—" Another blush came to Jeff's cheeks in confirmation of his words. "—and if they once establish that as fact, they'll scratch up his disappearance to 'lovers' spat' and forget about it, unless..." He broke off, not wanting to pursue the next most obvious line of reasoning.

"You mean if something's happened to Alfie, if he's ... he's dead..." Jeff swallowed hard again, forcing the word to form on his lips. "...then I'm going to be the big suspect."

"But that's not just because he's gay," Frank broke in. He had thus far remained a silent witness to the exchange, sitting next to Alice on the sofa.

"What's that supposed to mean?" asked Abe.

"Well, there was a lot of dialogue about it in my old TV series. Most murders are committed by spouses: husbands or wives, or by lovers. And it doesn't matter if they're gay or het. The point is, if something's happened to Alfie, they're naturally going to question Jeff. But that's as far as it's going to go unless they find some evidence to substantiate—"

"This is getting into a needlessly morbid discussion," said Bruce, interrupting as he watched the play of distress on Jeff's even features. "There's no reason to assume that anything's happened to Alfie. The problem right now is how to help Jeff cope with his present situation."

"Yes, Jeff, what *do* you want to do — assuming, you know, assuming everything's equal?" Alice asked. And seeing the youngster's evident indecision, she patted the place next to herself on the sofa. "You come over here and talk to Frank and me for a few minutes. We haven't had a visit since you were a little boy. Frank went through a difficult period when he first came to town, too. He certainly understands where you're coming from."

With only a brief hesitation, Jeff did as he was asked, settling on the sofa between Alice and Frank. Despite himself, he was soon in an animated, almost whispered conversation with his aunt and Bruce's lover. Sensing that Alice had probably guessed the most sensible approach, Bruce and Abe started their own discourse at the bar.

"So, I understand Frank's having a problem with that reporter, Monroe," said Abe.

"He was, back in New Orleans. So far, the asshole hasn't done anything out here. Not yet, anyway, although Frank thinks someone followed him to my place just this evening. But he's not a hundred percent sure."

"Monroe *is* out here," said Abe unexpectedly. "And that *is* for sure. He was at the Commission meeting, yesterday, and interviewed one of the other members afterward. He's been bugging my secretary for an appointment with me."

"You going to talk to him?" asked Bruce.

"I don't know," Abe replied. "Probably. Only because there isn't any graceful way out of it."

"Best be on your guard," Bruce cautioned.

"You know it!" Abe agreed. "For an up-front gay, he has some very strange political credentials. The bastard hates liberals — considers A.C.L.U. membership as about the same as belonging to the Communist Party. He thinks that Gay Republicans offer the only solution for the movement, but doesn't think a man should conceal his sexuality, even if it means losing his job. In a word, I think he's a bit of a nut."

"He's the kind of theoretically correct, but functionally misguided idiot who drove me out of active participation in gay politics," Bruce returned. "Hopefully, in fifty years, his ideas will be practical. Right now, they're just destructive."

"In the meantime, what are you going to do about him? If he really did tail Frank, your relationship might be enough to confirm his suspicions. You're just far enough out of the closet that Frank's spending the night at your house would do it — to say nothing of the scenes of domestic bliss he might observe around the swimming pool."

Bruce laughed. "If he ever sets foot on my property, Rudy'll tear him to pieces."

"That'll be the day. Silly mutt's never attacked anything more dangerous than a sausage since Frank got him."

"Are you making libelous remarks about my dog?" asked Frank from behind them. He had gotten up and come to the bar for a refill. "I'll have you know, Rudy's a reformed character — a certified graduate of doggie charm school. But that bastard reporter!" he said, abruptly shifting subjects — and tone. "Well it's such a nice evening, why don't we forget about Monroe the Misfit, and pump our inside contact for some poop on the neighborhood scandal."

"What scan—? Oh, you mean the Orsini murders?" Abe returned, moving behind the bar to freshen up everyone's drink. "I guess there's no secret. It'll be on the late news tonight. The detectives have given up on the Mafia angle, and although there's still some question as to whether it might be the Colombians, there isn't any evidence. They picked up the two kids this afternoon — the sons."

"The two boys?" Bruce reacted with some surprise. "That's really hard for me to accept, that they'd garrote their own parents. Shoot them, maybe, poison them, even. Anything that was either quick or overtly 'nonviolent.' But—"

"I know," Abe agreed. "I haven't been right on top of the case, just hearing the usual rumors. But I get the impression there's an enormous amount of pressure from the studio people — not so much to 'find the killers of their friends and colleagues,' but rather to resolve the organized crime issue. You know, Hollywood's very sensitive to this, ever since the Bugsy Siegel–Mickey Cohen era."

"To say nothing of that wonderful scene from *The God-father,*" Frank said, "where the producer wakes up with the horse's head in bed with him."

Abe smiled grimly. "Well, be that as it may, there was a lot of smoke and no fire, as far as the Orsinis' being involved with drug dealers was concerned. They were originally refugees from Castro's Cuba, and appeared to have financial ties to some suspicious sources in the Caribbean. But no one could make the connection with any funny money, let alone dope, which I think was the initial suspicion. So, eliminate the mob, and that leaves the boys, since it obviously wasn't a burglary. There just isn't anyone else. They were looking for a young kid who worked part-time around the house — the cook, or house-keeper's son — but he was never really a suspect. Might have seen something, though. In fact, they'd still like to interview him. The really serious suspicion, now, has fallen on the two sons — one or both. I don't think they've zeroed in on that, yet."

"That's interesting," Bruce remarked. "I hadn't been following the case in the papers, particularly, and I didn't pick up on the mob theories except that Dennie made some mention of it. But the garroting thing. That's an old Mafia murder technique, not something you'd look for from the Colombians or other Latin American dope merchants. I did a little piece on this in one of my FBI profiles. The practice has been common in Italy — Sicily, particularly, and, of course, in the Orient — in India by the Thugees, by some of the Chinese mafia equivalents. The point, though, Abe, is that the act of garroting someone is a physically difficult feat — especially if the victim is awake, conscious at the time. It would be a rather grisly thing for a kid to do to his parents."

"So," Abe said, "in your professional opinion, it's unlikely for a kid to garrote his folks?" Again the grim laugh. "I'm sure our investigators are aware of this — probably the reason they didn't pick the boys up sooner. But, of course, now that you've put your foot in it, how would you like to interview them — officially, for the Department? We'd just like your professional opinion as to whether either of them has the balls to have done it."

"You trapped me, you bastard!" Bruce's exclamation was just loud enough to attract everyone's attention. He laughed and continued in a more modulated tone: "Did you have this in mind all the time?"

"Actually, I hadn't really thought about it until just this minute," Abe told him, "but you *are* on retainer, so we might as well get our money's worth out of you."

"Okay," Bruce agreed. "But let's wait a few days and see if they elect to hold them or not. If the detectives decide to kick them loose, I'd rather interview them in my office than in the zoo."

"I think you may get your wish," Abe told him. "My best sense of this is that they're hoping to shake the kids up, just in case there *is* something to connect them. Or to jar their memories in the event they're innocent, but know something they haven't thought to tell us. There's nothing like a night or two in the slammer to make a guy regain his memory — fast!"

"That seems a rather extreme effort," Bruce remarked.

"It is," Abe agreed, "but the D.A. refuses to file charges, yet; so the chief ordered them to pick the kids up while the case goes to the grand jury. He's concerned they might skip, because there's apparently a lot of money stashed in several Latin American countries. Of course, it'll all come to nothing if they don't get an indictment."

"What's your make on that?"

"They'll get knocked on their collective asses," Abe told him. "I'd guess the kids are out in under a week. With Mickey Halloran defending them, maybe a lot sooner than that. And by the by, when you get them in your little leather-lined web, don't make the same mistake the shrink in the Menendez case made."

"Tapes?"

"Yeah, no tapes," Abe replied. "If there're no tapes, there's no physical evidence, no subpoena, no battle to the steps of the Supreme Court. It keeps it simpler all around."

"And cheaper," Bruce laughed.

"Much," Abe agreed.

"All right, you two," said Alice. "That's about enough professional nonsense for tonight. What are we going to do about Jeff's problem?" She paused and looked fondly at her nephew. "And I really don't like having you stay in that dreadful part of town," she added. "I know you probably wouldn't want to stay way out here in Malibu, but we have a lovely small apartment in Century City. You'd be welcome to use that. Abe sleeps there

70

once in a while when he has to work late, or we stay there on a heavy theater night."

"It's my 'official residence,'" Abe added, "for political purposes."

"Gee, that's real nice of you, Aunt Alice," Jeff replied, "but I've gotta stay where I am until Alfie gets back. Otherwise he won't know where to find me. And, well, if he needs help and tries to call — you know."

"I don't think it makes too much difference where you stay for the moment," Bruce remarked, "but I think it *is* important that you keep in close touch with your aunt, with all of us, for that matter. And you should also give some thought to easing your parents' anxiety."

"Jeff's already agreed to have dinner with us tomorrow night," said Frank. "That'll give us a chance to talk about things again." He did not have to add the unspoken thought that Alice — while having broken the ice, so to speak — was now a somewhat inhibiting presence for Jeff.

"Fine," Bruce agreed. "And if Alfie shows up by then, bring him along."

"Go early, and you can all have a swim," Alice added, her slightly malicious remark followed by a silvery tinkle of laughter. The fact that no one ever wore swimsuits in Bruce's pool made it clear she had also picked up on her dichotomous role — extending an invitation which, coming from any of the others, might have seemed slightly provocative.

■ ■ ■

Hugo drew his powerful body into a tight ball, making himself as small as possible. Lights from the neighborhood patrol unit were moving across the wall toward the window just above his head. They did this every night, usually several times; but they never tried to enter. They were also noisy, because their car had a defective muffler, and the iron gates at the foot of the drive squeaked when they opened. But that worried Hugo, because he knew the gates were kept locked, and if the patrol guys had keys for that lock, they probably could enter the house if they wanted to.

But, in a way, having them come by was a relief. Once they had been here, Hugo knew he had at least a couple of hours before they'd return. That gave him time to use the kitchen stove, and even to watch a little TV on the set in the dining alcove. Although he had the whole house to himself, he somehow felt more comfortable if he stayed in the kitchen and the small rooms connecting through the butler's pantry — the servants' quarters. It seemed not only appropriate that he should place this restriction on himself, simply as a matter of propriety; but he reasoned that should his presence be detected, no one would be as angry with him if they knew he had not intruded into the elegantly furnished rooms beyond the kitchen.

He had hardly left the grounds since the night he had fled the Orsinis' and taken refuge here, in the big house at the end of the cul-de-sac, next door to Bruce MacLeod. He had no car; but he had found a bicycle in the garage, and had used it a few times to pedal down to the small market–liquor store. It had taken him a couple of days to figure out that the best time would be at dusk, when he was less likely to be noticed in the dim light and during the rush of homebound commuters. In bright daylight, someone could recognize him more easily, and if he waited until later, he would likely be picked up by the police or private security patrols that were constantly moving through the area of large residences.

On the night when his former employers had been murdered, and he had needed a place to hide, he'd slipped through the alleys behind the big houses on the other side of the arroyo, and made his way up here. He knew this area better than some of the others, because he'd explored it with Paul Orsini all those many months ago. The old Tudor mansion on the dead-end street was closed up and deserted except for the security patrol and the groundskeepers who came three times a week. Hugo had no way of knowing it, but Bruce MacLeod's neighbors had decided to stay in their Hawaiian condo until the aggravating construction project was completed next door.

Then Hugo had been lucky once again, a couple of days after settling into the empty house. Hearing voices from the next yard, he had crept close enough to eavesdrop on the conversation. The plantings on both sides of the fence had been so heavy, there was little chance of his being seen. He heard the good-looking doctor who owned the place talking with the aged

Latino gardener. The old man was telling his employer that he had to quit, because he was getting too old to do the work. Both his sons were in school full-time, and now the immigration people were threatening to put a man in jail if he hired someone who didn't have a green card. So, at the moment he had no one to help him. He'd do the best he could to find Bruce a replacement, but he didn't know how successful he was going to be. And that had given Hugo the idea. He knew about the house and the people in it, because Paul had taken him up to the hill above the property one night the previous summer, well after the end of their affair, but as an effort to prove he still regarded the big, good-looking kid as a friend.

"I used to have a hideaway up here when I was a boy," Paul had explained. "I took a walk one night, and just out of curiosity I climbed the fence to see if it was still there. It wasn't, but I saw something much more interesting."

Paul had gone on to describe the various attractive men he had watched swimming naked on several different occasions. Nothing had been happening that particular evening when he took Hugo, but out of curiosity the big guy had started going back on his own, especially after Hugo and his mom had moved into the apartment above the Orsinis' garage.

For some time, Ruth Orsini had been trying to persuade Emma Fitzpatrick, Hugo's mother, to take over the small suite of rooms on the property. Emma had resisted, because she felt it would rob her of a certain autonomy. However, the old apartment house where she and Hugo had been living was sold, and the new owners planned to tear the place down. Finally, Emma agreed to move in, and thus Hugo became a resident on the estate.

For the first few months, this made things much easier for the two boys — Hugo and Paul — to get together and enjoy their rituals, with only an occasional interruption by Rupert. Finally, however, the affair began to cool down, at least on Paul's part. The final end came one night when he had submitted to Hugo, and asked to be gagged and hooded. This proved a serious mistake, because he was unable to communicate with the hulking youth, despite their having agreed ahead of time that his "distress signal" would be to make his body completely rigid. Unfortunately, this subtlety was lost on Hugo.

Once the smaller boy was strapped down, naked except for the leather hood on his head, and the bindings on his wrists and ankles, Hugo had proceeded to lash him with increasing intensity — first using a wide belt, then switching to a riding crop. This latter appliance was a new acquisition, and even the first, relatively light blow sent a searing pain through the bound and helpless subject. The second and third were enough for Paul to attempt signaling his distress, but the dull light and tight bondage would have made the rigidity of the body difficult to discern, even for a more practiced hand. It was completely lost on Hugo. And what sound he might have heard from the gagged and muted mouth was completely absorbed by the disco music.

As a result, Paul sustained such a severe beating, he was literally unable to sit for several days. His back was also seriously lacerated. At first he had been angry, but he knew he really had only himself to blame, and in the end he forgave his self-created Top. Still, he vowed never to submit to Hugo again, and despite an occasional craving for the big kid's touch, he stuck with his decision.

However, he still felt a certain responsibility for Hugo, and he employed him as helper in his burgeoning business of making department store mannequins. He had already rented the house in Echo Park, but had also maintained his workshop on the grounds of the family estate. In truth, he preferred to do his work at home, using the house for his sexual escapades, where neither his brother nor Hugo would know. Thus, the discontinuance of their sexual exchanges had a minimal effect on Paul, who was finding his solace elsewhere. For Hugo, it was more difficult. Living on the estate, and having no car of his own, it was nearly impossible to make other contacts, even if he had known how to go about it.

As a result of all this, especially when Paul became too preoccupied with other things to pay much attention to Hugo, the powerful youth had started going off by himself, climbing the chain-link fence, then lying on the bed of pine needles to watch the uninhibited goings-on in Bruce's pool. Once secure in the knowledge that he was unlikely to be discovered, he would strip himself as naked as his quarry, and slowly masturbate as he savored this private show.

Now, having persuaded the big bearded guy who ran the household to hire him as the replacement gardener, he felt a peculiar sense of closeness — almost a proprietary interest in the doctor and his very handsome lover. He had watched them so many times since the previous year, as they had disported themselves in the pool, that they seemed almost like his own personal possessions. After all, it *was* his secret, his alone, because Paul was completely disinterested. And no one else was even aware of the secret place above their backyard. In just the few weeks he had worked for them, he had come to feel very close to each of the three men who lived in the house. They had all been nice to him, and at one time or another each had taken the time to engage him in conversation — something no one except Paul had ever done at the Orsini place. And although they were all very openly gay, none had made a pass at Hugo. That, of course, was a two-sided coin. On the one hand, he took it as a sign of respect that no one sought to take advantage of him. On the other, he found each of them attractive, and would have enjoyed a little action.

Of them all, though, it was Frank for whom Hugo had developed a special feeling. First, there was the basic physical attraction, which in the beginning had been almost a painful lust. However, the big kid soon recognized the bond between Frank and the doctor as something very solid. The activities he had witnessed the previous summer, he now realized, were the initial stages of a relationship that still remained strong — and exclusive. Because of this, knowing how Frank felt about Bruce, some of the devotion he felt for the one was initially transferred to the other. Hugo could not have explained the finer nuances, but he felt a bond with both men. And although his feelings might change in time — as he became more fixated on the handsome young actor and came to perceive Bruce as a barrier to his lustful desires — for the moment, he felt something akin to love for the one, and a grudging sense of loyalty to the other.

The schedule Hugo had established for working at Bruce's house had been calculated to keep him next door while the gardeners who maintained the grounds about the empty house were on the property. In order to avoid these other workmen, he occasionally had to delay his departure from Bruce's house until Bruce and the others were finished with their daily labors, and came outside to relax. A few times he had even been invited to join them in the pool, or simply to use it on his own — as long as the doctor did not have patients or other visitors in the house. And these were fabulously exciting moments for Hugo. He enjoyed being naked, knowing that his body made other men envious. And he enjoyed seeing the others in a similar condition. So Hugo felt very contented, convinced that he had achieved a successful transition — sure that no one was going to discover who he was. His identity as the "Huey" who now worked for Doctor MacLeod was clearly not the "Hugo" who had once worked for the Orsinis.

Now, Mr. and Mrs. Orsini were dead, and both their sons were in jail. He'd seen that on the television, and it pleased him. Rupert had always treated him like a shit, and after the way Paul had been shining him on lately ... well, he deserved it, too. Fuck 'em both! Of course, the situation with Paul had been partly Hugo's fault. He knew he'd hurt Paul that last time they'd had sex. But how was he supposed to know? Stiffening his body! Shit! But that had been almost two years ago, and now Paul acted like he and Hugo had never been anything but friends, as if they had never had sex, had never been lovers. So now Hugo hated him!

And Hugo knew how to hate. In fact, his greatest pleasure was to get by himself — either when he was working, or when he was lying in bed, waiting for sleep to claim him at night — and picture in his mind's eye each of the people he hated. Then he would imagine the terrible punishments he would like to inflict upon them.

It was a wonderfully satisfying pastime, and Hugo never tired of it. There were so many potential victims on his mental roster — everyone he'd ever known, or almost everyone. Except the three guys in the house. They were the only ones whom Hugo might spare — them and Rudy, partly because the big Lab was Frank's dog and he knew Frank loved him. But also because Rudy really liked Hugo, and it was the first time in his life that any animal had responded to him with positive enthusiasm.

Hugo's other fantasy, more recently inaugurated, involved Frank. Although he had watched this object of his adoration from a distance, long before ever encountering him in person, this newfound passion had begun to develop only after their initial conversation. It wasn't simply Frank's good looks that inspired these powerful sentiments in Hugo. It was the perception of a spiritual, almost godly being contained within those glorious bodily contours that now held Hugo in total servitude. His passion — though undeniably physical — was even more strongly a true devotion. While in his intellectually barren life Hugo had absorbed little by way of formal education, he did know the great tales of chivalry — of Tristram and of Lancelot. From his mother's renderings he was intimately aware of these epics; then his own readings from the "classic" comic books — all those heroes who protected the innocent. It was thus his great fantasy grew more elaborate each night, as he continued to add further refinements. He saw himself as Frank's protector — his knight — albeit in somewhat tattered denim instead of gleaming armor.

In keeping with this dream to one day render Frank some life-preserving service, Hugo reasoned that he could accept Bruce as the physical companion of his hero, because Bruce made Frank happy. As long as that condition persisted, Hugo was content to watch from the sidelines without any attempt to fulfill his own physical cravings — again, because he knew that were he to do this he would make the object of all this devotion unhappy. It would probably also result in his being fired from his gardening job, and that would deprive him of the opportunity to observe his idol every day.

Instead, he would crawl into his bed in the servants' quarters next door to the house where he knew Frank was sleeping with Bruce. He would imagine Frank alone in some dank and overgrown wood. He would be naked and lost, unable to find his way in the darkness and pursued by some dreadful demon. After he had stumbled and fallen, exhausted and barely able to keep going, Hugo would appear from the shadows — also naked, except for his helmet and buckler, and carrying his huge, razor-sharp sword. He would take his stance between Frank and the pursuing horror, and after a ferocious battle, defeat the hideous beast.

Then he would lift Frank's slender, battered body in his arms and bear him into the golden hall, where Sir Hugo ruled as chieftain, and where his servants scurried to obey his every command. He would place Frank on a silk-covered dais, where beautiful unadorned slave boys would tend his wounds. Then the two of them would swim together in the warm, scented pool, their naked bodies pressing together, their lips meeting in a series of searing exchanges. His own powerful cock would press itself between Frank's thighs, until the smaller man would beg to take it.

Then Hugo would carry him from the underground grotto, into an opulent bedroom, furnished in black leather, with several hooded slaves to assist in their exchange. Hugo would order Frank to be bound upright into an open frame, arms and legs spread wide, so that every part of his body was accessible. As the benevolent Master he would then tantalize Frank's body, caressing the tightly corded muscles, teasing the nipples with his tongue, chewing gently on the nubs until he brought his beloved subject to the verge of pain, stroking the writhing body as it sought escape. He would go onto his knees, giving his lover the full benefit of all he had learned from the Orsini brothers. He would service the big ripe genitals, as he had always hesitated to do with the others. He would run his tongue up under the foreskin, tease the testicles, pull them into the base of the sac, then twist them slowly until the first spasms of pain caused the victim to twist away from him.

All these things he would do, and in the end Frank would fall into his arms, professing his love and his willingness to accept Hugo's protection from all the evils that might threaten him. The great, powerful body would always be there to assure Frank's welfare. And one day, Hugo knew, he would somehow find a way to display his devotion in reality, although he might never be able to equal the dramatic depths of his mental imagery.

S I X

Bruce's last patient left on schedule, just before three in the afternoon. Frank had stayed over when he and Bruce returned from the Javitses' the previous evening — since, as Bruce had put it, "You got me into having the kid for dinner. You better be here to help referee the match."

"What's the matter? Can't Beverly Hills' finest therapist handle one nineteen-year-old Greek god?" Frank had teased.

To which Bruce had replied, in a surprisingly serious tone: "Even if I weren't happy with what I have, and despite the kid's very obvious physical attributes, I'd be a bit antsy playing with him." And at a raised eyebrow from Dennie, who had joined them for a nightcap, he continued: "First, I'd bet the kid's been selling his ass for a couple of months in Hollywood, which would make me apprehensive about his HIV status. Secondly, his old man spent almost two months practically camping on my doorstep, hoping I'd pull off some miracle of sleuthing to find his little boy. I'd feel like a child molester."

"Dirty old man is more like it," Dennie had chided.

"Well," Frank had said, getting up and linking one arm through Bruce's. "I'm taking my dirty old man off to bed."

That had been the previous evening. Now, with the last patient gone and the house to themselves again, Frank joined Bruce on the deck beside the pool. "Well, what did you do with yourself today, while I was trying to make an honest dollar?" asked the doctor.

"I slipped out for a while this morning," Frank told him. "They were having sales at a couple of stores, so I went in to look around. I've been so busy for so long, I needed to pick up a few things to keep me from greeting my public in tatters." He laughed at Bruce's scornful expression. "Well, you can't expect a star to appear in the same outfit all the time," he responded. "Come on, let's go for a dip," he added, slipping off his shorts. He stood for a moment beside the pool, in profile to Bruce ... slender body outlined briefly against dark green foliage, heavy genitals swaying with his every motion. Then he turned and dove headfirst into the water.

He came up sputtering, kicking his feet frog-fashion to keep his head above the surface, as he used both hands to press back his hair. Bruce, who had been wearing his usual "counseling slacks and shirt," was standing crane-fashion on one foot as he slipped off a shoe. Frank laughed, and suppressed the urge to splash him. Then, spotting "Huey" at the side of the house in his denim cutoffs — watching, but trying not to do it conspicuously — Frank called out to him, inviting the young man to join them.

Huey/Hugo came up to the pool, moving lithely with an athletic, cat-like grace, despite his bulk. He grinned sheepishly at Bruce, who was now removing his shirt, then paused a moment at the edge of the water, seeming to await his employer's approval before accepting Frank's invitation. Bruce laughed and clapped him on the shoulder. "Go ahead, Big Boy," he said. "We've seen it all before."

Hugo blushed, forced a grin, and unfastened the waistband of his denims, allowing them to drop around his ankles. As he stepped out of them he couldn't resist a pulling adjustment at his cock and balls, unsticking them from his sweaty thighs, allowing his powerful, uncircumcised manhood to hang out at its full potency, an unspoken challenge to the display Frank had made just moments before. He walked the few feet to the poolside shower and rinsed the worst of the grime from his body under the cold stream, before stepping gingerly into the pool at the shallow end. He was still trying to lower himself into the chill water when Bruce tossed aside his slacks and briefs, then quickly followed Frank into the deep end. Although normally unconcerned about his own ability to make an adequate genital display, he could not help but feel a bit overwhelmed by the exceptional, uncut endowments of his two companions.

The two lovers swam for fifteen minutes or so, then climbed out to lie on towels tossed across the recliners at poolside, while Hugo continued to swim laps in the pool. As if on cue, Dennie arrived with a tray containing a pitcher of "slightly spiked" lemonade, glasses, and some guacamole made from the fruit off Bruce's avocado trees. Frank had sat up to accept the glass Dennie was holding out to him, when he happened to glance up, his attention caught by a sudden, brief flash of light on the hillside above them.

"What the fuck!"

"Frank? What's the matter?" asked Bruce, startled by the exclamation and the angry expression on Frank's handsome features.

"I think I just busted a crown," he said loudly, poking about his mouth with a finger; but as he lay back he added just loudly enough for Bruce to hear him, "Somebody's up on that hillside. Don't look up for a second." He reached for his mirrored sunglasses, put them on, and lay back on the lounge. "Just as I thought," he muttered after a couple of minutes. "It's that fucking son of a bitch Haven Monroe up there," he said, "taking pictures! I caught a reflection of sunlight off the camera. Get your fuckin' ass offa there!" he shouted, bolting to his feet. Rudy started to bark, charging toward the hill, where he ran back and forth at the base of the steep, ivy-covered slope in helpless frustration. The intruder had already retreated into the brush. Bruce's backyard stretched some twenty-five feet beyond the pool, at which point the ground made a nearly vertical ascent of about thirty ivy-covered feet, before flattening out onto the upper lot. The only way to reach this higher level from Bruce's house was to go around via several streets, and to approach the area from the opposite side.

"I'll take care of that!" said Dennie, snatching up his jeans and starting toward the side gate.

"It's no use," Frank told him. "He knows we've spotted him; he'll be long gone before you can get around the hill." The three of them shared a moment of silent frustration, standing in naked helplessness, staring up at the now-deserted hillside.

"Ain't that a pisser!" said Dennie, sitting dejectedly on a chair beside the water. "You sure it was that Monroe asshole?"

"Yeah, I only got a quick glimpse of him, but I'd know that shithead anyplace," Frank replied.

"Unfortunately, he also got a good look at us," Bruce added. "Of course, there's nothing very incriminating about a couple of guys skinny-dipping in a private pool. I just wonder how long he's been fucking around up on that hillside." Bruce was quiet for several seconds. "I don't know that there's been too much for him to see," he continued thoughtfully. "Not since Frank got back here, except for the first couple of days," he added, "but I doubt he'd had time to discover the place that fast."

"He's still out to crucify me," Frank sighed, "and even the little he's seen today, and for how many other days he's been up there, it's going to be enough to—"

"I should have guessed," Bruce growled. "Abe told me the bastard had been in town since before you got back, staying at the Fountaine Royale, that little hotel just over the line by West Hollywood."

"That puts him right on our doorstep, for sure," Dennie agreed. "But didn't you say he was supposed to be out here to do a number on the Orsini murders?"

"That's what Abe told me, and he's apparently done a couple of pieces — one, for sure. Abe told me about it last night. Monroe was claiming he had evidence that it was an organized crime — execution slaying. So, maybe that's his excuse for being here; but he's obviously obsessed with outing Frank."

"Why can't the fucking bastard leave me alone?" Frank wailed in desperation. "All these years of work and waiting ... and I'm right on the verge, and now this dirty, miserable bastard!"

"What did you ever do to the son of a bitch?" Dennie asked, his question obviously intended to be rhetorical.

To both his and Bruce's surprise, Frank replied: "Ugly little troll! He made a pass at me when I first got to New Orleans, and I told him to get lost." He dropped dejectedly onto the plastic chair beside Dennie's.

"Hell hath no fire like a troll denied," Dennie muttered.

All three of them grinned, despite their varying degrees of anger and outrage. "The guy is so far beyond any civilized limits," Bruce said, "it's hard to know how to handle him. But, since the cat's more or less out of the bag, anyway," he continued slowly, "why don't I go by tomorrow and see him? Maybe I can talk some sense into him."

Frank sat up, sighing again, shaking his head. "I think a lot of people have tried to persuade him to show a little decency in the past, and it's never done any good. But you're right, it can't hurt to try. Except, I'd lay money you don't accomplish anything. I'm afraid it's just a matter of time before he drops the bomb on me."

"What's he going to do?" asked Hugo. He was still in the pool, his chin resting on his arms as he hung from the rim. His bright, uncomplicated expression bespoke such open innocence that Bruce, who couldn't help smiling at him, had the urge to pat his head.

Instead, he petted Rudy, who had stationed himself beside the small table where Dennie had left the hors d'oeuvres. "The man who was up on the hillside," Bruce explained, "is a nosy reporter — a man who's gay himself, but tries to make everybody else who's gay admit it in public. He's after Frank right at the moment, and we're afraid he's going to publish a story on him."

"That's not fair," said Hugo.

"No, it certainly isn't," Frank agreed. "I've been trying to avoid him ever since I was in New Orleans. Now he's followed me out here." And even as Frank was speaking, Bruce thought he detected a subtle change in the big kid's previously open expression — the silvery eyes taking on a harder aspect, more like a wolf than the big puppy he had seemed a few moments before.

■ ■ ■

Jeff's pickup pulled into Bruce's drive a few minutes after 7:00 p.m. Alfie was not with him. Dennie answered his ring at the front door and led him back into the den, overlooking the pool. Although the three occupants of the house had all pulled on shorts and t-shirts, they were still attired in proper Southern California "poolside" informality.

"Well," said Bruce, rising to greet his guest, "you made it okay. Did you have any trouble finding the house?"

"No, Frank's directions were right on the mark. But, what are all the cop cars doing down that street a few blocks over from here?"

"Are they back again? That's the place where the Orsini murders took place," Dennie explained. "Every few days they get a wild hair up their butts, and come back to search for something they think they missed the time before."

"Boy, that's really a big case, isn't it?" Jeff responded, taking a seat in a big leather chair next to Frank's.

"It's got them running around, chasing their tails," Frank told him. "They can't figure out whether it was the kids, the Mafia, Colombian drug dealers, or some unholy combination of all the above."

"Have they come questioning you guys?" asked the youngster.

"No, why should they?" Bruce replied, somewhat surprised at the naivete of the question.

"Well, you live so close. I thought they might have come to ask if you'd seen anything ... you know."

"Actually, they did," Dennie replied unexpectedly. "Informally. I was just taking Rudy out for his evening constitutional — when Bruce was down at the Center with his counseling group. This black-and-white stopped me about a block from the house, and they wanted to know if we'd seen or heard anything on the night of the murders. I talked to them for fifteen minutes or so. Kid driving the car was kinda hot, so it wasn't too painful an experience."

"You're becoming a notorious lecher!" said Frank, getting up and turning toward Jeff. "We don't often entertain a minor," he continued, "but what can we offer you to drink?"

"Well, if you don't think we'll get raided, I might have a brew." He grinned at Dennie, who had moved into the doorway to the kitchen. The big man looked a bit uncertain.

"I think we can risk it," Bruce said.

"I promise not to get drunk and take advantage of you," laughed Jeff, his gaze still locked on Dennie's muscular bulk.

With a grunt of feigned displeasure, the big man turned into the kitchen, where he was soon rattling ice and glasses, pouring beer for Jeff, and mixing drinks for everyone else. Bruce broke this momentary pause in the conversation with a more serious comment. "I guess you still haven't heard from Alfie?"

"No," Jeff told him, "and I'm really worried. He's been gone almost five days; I can't imagine where he could be."

"I surmised — at your aunt's house — that you were being a little evasive regarding your ... er, activities since coming to town," said Bruce. "Since we went to quite a bit of trouble trying to find you — both of you — I assume you weren't 'on the street.'" He paused, then, hoping Jeff would trust them enough to open up a bit.

"You know, Bruce, I don't care if you guys know the whole story, but please don't tell Aunt Alice or — God forbid — my father. See, he thinks Alfie and me, that we were involved in some kind of S&M ring back in Iowa. At least that was his term, all because he saw some drawings I did. But that's not the situation at all. I mean, on my own ... oh, shit. I don't know how to say all this."

"Maybe if we explain a little more of our own situation, it'll be easier for you," Frank suggested, glancing at Bruce, who nodded agreement. Jeff was watching him expectantly, and Frank continued. "You know we're all gay," he began, "but more than that, all three of us are into the types of things you depicted in your sketches," and at a look of consternation from the youngster, he went on: "Not in a *ménage à trois*. Bruce and I have been together for a little over a year. Dennie's on his own."

"But seldom alone," Bruce quipped. "In other words, we're not a group to be shocked, no matter what you've done, or had to do." He stopped and waited for Jeff to respond.

"Just by accident, right at the beginning," Jeff began, "I got it on with a guy who was really into some very weird SM action. He had a place down on the other side of town, a real dungeon setup in an old house, lots of equipment, mannequins all over the place. Very strange guy, good-looking in a dissipated sort of way, plenty of money, I guess. Anyway, he got me to Top him with all this stuff, and when I left he slipped two hundred-dollar bills into my pocket. I didn't even realize how much it was until I got home."

"And you hadn't asked for anything?" Dennie said.

"No. And then, the next night, another guy asked me up to his place. Wasn't an SMer like the first one, but he ... well, he swung on my cock, jacked me off, and gave me forty bucks without my asking for anything, either. So, the long and the short of it was that Alfie called several of the model agencies — those places that advertise in the throwaway newspapers they have in racks in front of a lot of businesses in Hollywood. Anyway, he checked out a few of them, and finally said he'd found a man who seemed legit — or at least honest. He took me to see this guy in a big house up above Vermont Avenue. It wasn't sleazy at all, not like I expected."

"I bet the guy about dropped his dentures when he saw you two walking in," Dennie remarked.

Jeff grinned, blushing again. "Well, he was very friendly, but he was also very professional, in a way. I mean, he didn't try to put the make on us. And we met a few of the other guys, and they all said the same thing. 'Madam,' as we all called him, might keep one of the guys around the house for a while, but he was really more interested in the money than trying to get into everybody's pants."

"But he sent you out on sex calls?" Dennie urged.

"Yeah, but they were all with pretty decent guys. None of them was real ugly. A few were older men. But we made at least a hundred-fifty on every one, sometimes two hundred. And it was all safe sex, and nothing, uh, leathery. Just plain, you know ... mostly just oral sex, or maybe the guy'd want to get fucked. If he did, we always used a rubber. Madam — Howard was his real name — he made sure we all understood the safe-sex rules, and if he heard that any of his boys weren't following them, he'd drop him."

"He sounds like an unusually ethical pimp," Dennie quipped, getting sharp glances from both Bruce and Frank for his trouble.

"And I assume he kept you busy enough that you weren't out looking for anything else?" asked Bruce.

"No, we were pretty pooped a lot of the time, and besides ... well, we had each other. We aren't really lovers, but we ... we always have a good time together."

"But you didn't play bondage games?" asked Frank.

"No, just once in a while when Alfie really wants to turn me on he'll, like, maybe tie my hands behind my back, but he'll never do it tight enough that I can't get loose. It just isn't his thing, unfortunately. And that's really why we aren't lovers."

"That's also why we weren't able to find you," Bruce remarked. "You weren't out where my friends would see you, and you weren't staying in a hotel-motel right in Hollywood. But, be that as it may, Jeff, what do you want us to do about your father? You know, he's really climbing the walls, trying to find you."

"He's into a heavy guilt trip," Dennie added.

"That's not all of it," Jeff replied; then, to everyone's amazement, he added: "Alfie was into dope — selling it, I mean — and I'm sure Dad knew it. In fact, I kinda suspect he might have been playing some kind of games himself."

Dennie was the first to recover his voice. "You mean, dear old four-square Daddy was a dope peddler? That's pretty hard to swallow."

"No, it wasn't quite like that," Jeff told him. "Dad couldn't actually sell the shit, but I'm pretty sure he let people use his buildings for storage. I know he rented to some very strange characters, and I suspect he got some big bucks for letting them use a place for just a few weeks. I know, too, that there was a lot of crack and cocaine — and grass, of course — all being sold on some of his big construction projects. He always acted like he didn't know anything about it, but I think he was afraid to try and stop it, for fear of having trouble with the guys who were paying him to use his storage facilities."

"That's quite an indictment," Bruce said. "Do you have anything more than just suspicion?"

"Not really, I guess. Just rumors, plus what little I saw for myself. But I didn't ever make a real effort to find out. It wasn't so much that I didn't care, as that I really didn't want to know. But it was bugging me, and when all the fireworks started over my supposed gay and SM stuff ... well, maybe it was just a good excuse."

"So you really weren't into heavy SM activity?" Dennie asked. The forced casual tone of voice was not lost on Bruce, who now watched in amusement, knowing his friend was responding strongly to the young man sitting across from him.

"No, just one guy I played with once in a while," Jeff told him.

"Your dad said you illustrated some rather complex bondage scenes, depicting a lot of equipment," Bruce suggested. "You didn't actually have any?"

Again, the innocent blush. "I didn't have many things," Jeff replied. "I got hold of some mail-order catalogues, and I ordered a few toys. Most of it's never been used, except by myself." His face was now burning red, and Bruce was painfully aware of his embarrassment.

"It's too bad you couldn't have told your dad all this," Frank suggested, speaking before Bruce could say anything.

"I would have if he'd'a shut up long enough. But he didn't want to hear anything I had to say. Mostly, I think he was going bananas because he could just as easily have flipped my sketchbook open when some of his men were around to see what was in it. That would have really been a put-down for him, and just the thought of it was enough to drive him bonkers, I guess."

"Then you took off with Alfie, whom Daddy knew was dealing dope," Dennie added, "and that sent him over the top."

Jeff paused uncomfortably, obviously trying to choose his words before answering. "I'm just guessing at what Dad knows," he replied at length, "but Alfie's been selling stuff all through high school — grass, mostly, at least in the beginning; but he was peddling some of the heavier stuff into our senior year — cocaine, ludes, crystal. I'm not sure what else. And I can't be sure how much Dad knew about it, the details, I mean. But I'm pretty sure he must have known, or suspected something."

"Why?" Frank asked, and in reply to Jeff's questioning look: "I mean, why do you think your dad knew, when — presumably — your other friends' parents didn't know? This is what you're saying, right?"

"I don't know how Dad knew," Jeff replied helplessly. "I'm just about ninety-nine percent sure he did know, because he made several remarks about my 'drug-dealing friends,' during that last scene I had with him, and I knew he meant Alfie."

"Okay." Bruce spoke after listening to the others' discourse. "The next logical question would be your own involvement," he said matter-of-factly, his tone betraying no emotion. "I'm sure this would have been your father's greatest concern."

Jeff moved uncomfortably in his seat, tossing down the last dregs from his glass. "I smoke grass sometimes," he admitted. "Not unless I'm with other guys, though. I've tried the other stuff, but I'm scared of it. I did have those couple of nights when we first got out here, when I was still real uptight over everything. I used the stuff the first two guys — the ones I told you about — what they gave me. I'm really not a doper, Bruce," he added more stridently, looking up abruptly and fastening his innocent blue-eyed gaze on the psychiatrist's face.

"What about Alfie?" Bruce pressed.

"I don't think he ever used anything heavier than grass — maybe some speed when he didn't get enough sleep and needed the extra energy," Jeff replied thoughtfully. "He didn't like for me to use any of the heavier stuff, either. He really got on my case when he thought I might start doing it out here, when he knew I used the stuff the guys had given me. 'Course, part of that mighta been that he was jealous, because I'd gotten it on with someone else. See, he was ... I guess you'd say, he was in love with me. And if he'd just been into a little kinkier action, well ... Anyway, he has a kinda superior attitude, you see, really looks down on guys who get hooked. He doesn't go for this 'I can take it or leave it' crap. He says he's heard too many assholes saying it, when they'd kill their grandmothers for another fix. We were both on the gymnastics team, and he even got upset when he knew a guy was taking steroids."

"So, except for that period of depression when you first came out here, you aren't using anything?" Bruce asked.

Jeff nodded. "I've shared a joint with a john a couple of times," he admitted, "but nothing else."

"And alcohol?"

Jeff smiled, holding up his empty glass. "Just a couple of beers," he said. "Like now, if Dennie doesn't mind contributing to my delinquency."

■ ■ ■

Hugo hunkered down on the service porch, waiting for the flashlight beam to touch the curtained window above him. The patrol was later than he'd expected, and it had held him up. He had wanted to leave before midnight, but he had been afraid

89

of running head-on into the rent-a-cop patrol car. Now the fuckers were taking their time, poking around the grounds.

A flash of light passed across the glass, and the heavy footfalls drifted away — no more motion visible to the crouching figure. But he knew they were still there, because the faint rumble of the car's engine remained just on the threshold of his hearing. Impatiently, he shifted position, finally stood up and stretched. The fuckers were staying much longer than usual, and Hugo felt the stirring of fear in his gut. What if he'd left some evidence of his presence? But he'd been very careful. All the wrappers and containers of the food he had either brought in or taken from the well-stocked pantry shelves and freezers ... all this had been dutifully stuffed into neighboring trash cans — Bruce's, for the most part. He'd always been sure to place the bicycle back in its exact place each time he used it, and he never left a door open that should have been closed.

Finally, his impatience got the better of him and he risked a peek through the window, above the curtain. He could see one of the patrolmen standing some twenty feet away, at the edge of the kitchen herb garden. He was just milking the final drops from his cock, as he finished urinating on the owners' plants. That was a degree of vandalism that bothered Hugo, made his mind flash red with anger. Even as an uninvited interloper, a wanted fugitive, he would not have done such a thing. The people who owned this place were paying that asshole to look after it, and there he was pissing in the vegetable garden. Hugo felt his hands contracting into fists, wished he dared use them.

But he had a better use for those powerful hands, and he was about to risk discovery in order to serve his chosen. He chuckled to himself. His chosen ... what? Just *Chosen*, he told himself. Frank was sure no lady fair. He was a man, a real beautiful man in more than just the way he looked. He was Hugo's hero, his secret idol, the lord he'd sworn to serve. And tonight this serf was going to do his *Chosen* the greatest service any man could do for another. No knight in all his shining armor could have done more, either for king or lady. He forced a pause in his rhapsodizing, and brought his mind back to the present. He could hear the patrol car backing out of the drive, and a moment later the electric gate clicked back into its closed position. It was time to leave, time to mount his wheeled charger and slip through the enemy lines to serve his *Chosen.*

■ ■ ■

"That was strange," said Dennie, coming back to join Bruce and Frank on the patio after taking Rudy out. Jeff had returned to his Hollywood apartment. "The patrol went down the hill as we were coming back into the driveway. Must have been at the Rushes'. Then, I'd just unsnapped Rudy's leash and started to open the door, when I'd swear a bicycle went zipping past the front of the house."

"Don't people ride bicycles around this neighborhood?" Frank responded. "I thought it was all the fad these days."

"It may be," Bruce said, "but not at midnight, not in a cul-de-sac with one empty house and one other under construction, plus our own. Did you see who it was?" he added, looking over at Dennie.

"Looked like a pretty good-sized man, but he went by so fast I wouldn't swear to it."

"I hope it wasn't that Monroe asshole," said Frank. "Better make sure the house is locked up tight, tonight. I don't want him shooting videos in the bedroom."

"I'll set the alarm before we go to bed," Dennie assured him. "And I'll leave our menacing beast loose in the house," he added, petting Rudy, who sat next to him, nudging with his nose for attention. "I wish the kid would get over worrying about his friend. I think he might have stayed over, if he hadn't been so concerned about 'getting back for Alfie.'"

"Talk about old lechers," Frank quipped, repeating the familiar line. "I hesitate to think what might have happened to that innocent young thing if you'd taken him back into your den of iniquity."

"I think he'd have been perfectly willing," Bruce told him. "The kid's been fantasizing about SM all his life, and he's only had a couple of cracks at it — almost always being forced to play Top, when he really wants exactly what Dennie would give him."

"How do you read him?" Frank asked.

"He's a kid who was probably considered fairly sophisticated back on the farm, but he's a novice out here. On his own, the

91

street would eat him up. I just hope it hasn't already done that to his buddy."

"You think Alfie's in trouble, don't you?" Frank said.

"He's been missing too long, and he's apparently had his hands in too many pies," Bruce agreed. "Yes, I think it's possible that he's in very serious trouble."

■ ■ ■

Haven Monroe was no beauty. At thirty-four, he had developed a paunch, and his scrubby hairstyle had gone out with the sixties. He looked a good ten years older than he was. But he was very pleased with himself this evening. His second article on the Orsini killings had just been published, and there was already a pained outcry from every imaginable quarter. And that's how he liked it: controversial.

Then he had just emerged from the bath — his makeshift darkroom — and the pictures of Frank DeSilva were great! He and his friends would be a big hit in any of the porno mags, and tomorrow Haven would write the article to go with them. The pretty boy was going to get his comeuppance — *turn down my invitation, the conceited little shit!*

There was a gentle tap at his door, and the reporter gave his disheveled hair a quick pat as he hurried to answer the summons. The hunky little bellhop stood grinning at him, and Monroe quickly ushered the kid inside. He hadn't asked the boy his age, but he knew the youngster couldn't be over sixteen, seventeen at the most. But he knew his way around, had his clothes off almost as soon as he entered the room, and as the scrubby reporter took hold of the boy's naked shoulders, the kid reminded Monroe that he'd promised him fifty bucks.

Grumbling, the reporter fumbled in his wallet, placed the bills on the dresser, then hustled the kid onto the bed. He turned off the light and quickly stripped off his own clothes, slipping under the covers before the kid's eyes could grow accustomed to the dim illumination. No use letting him see the sagging flesh, or the purple splotches on his legs.

He rolled on top of the youngster, driving his lips hard against the boy's. Feeling some resistance, he grasped either side of the kid's head and forced himself more strongly, until the lips parted and the reporter's tongue could probe the rows of even teeth. He teased and tormented the young man's body, trying to create a responding hardness; but the kid seemed unable to reciprocate the passion of the older man. Finally, Monroe turned him on his belly and started probing at his asshole.

"If you wanta do that, use a rubber," the kid whispered.

Monroe continued his explorations, testing the firm roundness of the youthful buttocks, sliding his fingers into the crack, lubricating it from a tube of gel. Slowly, he eased himself up on the naked backside, allowing his cock to trace the slippery warmth.

"Use a rubber," the kid demanded again, and twisted partially onto his side.

"I don't have one," Monroe replied.

The kid started to struggle free. "Then you can't fuck me," he said, trying to extricate himself from the reporter's grasp.

Monroe's response was to slap him — hard across the face, but the kid was not inexperienced. He was almost eighteen, and he'd been turning tricks for a good two years. He pulled his legs up tight against his body, then flexed them both — hard against the reporter's chest. In the few moments while Monroe was powerless, trying to catch his breath, the kid grabbed up his clothes, snatched the crumpled pile of bills from the dresser, and bolted out the door.

It took three or four minutes for Monroe to regain control of his breathing, and by then he was furious! Naked, unconcerned that someone might see his scarred, ugly body, he yanked open the door, and ran head-on into a tall, powerful form. The man grabbed him, twisted him around, and forced him back inside the room. Within the space of a heartbeat, a silken rope was wound about his neck, and before Monroe could gather his wits to resist, he felt himself falling into blackness, felt the rush of blood through his neck, a pulse that strained, and stopped abruptly. But that last whisper, of course, he never really heard.

SEVEN

"Bruce, I've got Abe's office on the line. He'd like to speak with you. Says it's important." Dennie's tone indicated his uncertainty, knowing he shouldn't interrupt, but afraid not to.

Bruce frowned in displeasure. He was in the middle of a session with a young woman who had just begun to relate, and he was sure she would react negatively to his taking a phone call, possibly perceiving it as a form of rejection. "I've got to call him back," said Bruce. "But you can take the information."

He hung up, feeling guilty. *Well, better to offend your best friend than set a client back in her therapy.* But the woman was definitely beginning to wear on him. She was also evidencing signs of sexual interest. By the time he terminated her session he was more than a little frazzled — and very anxious to speak with Abe.

"He says the Orsini kids are out of the slam," Dennie told him, "and he's persuaded them to see you. I don't know how he did it, but he definitely wants you to call him. Says there's something else, but he wouldn't give me a clue."

"I've got Peter coming up next, haven't I?"

"Yeah, but you know he's always ten minutes late. I'd say you have half an hour. Want a sandwich? It's going on two, and you didn't eat much for breakfast."

"Why don't you make me one of those diet shakes? Chocolate, if you've got it." Bruce settled back behind his desk and picked up the phone. "Oh, Dennie. Where was Abe? Which office?"

"Must be his regular one ... Century City. The girl said 'Mister,' not 'Commissioner Javits.'"

Bruce punched in the button on his automatic dialer, and Abe answered the phone himself. "Sorry to put you off," Bruce told him, "but it was a bad time."

"No harm done," replied his friend. "I was just so pleased with myself at getting those two spoiled punks to agree to see you, I couldn't wait."

"How did you do it?" Bruce asked. He knew that Abe was fully aware of his aversion to working with clients who were coerced into seeing him.

"I told them I personally didn't believe they were guilty — which I don't, by the way. I don't like them, but I still don't think they did it. They're out, as you may have heard, because the grand jury refused to indict them."

"I didn't know that," Bruce told him. "I've been with a steady stream of patients all morning."

"Yeah, the news came down around eleven, and the kids' lawyer had them out by noon. But I'd already gone in to see them — separately, of course, and I convinced them that you would not only be able to help their cases, if it came to that, but that you were sure to help ease some of their emotional woes. Paul, the younger one, was easy. He's all hot to see you, especially when I told him you lived just a few streets away. Rupert was a little more difficult, but he agreed, too. I may have to call and remind him, but I'm sure he'll make it onto your couch."

"That sounds like quite a job of persuasion. In fact, I'd lay money you're not telling me all of it."

Abe laughed aloud. "Okay, I'll admit I talked to Mickey Halloran first," he said, mentioning the name of the boys' very prominent defense attorney. "He's also a client of mine, and I guess what you'd call a 'business friend.' He seems to honestly believe the kids are innocent, by the way. He asked me to recommend a shrink, and when I mentioned you he all but did an Irish jig! 'Just what I should have thought of myself,' he tells me, and says he'll pass the word to his clients."

"So I see them with proper blessings all around. But I'll have to admit I'm looking forward to it. It'll certainly be more interesting than the general run of patients I've had lately."

"Okay, now we have that settled," Abe continued in a more serious tone, "I've got what may be some bad news, at least some disturbing news."

"Alfie?"

"No, not that bad. It's Haven Monroe. They found him dead in his hotel room this morning. He'd been garroted."

"Well, I can't rejoice at anyone's untimely passing, but I won't shed too many tears over this one."

"Maybe not, except that yellow rag he works — worked for — knows why he was out here, and ... well, you know how the print media people react to this sort of thing. They may fight like cats and dogs over one issue or another, but let someone injure one of the brotherhood — like a judge tossing one of them in jail for refusing to reveal a source — and they all stick together."

"You mean, you think the shit's going to hit the fan about Frank?"

"I think it could. Fortunately, your old friend Pete Jackson is the detective in charge of the investigation."

"I thought Monroe was staying in West Hollywood."

"Yes and no," Abe told him. "West Hollywood is a peculiarly shaped piece of real estate. Monroe's hotel was in a little patch of Los Angeles, which technically makes it our baby. But...," he continued, after a significant pause, "...there's real coopera-tion all around on this whole thing: L.A., Beverly Hills, the sheriffs — who, as you know, police West Hollywood under contract to the city."

"What 'whole thing'?" asked Bruce, now really puzzled.

"I'm not alone in believing that the kids didn't do it," Abe replied. "And if they didn't, who did?"

"We're back to the mob, again?"

"I don't think we ever got very far away from it, and now with an investigative reporter who was sent out to cover the case also getting throttled with a silken rope around his neck, the odds have shifted back heavily in our favor — that's to say, those of us who adhere to the organized-crime theory."

"I just hope the emphasis stays on that angle, instead of Monroe's other reason for being out here."

"That's why I did a little manipulation to get Jackson on the case. He won't conceal any significant evidence, but he also knows how to handle sensitive, extraneous information. Of course, you already know that; you've worked with him. The media guys don't particularly like him, because he's known to be tight-lipped about anything that isn't supposed to be leaked."

"What if he just comes across Frank's name on something by accident?" Bruce asked. "What's he apt to do?"

"I've already taken care of that," Abe told him, "and that's an example of how much I trust his discretion."

It took Bruce a moment to connect on that one, and Abe — thinking he had been obtuse — explained: "I mean, Bruce, although you've never gone into the gay issue with him, I assume he's been perceptive enough to sense it. Like most cops, he isn't exactly on the side of Gay Liberation, but as a black man he has a lot more compassion than some redneck bigot."

"Yeah, I'm with you," Bruce agreed, although he spoke with a note of hesitation. "I'm sure Pete's been on my wavelength for a long time, and as you know, I don't really care — not for myself. Thanks to you, they can't hurt me financially, and a good portion of my professional activity involves the Community, anyway. But Frank has a lot to lose if someone outs him right now."

"I'm sorry, Bruce. I hope I didn't put my two cents worth in where it didn't belong."

"No, I trust Pete Jackson," Bruce agreed. "I've always liked him — and respected him; and I think it's mutual. But, Abe ... do you really think the mob killed Monroe? I can't imagine that he dug up enough to make him a threat to them, at least not this quickly. He hasn't been out here that long."

"You obviously don't read the supermarket yellow journals," Abe laughed. "The stupid bastard started tossing some of gangland's biggest names around in an article just last week. And as if that weren't enough, in his latest piece he made references to several Colombians, one U.S. senator, two representatives, and half a dozen prominent leaders in both the black and Chicano communities. He even took a potshot at Mickey Halloran, the Orsini kids' lawyer."

"My God, that's an article I've got to see. He's antagonized everyone but the president."

"I'll fax it over to you. Let me know how you do with the Orsini brats."

■ ■ ■

Bruce's last appointment ran late — something most therapists try to avoid, but which seemed appropriate in this case: a physically unattractive young man, struggling with his sexual identity. He had originally come to Bruce as a referral from the suicide prevention hot line, but was now making exceptional progress. Bruce saw him to the door a little after six, and was surprised to find Jeff just pulling into the circular drive. He could see his patient's eyes bulge as the handsome youth slid out of the cab and started toward them. Bruce introduced them, something that was also unusual, and Jeff beamed a pleasant greeting.

Bruce remained on the doorstep until his patient had driven away, then turned to Jeff. "You made the poor guy's day," he said casually, to which Jeff made a startling reply: "He knew me; he'd seen me, anyway. He was one of Madam Howard's customers, went with Alfie one night."

Cliches such as "small world" and "close community" were swirling in Bruce's mind as they went inside. He remembered his patient's mentioning a hustler service. *Never connected it. No reason why I should, but this whole situation is coming full circle, and then going around again. Merry-go-round!* "You know, Jeff, your old man's going to call here any time," Bruce said, forcing his thoughts into a more comfortable set. "In fact, I'm surprised he hasn't been on the horn before now."

"I know. He's already called Aunt Alice, yesterday. She told me, and she's on my case to call him before he discovers that she's 'harboring me,' as she puts it. But I don't know what to say to him. Would you ... would you call him and tell him I'm okay? You wouldn't have to say I was here. I *would* like to talk to Mom, though."

"Why don't you pick a time of day when your dad's most apt to be out working, and call your mother? Better yet, pick a time; I'll call, and if your dad isn't home I'll put you on the line. I'm not comfortable letting them go on worrying about you."

"Yeah, I will. Mostly, I was waiting for Alfie to show up before I called. Everything's just kind of up in the air until I know he's okay."

They had reached the den, in the rear of the house, and Bruce was uncertain how to handle his visitor. As far as he knew Jeff had not been invited. Although the kid was certainly not unwelcome, Bruce wasn't too sure he wanted to have him stopping by unannounced — perhaps at some other, less convenient time. He was about to raise the question, when Dennie emerged from his wing of the house.

"I thought I heard you drive up," he said to Jeff, and to Bruce he added: "Jeff and I are going to grab a bite to eat and take in a show." As an afterthought he added: "If you and Frank want to join us, we thought we'd try the Beverly Center Cineplex."

"No, you guys go on. Frank has a late appointment at the studio with Rufus and some producer ... all very hush-hush at this point. He wanted to have dinner at Alouette — that little French place on Santa Monica Boulevard. They've got a special on Santa Barbara mussels this week. You know how crazy he is about them."

"Okay. Oh, by the way, your schedule's clear for tomorrow morning. Chester canceled, and Marje Wilson's out of town until Friday. I rescheduled her for Monday afternoon."

"Good, I'll get an extra hour's sleep. Jeff, if you want to try the phone calls, tomorrow might be a good time. Want to stop by in the morning?"

Jeff grinned somewhat sheepishly, and looked at Dennie, who in turn placed one arm across the youngster's shoulder. "I expect he'll be here in the morning," he said.

■ ■ ■

Paul Orsini pulled the door shut on his room — suite, really, since each of the brothers had a sitting room, bedroom, private bath, and dressing room — all quite spacious, and very private. God, how he'd missed all this — not the comfortable setting, so much as the privacy. He had been in a high-security, antisuicide cell, which meant that although he had no cell-mates, he was under constant surveillance. *Couldn't take a crap without someone watching me ... couldn't even jack off. Made me feel like a fucking zoo exhibit.*

He kicked off his shoes, and quickly stripped the rest of his clothing, making one quick side trip to the bathroom as he unbuttoned his shirt — then turned on the hot water in the sunken Roman tub, and closed the bathroom door so the steam would build up. *Can't wait to get the stink of that fucking jail off my skin! Whole place smells like a men's room on a summer day. Even when they let you take a shower you come out sweaty and have to put your clothes on before you can dry yourself. God, I never want to go through that again!*

Sure hope Commissioner Javits is right ... that they're going to follow up on some other leads and leave me alone for a while. But Rupert, dear brother Rupert. I don't trust you, you fucking bastard! I wouldn't put it past you to have killed Mom and Dad. Sneaky fuck-ass! The way you've been spending money ever since, and hanging out with Paco and those other South American pukes...

He knelt down beside the tub, running his hand in the water, mixing the newly added cold to the hot, bringing the temperature to a level where he could ease himself in ... gingerly, barely able to stand the heat. *Oh, shit, I've been dreaming of this ever since they hauled me off to the pokey. Never thought I'd get out this quickly.* He stretched out full length, letting his head come to rest on the padded ledge. He reached for a small towel and dried his hands, then took the remote control from its niche above him and flicked on his sound system. He'd left some heavy metal on the CD changer, and started it going, adjusting the volume to a high enough level that the waves of sound seemed to envelop him as surely as the hot water, foamy now as he started the Jacuzzi and poured in some bath powder.

Oh, man, that feels good! I'm allowed to touch my dick for the first time in ... shit, felt like a couple of weeks, but it wasn't much over forty-eight hours. Halloran sure got us out in a hurry, once the grand jury fucked up the D.A.'s day. That bastard! Another asshole looking to make the headlines. But that Javits guy, imagine him coming into my cell. Twice he came by, telling me he knew I didn't do it and talking me into an interview with that MacLeod shrink. Wonder if Javits knows his psychiatrist's as queer as I am. When he started telling me about him, and how he lived so close, I wanted to tell him, "Oh sure, man, that's the guy lives up on the next hill, with the pool where all the hunky dudes go swimming in the buff, and sometimes have sex in the water. I started watchin' 'em a couple years ago, man.

I'd climb up the hill, over the fence, and lie up under the trees. Best after dark, warm summer nights, and especially last summer, when that pretty dark-haired guy appeared on the scene." He laughed, hugging himself in delight. He wondered which one of the guys he'd watched would turn out to be the doctor. *The big guy with the beard, I bet. He looks most like a shrink. The other ones are too pretty, especially that new one. Looks like a character on one of those TV cop series. Always did turn on to him. Wonder if he could really be the actor...*

Paul began gently stroking himself, bringing his cock to full erection as his mind reproduced these visual images from the previous summer. He had been almost obsessed by Frank's hard, slender body and the very substantial uncut cock, so dark and potent against the untanned area where his swimsuit had kept his skin lighter than the rest of his body. Then, as the weeks had passed he had seen that area gradually darken, as the young man spent more time soaking up the sun without a swimsuit.

As the passion began to well up in Paul's groin, and his mind drifted into the most familiar, well-defined tracks, he gradually allowed Frank's image to give way to the other, more immediately sexual moments in his life, the true high points: the first sessions with Hugo, until the stupid jerk had gotten so heavy Paul couldn't trust him any more ... had become afraid to let the kid tie him up. But those first nights ... *man, the greatest ... except for* that *night, the night I met that hustler from Iowa. Same night the folks got killed. Fuck, if I could just find that guy again, I'd be off the hook!* His hand slowed its motion, as the familiar theme echoed through his mind, and the familiar dread began to pound inside his skull, momentarily obliterating the well of sexual arousal.

But he had been down this same mental path too many times, and he'd learned to turn it off. *Probably never find the kid, but shit, not just for an alibi. I'd love to feel his hands on my body again. He seemed pretty green, really inexperienced, but so willing! If I could get it on with him again ... a few more times. I know I could teach him how to be the best Top in the business — best-looking, anyway. Have to get him before he's been kicked around too much, before he's infected with AIDS. Nice fresh-off-the-farm stud-boy. Big uncut dick, like the little*

guy in the pool. Only I actually had my hands on that farm boy!
Mouth, too ... that hard young body pressed up against me when
I was strapped up on the X-cross, face against the wood, back
and ass touching his cock and his hard belly when he leaned
up against me. Then the belt. Oh, fuck, what a session! Wonder
where that kid got to? Still out here? Back on the farm? If I could
only find him, get him to work me over again before we go to the
cops and let him tell them we were together.

Maybe if I tell the shrink about it. But Halloran didn't want
me to say anything until we found the kid. Wouldn't do me any
good, he said, and the homosexual angle would just make a
jury less sympathetic to me, if it came to that, especially if I said
anything about the SM and bondage. But the shrink ... get the
feeling he's into it. Never actually saw anything, but just
snatches of conversation I was able to hear. Yeah, tomorrow I'll
call and make an appointment. Maybe I'll tell him what I've seen
from his vacant lot. I'll be like the old lady in the dentist's chair,
grabbing him by the balls and telling him: "Now, we aren't going
to hurt each other, are we?"

He laughed aloud and forced his mind to regain its images of
the house in Echo Park, of his dungeon room with all the equipment and mannequins ... and Jeff. *Yeah, that was the kid's*
name, Jeff. Oh, to get my hands on that swinging dick again!

■ ■ ■

Looking out the window, Bruce could see that Jeff had, indeed,
spent the night. His red pickup was still parked off the drive,
under the overhang near Dennie's bedroom window — just
where he'd left it when the two of them had driven off in
Dennie's Buick, now parked in back of the pickup. *Bumper to*
bumper, Bruce thought — *probably just the way they're lying*
in bed right now.

"Did Jeff spend the night?" asked Frank, lifting one eye
above the pillow.

"Looks that way."

"You going to call Daddy this morning?"

"I hope so," Bruce replied. "I'm really beginning to feel guilty
about letting it go this long. The poor guy spent all that time
out here, never found the kid, and now I'm sure he's home
stewing. And the mother; she must be more than frantic."

"I thought you didn't like Old Man Donovan," Frank remarked, sliding out of bed and padding naked toward the bathroom.

"Oh, he's okay, for a square. What's that wonderful word Rufus uses?"

"Schmeckel?"

"Yeah, schmeckel. I'm not sure what it means, but it sort of fits Dan Donovan. If I ever met a schmeckel, that's him — kind of silly, but harmless."

Frank pissed with the bathroom door open, looking over his shoulder at Bruce. "'Course, Donovan was just the opposite of most guys we run into — smart, but street-dumb. Remember what you told me about the day Henry van Porter took him — and you — through the deserted buildings in Hollywood?" He shook off the final drops and returned to the bedroom, gently massaging himself, watching impishly as Bruce's gaze fastened on his groin. "You said Dan'd all but shit his pants when he saw how those kids were living, and had to imagine that his own son could be in similar circumstances." He was now standing over Bruce, who had been working on the sit-up board. "If you lift yourself up here one more time, I'll give you a candy bar, little boy," Frank teased. He stretched his foreskin out on either side of his cock and stood so close that Bruce would have to bump his head against the tumescent organ if he did another rep.

Looking up from his canted position on the board, Bruce grinned at his lover. "We've got all morning," he said. "And I have a couple of new toys I picked up while you were away. Been saving them for a special occasion."

"We haven't celebrated the Great Execution," said Frank. "Isn't that special enough?" He stepped back to let Bruce swing his legs free of the board, but his friend remained in place.

"Don't even joke about that! They haven't figured out who killed him, yet. I don't want them coming here to question you."

The idea seemed to freeze Frank in place for several moments. "You don't think they really would, do you?" His tone implied a genuine, suddenly realized fear.

"No," Bruce laughed. "You were with me, anyway. And Dennie also knows you were here. Pete Jackson's investigating the case."

"Then, since I don't got no worries, how 'bout a little toss in the hay?" He swung his leg over the top of the slant board, straddling it, so that Bruce lay looking up at him. He fingered his cock, again stretching the foreskin out to either side, tauntingly. Bruce's face would come in direct contact if he did another sit-up. "Come get this candy, little boy. Daddy's big pee-pee's all ready for you."

Even as he spoke, the ruby cockhead had thickened to fill the void in the tunnel of skin. Frank laughed again, then squatted down, his ass coming to rest on Bruce's chest. He flopped his cock up and down, striking it on the breastbone, just a couple of inches from Bruce's chin.

Bruce licked his lips, grinning. "Come on," he whispered. "Gimme that big floppy; let's see if I can't get it hard."

Frank moved his body lower, pinning Bruce to the board as he flapped his cock against the eager lips, not allowing a long enough pause in his motions for the other to grasp the prize. Then, as Bruce tried to bring his hands up, Frank grabbed his wrists and forced both arms down. He held Bruce's wrists against the carpet as he allowed his cock — now at full-mast — to rest against his lover's lips.

"Guess who's going to be boss, this morning?" Frank teased. And with that, he pressed down with his cock, allowing it to slide deeply into the waiting throat. He was still holding Bruce's hands tightly against the floor. "What kind of new toys did you get?" he asked, and as Bruce tried to answer, he added: "It's not nice to talk with your mouth full!"

■ ■ ■

When they emerged an hour later, Dennie and Jeff were already in the kitchen. The big man was wearing just a pair of walking shorts, but Jeff had on a t-shirt and jeans — the remnants of his costume from the previous evening. Both looked somewhat disheveled, obviously not yet having showered and prepared to meet their public, as Frank put it. "And I hope you both had a good time," he added.

"Ye-ah-h-h," said Jeff, grinning like a fox.

"We had a very pleasurable learning experience," Dennie told them, "and that's about all we need go into at the moment," he continued, giving Jeff a meaningful glance.

"Well!" Bruce said. "I think we all need a bit of orange juice, coffee, and a quick dip in the pool. Then we can get to work — first off, your parents, kid."

"I already did it," Jeff announced smugly, looking at Dennie with an expression that could only be interpreted as devotional.

The old lecher's made another conquest, Bruce thought. Aloud, he asked: "So who did you talk to?"

"Both of them," replied the young man, proudly. "And Dad says it's okay with him if I stay out here a while. He'll even send me a few bucks if I need it, but he made me promise to keep in touch with them."

"I think they were so relieved to hear his voice, they'd have agreed to anything," Dennie said.

"I think it's a big relief for Jeff, too. Wasn't it?" asked Bruce.

"It was," the young man admitted. "You know, though, it's typical of Dad to think of money right away. I suppose it could be a problem as time goes by, because I don't see us keeping on the hustling thing. But between the two of us Alfie and I made quite a bit — enough, in fact, that it became a problem keeping it secure. We didn't want to open a bank account, you see, because we really didn't want to be found. And keeping it in the apartment wasn't safe."

"So what'd you do?" Dennie asked.

"We rented one of those 'store it and lock it' places. I also left some of my SM toys there, just so they wouldn't get stolen out of the room if we were both away for any length of time."

"Did you both have a key to the locker?" asked Bruce.

Jeff nodded. "Sure ... Oh, I see what you're getting at. I oughta go see if Alfie's been into the stash."

"It might be a good idea," Bruce replied. "When was the last time you checked it?"

"The day before he disappeared. We went together."

Bruce glanced at his watch. "We've got about three hours before my first appointment. Let's finish up here and go by your locker."

■ ■ ■

They had decided to take two cars, because Jeff wanted to go home afterward — again concerned lest Alfie show up when he wasn't there, although even he was beginning to lose hope of his friend's ever returning. Bruce and Frank were in Bruce's Mercedes, following Jeff in his red pickup. Dennie had stayed behind to tidy up, and to receive any calls or visitors who happened by.

"It looked like Dennie really gave the kid a working-over," Frank said. "He was marked up from neck to ankle."

"Just about," Bruce agreed, "but it certainly seemed to agree with him. After the two of them stopped playing grab-ass in the pool, the kid came out with a full boner. And in our cold water that takes some doing!"

"He certainly lost all his inhibitions in a hurry. The first time I met him he seemed to blush if you mentioned the word 'sex,' let alone 'SM.'"

"I think it was the combination of Dennie's working on him, plus calling home. I know he'd been dreading that, and getting it done must have lifted an enormous burden from his mind. Ah, looks like we've arrived."

They pulled up by the pickup in the parking stalls beside a large public storage company building. Jeff led the way, and they moved inside, past a uniformed guard who waved them along when Jeff flashed his key. They walked up one flight of stairs, and entered an area that reminded Bruce of a cemetery, where the ashes were stored in a series of compartments, aligned by row and column. Jeff unlocked one of the lower bins, and pulled open the door. Inside was a cement cubicle, about three feet square.

"Well, my bag's still where I left it," he said, pulling out a canvas gym duffel. He unzipped the side pocket and pulled out a wad of bills. He quickly flipped through it. "I think it's all here," he said slowly, then: "Listen, can I send this home with you? I'm sure Dennie'd keep it for me — probably safer than here ... certainly more accessible."

He had placed the money back in the zipper pocket and held the small duffel bag out to Frank, who took it from him and asked, "What's that other thing in there?"

"I don't know. Alfie must have put it in after we were here together."

"We'd better take a look at it," Bruce told him.

Jeff reached in, and pulled the brown-paper-wrapped parcel to the edge of the locker. It was a little larger than a pound box of sugar, carefully sealed with paper tape. Jeff tore open one corner, then stepped back in surprise, and horror. "Oh, shit! He told me he wasn't going to do this!"

Inside they could see several plastic bags of dried leaves — obviously marijuana, but there was also a small package of white powder, and another of red-and-white capsules.

"Jesus fuckin' kee-rist!" Jeff was almost in tears. "What am I supposed to do with this shit? I don't wanta get Alfie in trouble, but..."

"We've got to turn it in," Bruce muttered.

"No, we don't," said Frank.

"Look, none of us can afford..." Bruce began.

"That's not the issue," Frank insisted. "Right now, none of us has committed any crime, because whatever those materials are, they don't belong to us. They don't, do they?" He directed the last part of this to Jeff.

"You mean, did I know this stuff was here? Honest to God, I didn't."

"Then you've got no liability for it," Frank assured him.

"Is this more of your TV-crime-fighter experience?" asked Bruce.

"Yeah, I guess it is," Frank admitted. "But they hire some of the best criminal lawyers in the country as legal advisors. Just hear me out. None of us has ever seen this crap before, and we don't know what it is. As far as I'm concerned, it looks like a package of oregano and a few packets of scouring powder. And those pills — they look like some plant food capsules I bought last year."

"You're right," Bruce picked up brightly. "But it all looks kind of old and spoiled to me. Jeff, didn't I see a men's room down the end of the hall?"

Up to this point, the youngster had been watching his two companions with something approaching open-mouthed awe, frozen in place by the shock of finding what so obviously had to be Alfie's stash. But he heard Bruce's question, and nodded dumbly in assent.

"Well, in that case," Frank continued, "I think we ought to just dump it all down the john. Isn't that what you were thinking, Bruce?"

His friend nodded. "Yeah. What do you think, Jeff?"

107

"I ... I guess ... I ... but what if Alfie...?"

"I don't know why Alfie'd want some rancid herbs and a few old garden pellets. Do you?" Bruce insisted.

"No, I guess not," Jeff agreed, and as this simple solution to the immediate dilemma penetrated his previous immobility, he looked back and forth between his two companions, gratitude giving way to relief. "If one of you will make sure the coast is clear, I'll go dump this trash."

EIGHT

aul Orsini arrived promptly at eleven Friday morning for his appointment with Bruce. He had spoken with Mickey Halloran's assistant only an hour before, and had been reassured by the paralegal that he really had nothing to fear from Bruce MacLeod — unless he indicated some propensity to commit an additional crime. And in fact, he need not have called, because the first thing Bruce did was to establish the ground rules, giving him the same advice as he had gotten from his attorney's office.

"You're here, officially, at the request of your own lawyer," Bruce explained, "and we've been instructed to bill his office. This makes you my patient, and places a seal on most of our conversation."

He paused, gathering his thoughts, giving Paul a chance to interject one of his own questions. "But if I want you to testify about something I tell you?"

"That's a tricky area. In most circumstances I wouldn't be called upon to testify about anything you say to me, except by the prosecution if they think you may have incriminated yourself, and done it in a way that circumvents the veil of silence. After all, if you tell me you didn't commit a crime, that isn't evidence. It could be evidence if you confessed to me. But I don't think this is going to be an issue, because I don't want to get into this sort of thing with you."

"It doesn't matter, Doctor MacLeod," Paul told him, with an almost imploring expression. "I didn't kill my folks. I didn't have anything to do with it, and I don't know who did it. I ... well, look, I've lived just a few streets away from you for as long as you've been here. I know something about you, so I feel I can say pretty much what I need to, although I'd rather you didn't pass it along to Mr. Halloran's office."

"That's a somewhat obtuse statement. I'm not sure I follow you."

"I'm saying that I'm a gay man," Paul answered evenly, "and I know that you are, too. Not only am I gay, but I'm into SM, and ... well, I sort of think..."

Bruce could not suppress a grin at his patient's overtly blunt statement, accompanied by an unmistakable quiver in his voice, as well as a breathiness that bespoke a nervous response. "That's quite a bit to deduce about a neighbor you've never met. Is this pure deductive reasoning, or have I been the subject of extensive neighborhood gossip?"

"Oh, you know how this neighborhood is." Paul tried to make his tone sound casual, but succeeded only in arousing Bruce's curiosity. "Most people don't even know their neighbors, except maybe to wave at them as one goes by another in his car." He looked up nervously, working his hands against each other in his lap. The body language was definitely trying to communicate something, but the psychiatrist was not able to interpret it.

"Maybe you'd better just tell me what's on your mind. I'm not going to tape this session, by the way," he added. "I'd rather not create a piece of evidence for the legal hounds to fight over."

"Do you really think that could happen?" Paul asked, genuinely concerned now, his anxiety building until the side of his mouth began to quiver.

Observing the tic, Bruce tried to calm his patient. "I don't think you have much to worry about, at least from the legal standpoint. If Commissioner Javits believes you're innocent..."

"I'm not so worried about the cops. But whoever killed my folks — well, I hate to admit it, but I felt safer in jail than I have since this happened. I sleep with my door locked at night — at the house, I mean, and I ... I just don't trust anybody."

"Do you think someone's trying to harm you?"

"Not physically, but someone would sure like to frame me for the murders."

"Do you have evidence of this, or are you just assuming it?" Paul regarded the therapist with an expression of discomfort, squirming in his seat again. Then he grinned, and continued in an almost challenging tone: "You haven't asked me how I knew you were gay."

"Do you want to tell me?" asked Bruce, forcing his voice and expression to remain neutral, although the young man had definitely piqued his interest.

"Sure. I spied on you," Paul told him, and in response to Bruce's quizzical expression, he added: "I used to climb over the fence onto that lot above your house, and I'd watch the goings-on around the pool." He leaned back in his chair, then, an expression of triumph on his face. "You didn't expect that, did you?" he added, noting the trace of a frown that Bruce allowed to darken his brow.

"It wasn't that, so much, although it is disturbing to suddenly discover that your home isn't as private as you'd thought it was. But, this is the second time in less than a week that I've discovered we've had visitors up there."

"I never told anyone, just Hugo. Honest, Doctor MacLeod." Paul's defensive denial was so childlike, Bruce found himself changing his perception of the young man sitting across the desk. Although he had read enough of the material sent over by Abe's office to know that Paul Orsini had conducted himself quite responsibly in all of his recorded contacts with the authorities, Bruce knew he was seeing a different facet of the patient's personality. For some reason, he seemed to be retreating into a childish affect.

"So, how long were you sitting up there watching us?" asked Bruce, not unkindly.

"Oh, about four years, I guess. I mean, I first climbed up there four years ago, but I haven't been there in quite a while — not since last summer." He was decidedly regressing, Bruce felt. Even the pitch of his voice had gone up, and his entire behavior was like a younger child, trying to please an adult.

"You said you only took 'Hugo' up there. Who is Hugo?" Bruce half expected his patient to tell him that Hugo was either a teddy bear or an imagined playmate.

Instead, Paul cleared his throat and forced his voice to assume its normal timbre. "Hugo was a guy who worked for

111

us," he said, "... big, good-lookin' dude, with a big dick. I used to get it on with him until he got too heavy for me."

"In what way, 'too heavy'?"

"In ... you know ... in a bondage game. I'd let him tie me up and work me over, but he wasn't too smart and he never knew when to stop. He scared me so badly once, I broke it off for good."

"Is this the kid the police were trying to find after the murders?"

"Yeah, that's the guy. Never have found him, but they don't seem to be real anxious about it. Probably not a suspect, just figure he might be a witness to something."

"Do you think he might be?"

"I'm not sure," Paul answered thoughtfully. "Maybe. But like I say, he's real stupid. Good-looking, tall-dark-and-handsome, but dumb, man, real dumb."

Bruce glanced out the window, the thought having struck him that Paul's description of Hugo came pretty close to their own Huey. The kid normally came on Fridays. In fact, Bruce had seen him an hour or so previously. He made mental note to watch for Paul's reaction if the big kid put in an appearance.

"Okay, Paul," Bruce said abruptly. "Let's get to work, now. I let you guide us away from the issue a few minutes ago, when we were going to discuss why you felt someone was trying to frame you. Want to tell me a little more about that?"

"Gee, Doctor, I don't know that there's all that much to tell."

"But you made the statement, Paul, indicating that you thought this was happening. Why? Who do you think is doing this?"

"My brother," he replied without hesitation. "I think Rupert wants to see me convicted for it." Then, going on before Bruce had a chance to ask the obvious question, he said, "But I don't know if Rupert had anything to do with it, or not. He says he didn't, a'course, but he can't prove where he was, and ... I don' know."

"How about you?" Bruce asked. "You've never told anyone exactly where you were, either, just that you had been in your workshop, over near Echo Park. But you weren't sure of the time? That seems a little strange, doesn't it?"

"Well, I couldn't tell 'em, Doc. That's why I made the issue about us both being queer for SM. I can tell *you*, but I can't tell the cops. I did tell Mr. Halloran, but he told me to keep quiet about it. 'Fact, I think it embarrassed him, 'cause he didn't want me to go into detail about what I did, the way he wanted me to be so specific about everything else I told him. Don't get me wrong; he's a great lawyer, and all that, but he's a real Catholic harp when it comes to sex. We had lunch with him one day, and just the way he talked, I wouldn't wanta discuss this sort of thing with him, even if he wanted me to." He broke off, fixing Bruce with a pleading expression that was both disconcerting and unaccountably appealing. "You haven't told me, yet, Doctor MacLeod. I mean, can I talk to you about this stuff?"

"You can talk to me about anything you like," Bruce assured him, "and if you don't want me to tell anyone else, I won't."

"I was having a scene," Paul told him. "I'd picked up this really good-looking hunk and brought him back to the house I use for a workshop. I got a dungeon all set up in the basement — real hot, with lots of equipment and stuff. I think the guy was kinda inexperienced, but real willing, and seemed real turned on by all the goodies. So, I got him to strap me onto the Saint Andrew's cross, and kept telling him how he should do it, and all. And he's real nice, real cooperative. And we're there for almost five hours. So as for time, I don't know, exactly. But it wasn't very late when I first met him, maybe about ten o'clock."

"Almost the exact time of the murders," Bruce observed. "If you have such a solid alibi, why not use it?" he asked.

"I would if I could find that hustler again," Paul replied helplessly. "If I had him to testify for me, then I'd admit what I was doing. Shit, it's better to have it all over the newspapers and television that I'm a queer sadomasochist than to sit out the rest of my life in the can. But I don't know where the guy is, or how to find him. And unless I can, then why tell the cops and go through all that embarrassment without it doing me any good? And that was Mr. Halloran's thought, too."

"If it got into the press, it might make the guy come forward," Bruce suggested. "He may just not realize he's a potentially important witness." As Bruce said this, his mind was already probing the recesses of memory: Jeff's account of his first night in town. Did it fit? *The small-world theory again. Of course, it*

113

all seems moot at this point. Paul doesn't need an alibi any more.

"I've thought of that," Paul admitted, "but it seems such a long shot. I just can't bring myself to face the additional notoriety, and all the phony shrieks of horror on the six-o'clock news." All traces of the little-boy syndrome had now disappeared, and as Paul warmed to his subject, his intellectual status became more apparent.

"You know that pair on Channel 3, the ones who go through such moralistic crap every time they discuss something to do with sex or porn, or dope? Well, they were each married to someone else less than a year ago — and since got divorced and married each other. But until all that was settled, they were fucking like mink all over town. She even got caught sucking him off in an elevator, once. No, Doc, I can't see myself the subject of their hypocrisy — theirs, and others like them, if it isn't going to do me any good."

"I can understand your feelings," Bruce admitted. "And under the present circumstances, it doesn't look like it's going to be necessary."

"Maybe not, unless my dear brother has his way, and convinces them to arrest me again. You know, some 'new' evidence might pop up, and all of a sudden they're ... Jesus Christ! That's Hugo!" Paul shouted, standing up and pointing at the near-naked figure who was starting to strain some leaves from the pool.

Before Bruce could intervene, his patient had run to the sliding glass panel and was pulling it back, shouting at the big kid outside. Huey/Hugo looked up and stared in open-mouthed surprise — horror? — as he recognized his former friend. Then, before Paul could get the door open far enough to squeeze through, Huey/Hugo had bolted from the backyard and disappeared.

■ ■ ■

"We've got to do something about that lot," said Bruce, inclining his head toward the steep slope beyond the pool. "We've been putting on shows for God knows how many interlopers."

Frank shaded his eyes with his hand and looked up. "Doesn't seem to be anyone there right now," he said. "But you're right. Can you have it fenced better, or something?"

"I've already had Dennie call the company to see if they can put in a higher fence, with barbed wire on the top. The only other answer is to put a fence along the top of the hill, above the pool, and set lights around the base of it, pointing into the fence. That way, if someone tries to see in at night, all he gets is a faceful of spotlight."

"That wouldn't look very nice from this side, though," Frank complained. "And wouldn't it make the backyard awfully bright? What if I wanted to suck you off, right here on the deck?" He grinned mischievously.

"You'd have to do it under proper stage lighting conditions," Bruce told him.

It was just past four in the afternoon; both men were wearing shorts and nothing else, as Bruce ran the skimmer over the surface of the pool. "I'd like to know where Huey ... Hugo, if that's really his name ... like to know where the fuck he went in such a hurry. One minute he was out here cleaning the pool, and the next he's long gone. Ran like a terrified rabbit the second he saw the Orsini kid."

"Why's he so scared? Did Paul give you any clues?"

"No," Bruce told him. "Only that the police wanted to question him — apparently not as a suspect, although I don't know how much of that Huey understands."

"You mean he might think they're after him to arrest him?" Frank asked.

"Either that, or he saw something he's afraid will get him into trouble — with the law, or maybe with whoever actually killed the Orsinis."

"Are you going to tell anyone? Abe, I mean, or any of the other guys you know on the force?" Frank had now moved behind his friend, as Bruce edged along the water, lifting out the bits of leaves and other debris. He pressed himself against the naked back, allowing the hard outline of his cock to press into the valley between the other's solid rounds.

"Um, that feels good," Bruce told him. "But you can't get me all hot and bothered right now. Pete Jackson called a few minutes ago, and he wants to stop by to give me something."

"Oh, too bad," Frank temporized. "I was going to give you a quickie before the crowd arrived — up in the bleachers," he added, pointing to the spot where Haven Monroe had observed them. "I have to laugh when I think about Huey, or Hugo, having watched us from up there," he continued. "Remember, it took us a week before we felt comfortable skinny-dipping when he was around? We sure weren't showing him anything new."

"You know, I think he really liked you. In fact, I'm hoping he trusts you enough that he'll come back and talk to you, maybe tell you what he saw, or what he knows about the murders."

"You think he'll come back?"

"He might. I doubt he works anyplace else, and he'll need money to survive. As it is, I don't think Dennie paid him yet for this week."

"Well, I hope you're right," said Frank, perching on the edge of a plastic settee. "I wouldn't want anything to happen to him, and I'd certainly be willing to help him if I could."

They heard the front-door chime, and Dennie poked his head out the kitchen door. "That'll be your cop friend," he warned them. "Just wanted to make sure you were behaving yourselves."

A moment later Lt. Pete Jackson came outside, through the den next to Bruce's office. The tall, black policeman was dressed in a somewhat rumpled gray suit, the tie pulled down from his collar. He was carrying a battered black attaché case in his left hand.

"You look like you could use a drink," Bruce told him.

"Thanks," he replied. "Dennie already took my order."

He sat on one of the white plastic chairs beside the pool, watching Bruce as he scooped out the last of the flotsam from the water's surface. "You guys really have it made back here," he said, "...all this privacy." But his gaze traveled up the slope, and he seemed to be considering just how private they really were. "You own that land up above, don't you, Bruce?" he asked.

MacLeod nodded, wondering just what had occasioned the sudden interest, and for a fleeting moment fearful that yet another unsuspected set of eyes had observed them. He kept quiet, knowing that whatever Jackson had in mind, he'd soon tell them.

Dennie arrived with a tray of drinks, which he set on the white wicker table, and handed out the glasses. He was about to sit down with them, when Rudy shoved his nose into the big

116

man's crotch, and made the whining demand for his late-afternoon walk. Dennie glanced at Frank, who started to get up. Rudy was his dog, after all, and Dennie had merely been baby-sitting him while the actor was away on location.

However, Pete Jackson, observing the byplay, waved Frank down. "If it's okay with everyone, I've got something to talk to Frank about," he said.

"Okay, I'll go with Dennie," Bruce suggested.

"Well, no, if you'd stay, too..." Jackson fumbled.

"Humph! I guess we know when we're not wanted," said Dennie, speaking to Rudy and leading him into the house.

"I suppose it really doesn't matter if he knows I'm doing this," Jackson continued, "but I'd just as soon he not actually see me do it." With that, he pulled a nine-by-twelve manila envelope from his attaché case and handed it to Frank. "These are some publicity shots I think you'd just as soon not have published," he said.

"Monroe's?" asked Bruce.

The detective nodded. "Yeah," he sighed. "I picked them up along with a bale of other stuff from the creep's hotel room. Can't see as they're of any value in our investigation, so be my guest." He grinned at Frank and took a deep pull from his glass. "This is, of course, *very* strictly off the record," he added.

"Pete, I don't know how to thank you," Frank said. He had pulled out the thin stack of prints, glanced at the two or three top pictures, then shoved them all back into the envelope, which he now carried to the barbecue. He placed the packet on the bed of cold ashes, and stood helplessly as he realized he didn't have anything with which to start a fire.

"Your old man'll owe me one," Jackson said, winking at Bruce. "Permit me," he added, getting up and holding his Zippo under the corner of the envelope. "The negs are in there, too, under the rest of the stuff." He stood back as the paper flared briefly.

All three were silent for a few minutes. It had been the first open acknowledgment of Frank's relationship with Bruce to be expressed by Pete Jackson, and no one seemed quite up to a proper follow-through.

"You know we both really appreciate this," Bruce said at length.

"Don't worry about it," said Jackson. "That Monroe character was such an asshole it's a wonder he lived as long as he did. No need to let him reach out from the grave to fuck up anyone else's life. He was sick, too, in case you didn't know — AIDS, Kaposi's all over his legs. And the coroner's preliminary indicates he wasn't in such good shape inside. Maybe that's what made him so bitter."

"Any ideas on who did him in?" Bruce asked.

"No, except a couple of people claim to have seen a young guy hanging around the hotel who fits the description of the kid we've never been able to find, the one who used to work for the Orsinis. May be just a coincidence, but I wish I could find him and ask him some questions."

"By 'hanging around,' do you mean earlier in the day, or...?" Bruce broke off as they heard the telephone ring inside the house, but Dennie had apparently just come back inside. He answered it.

"No, just about the time Monroe got it," Jackson said, in answer to Bruce's question, "sometime between midnight and one-thirty. Strange, you know, in all the time I've been on the force this is the first case where the victim was garroted, and now we've got a third one."

"You've got a fourth," said Dennie, joining them. "That was Abe Javits on the phone. It looks like they found Alfie."

NINE

L t. Pete Jackson had gone into the house to call his office, leaving the other three men in the yard, beside the pool. Dennie's announcement — while not totally unexpected — had nonetheless left them all momentarily speechless.

"I'd been so hoping this wasn't going to happen," said Bruce at length. "But, somehow, I just felt it had to."

"Yeah, the longer he stayed missing, the more I felt sure he wasn't ever coming back," Frank agreed.

"It happened several days ago, from what Abe said," Dennie told them. "He was in a hurry, by the way, said he'd give you a call later in the evening." This last was directed at Bruce, who nodded absently, his mind already on another tack.

Jackson rejoined them a moment later, and everyone looked up at him expectantly. "I checked on the Alfred Stimson killing," he said, "and pending the coroner's report, the time of death is tentatively listed as 'in excess of one week.' The body'd been dumped up in Griffith Park, and ... well, he'd been strangled, probably with some kind of a rope. He'd also been in a fight before he died — most likely a struggle with whoever killed him."

"But Abe told me he'd definitely been garroted," Dennie said.

"That's what it appears to be," Jackson replied, "but it'll take a lab analysis to determine if the killer used that same kind of silk cord as in the Orsini murders. It for sure wasn't robbery, though. The kid's wallet was in the grave with him — thumbprint on the driver's license gave us the I.D." He took a deep swallow from his glass, leaving it empty except for some ice.

Without asking, Dennie took it from his hand and went inside to make him another drink.

"So that gives us a possible tie-in between the Orsini killings, Haven Monroe's at the hotel, and now Alfie," said Bruce. "Except that Alfie would have been the third victim, and Monroe the latest."

Pete Jackson nodded agreement. "But the connections don't make too much sense," he replied. "The Orsini killings were presumed to be either a mob hit, with classic execution trappings — or an attempt to make it appear as such. We're still not completely clear on that. I think the consensus is leaning back toward some kind of organized crime connection, but only after being unable to develop a case on any other basis."

"In other words, the police are what the media likes to call 'baffled,'" Dennie remarked, returning with Jackson's glass.

The lanky detective shifted uncomfortably in his seat, nodding his thanks to Dennie for the drink. "Our problem with the Orsini murders is that they took place on that damned estate, behind iron gates, and with no witnesses to any goings or comings. Nobody even heard anything. We've interviewed everyone who'd been on the grounds that day: servants, workmen, delivery people, everyone except that half-witted kid who disappeared the day of the murders."

"That would be Hugo?" asked Bruce.

Jackson almost slopped his drink, as he jerked sharply around to face his host. "How did you know that?" he started, then grinned. "Commissioner Javits?"

"Partly," Bruce admitted. "But it was on the news, too."

"Not the name, just a description," Jackson corrected him.

"Well, I think we may have unwittingly had him here at the house," Bruce admitted.

Jackson raised an eyebrow, giving Bruce his best Walter Matthau quizzical expression. "So, tell me."

"This kid came to the door looking for work, right after our regular gardener had given notice," Bruce explained, "so I told Dennie to hire him. Then, when I had the initial session with Paul Orsini this morning, he spotted 'Huey' — as we knew him — out in the yard, and ran out to talk to him. Only, the kid saw him coming and bolted."

"So he took off?" Jackson asked. "What kind of a car?"

"That's the strange part of it," Bruce told him. "He never had a car. Always arrived on foot."

"Didn't that seem odd enough to you that you'd question him about it?" asked Jackson.

It was Dennie who answered him. "I don't think any of us were concerned enough to question him," he said. "He always arrived when he was supposed to be here, did a good day's work. He did mumble something, one day, about his mother working in the area, so I assumed he rode with her."

"His mother *did* work in the area," Jackson told them. "She was the cook at the Orsinis' — been having hysterics, by the way, because her kid's disappeared. She was on vacation at the time of the murders — back in Texas visiting her family. At first we thought Hugo had gone with her, but it turns out he stayed here. He had a room next to his mother's, over the garage on the estate. Trouble is, we don't know if he was there that night, and we can't find him to interrogate him. I personally doubt he knows too much — retard, apparently. He's never been a suspect, because the whole scenario smacks of too much subterfuge; but the brass would sure as hell like for us to ask him some questions."

"Yeah, I'm really sorry, Pete. If I'd had any idea we might have been harboring a material witness..." Bruce spread his hands in a gesture of helplessness. "And by the way," added the psychiatrist, "he's not retarded ... in fact, he may have fairly normal intelligence under all the dull exterior. I'd say his problem was emotional, not retardation. Maybe in some respects, a classic *idiot savant* — gifted in some areas of ability, limited in others."

"Not just a moron, then. Interesting," replied the detective thoughtfully. "But as to your harboring the kid," he assured them, "I understand that you had no reason to suspect him. Besides," he added with a grin, "he was a pretty good-looking guy."

"Only if you like classical Greek gods," Dennie muttered. But other than this, the lieutenant's second reference to his awareness had again stopped them for a moment.

Seeing that he had provoked a strained silence, the policeman did the best he could to alleviate the anxiety. "Sorry," he said, "I didn't mean to step on anybody's toes. But we've been friends a long time, Bruce, and you know, I've *gotta* know what's going on."

"I think it's because of the problems I've been having with Monroe," Frank said softly. "It had us all on edge."

"I can dig that," Jackson said sympathetically, "and it's a good thing I know what I know, or you'd have cops hammering on your door, looking for more than a drink."

"You mean they might have suspected me?" asked Frank, his dismay obvious in his tone and expression.

"I don't know that they'd have suspected you — not seriously — once it had been established where you were. But along the way, they would've uncovered a few dust devils under the bed, let's say."

Bruce nodded. "Yeah, we were lucky to have you there, Pete. And all of us really want to thank you."

"Tell me about Paul Orsini," he replied abruptly. "I assumed he'd open up to you, if he would to anyone."

"You mean, because you think he's gay?" asked Bruce.

"Oh, we *know* he's gay," Jackson assured him. "More than that, we know he plays bondage games, maybe some fairly heavy ones. We had a warrant and went through the house in Echo Park where he has his workshop. That basement is somethin' else."

Bruce grinned to himself, wondering just how much Jackson knew, or had deduced about his own activities. "I don't think I discovered anything you don't already know," he began thoughtfully. "I will say that I'm ninety-nine percent convinced the kid's innocent."

"Oh, I am, too," Jackson replied hastily. "I never seriously considered him as a suspect, although I'm sure he knows more than he's telling us. But whether he *knows* he knows...?" He shrugged his shoulders, splaying his long, thick fingers as he spoke.

"How 'bout the brother?" Bruce asked.

"Now, that's — as they say — a horse of a different color," Jackson told them. "You haven't talked to him yet, have you?" he asked, and at Bruce's shake of the head, he continued, "Well, this kid's a real little shit. Sneaky, you know. He's a nerd, although he looks more like a high school athlete. But he's

twenty-three years old, no close friends as far as we can tell —
no girl. No boys, either, for that matter. He's a neuter as best
we can define it. In graduate school, working with computers
and such."

"You suspect him?" asked Frank.

Jackson nodded thoughtfully. "Yes, but not as a top-of-the-
line first-rater. He's a possibility, though. See, if he's really
involved, it creates more questions than it answers. He's not
very big, although he's probably stronger than he looks. Still,
he'd have had a hell of a time hanging on to his old man long
enough to strangle him. Felix Orsini outweighed him by at least
thirty pounds, and was in very good physical shape for a man
of his age. Then there's the situation with his mother." Jackson
paused long enough to sip at his drink, and eat a couple of the
peanuts Dennie had put out.

"The one thing we've discovered for sure about this kid,"
Jackson continued, "is that he was very close to his mom. The
idea of his killing her is very hard to swallow. Even the money
angle doesn't add up, because she'd give him anything he
wanted — and that was plenty! You know, it's hard enough to
conceive of any kid killing his mother, but this one ... I just
can't buy it."

"How about his relationship with his father? I have an
appointment with Rupert tomorrow, so I'd be interested in
anything you might know about him."

"That's another tough one," Jackson replied. "They seemed
to get along fairly well, went a lot of places together, played
chess and backgammon with each other, that sort of thing. No
evidence of a strained relationship, and the old man appeared
to have been grooming the kid to take over the business, or at
least to get involved in it."

"So you're saying that you can't see any motive for Rupert
to have killed either of his parents, but — unlike brother Paul
— he might have been emotionally capable of doing in the
father, less so the mother," Bruce concluded.

"That's it, more or less," Jackson admitted. "But we're
hoping you can give us a more educated guess as to his
capabilities."

"Baffled," said Dennie.

■ ■ ■

Hugo squatted in the darkness by the fence, wearing just his cutoff jeans, aware of his own odor, secretly enjoying it. He was dirty and he stank, but he had heard enough of the conversation next door to know that Frank was concerned about him, had even offered to help him, if he could. He felt a surge of affection, a stirring in his balls which belied his self-imposed denial. He reached into his crotch, wriggled two fingers under his sac, and pulled his genitals loose from their sweaty contact with his thigh. He experienced the usual thrill of pride as his heavy sex fell free of its confinement, cock and balls swinging loose through the left side of his shorts.

His legs were beginning to ache, and he stood up. No need to hunker down. No one was looking for him, and the patrol had already been there. Despite the circumstances, he was strangely happy. It was this proximity to Frank, he knew. He wished there were some way he could be sure that, if he did reveal his presence, this man whom he held in such high esteem would keep his secret. If he told Bruce — or even Dennie — there was a good chance they would pass the information on to the police ... that black lieutenant, for instance. The guy had stayed there a long time, and sure seemed cozy with them. Said a lot of things that maybe shouldn't have been said, unless ... Yeah, the doctor. He was in cahoots with the cops, somehow. Hugo wasn't exactly sure what it meant to be "on retainer," but he figured it somehow put Bruce on their team.

He watched, now, through the bushes that shielded both sides of the chain-link fence. It was hard to see, unless you got your face right up against the heavy weave of metal fabric, and moved frequently to keep a clear view through the dense growth on the other side. But he had found a spot where it was possible to keep a nearly unobstructed view of the pool area, where Bruce and Frank were now moving about naked. Once the black guy had left, Dennie had gone inside to clean up. The young, pretty guy was coming by to see him, he'd said, and they were going to have to tell him about his friend who got killed.

Hugo shrugged at all of this social interaction. It made no difference to him, except that his loins were on fire. As long as he had been free to enter the grounds next door, even to strip and swim naked with this guy he adored, he had somehow managed to keep it all under control, like a noble knight who sought to serve, but who would never break the rules of chivalry. Only now, he was experiencing lust such as he had not known since those days right after Paul told him to get lost. *That fucking little bastard! What'd he have to show up for? Fucked up my new job, almost got me caught. Wonder how long before one of them thinks to come looking for me. Bruce. He's the one, so fuckin' smart. He'll figure it out, if anyone. Thought he liked me, acted like he did. But now? If it wasn't for him, maybe Frank...*

His big, beefy fingers stroked his cock as he watched the two men through the verdant frame along the fence. He slid one digit inside his foreskin, and teased the sensitive flesh of his cockhead, wishing it could be Frank's tongue working up inside the folds. *Like Paul used to do, before he decided I was too much of a man for him ... little faggot! But he knew how to make it feel real good when he got his lips around my cock, used his tongue, showed me how it should be done. Screamed and yelled like a little girl when I fucked him. Always said I was too big for his dainty little asshole, but he sure kept coming back for more, until that day I opened up his back with the riding crop. Wasn't my fault. Usually kept begging for more, all except that day. He was the one who wanted to use the hood. Then, when I took it off him and he saw that little bit of blood he went bananas! Called me a barbarian!*

Hugo laughed at the recall, despite the anger it caused him: the sight of Paul, naked and bleeding, crying and blaming him for possibly doing him some permanent damage. But all the while, the guy's skinny little dick had stayed hard, dribbling pre-cum, while he tried to convince Hugo how he'd been wronged. Of course, it wasn't funny ... *not what any of them been doin' to me. Paul deserves whatever happens to him. And Rupert, that creepy little fuck! All the things he made me do, because I was afraid he'd tell on me. But ... never thought about it, until Paul figured it out. Once he made me get down on my knees and suck him off ... once I'd done that, then Rupert was as much to blame as I was. If he told on me, I could tell on him. And it'd be worse for him than for me, 'cause his old man might cut him off.*

Hugo unbuttoned his shorts and let them fall around his ankles. He stood naked in the shadows, peering through the leafy barricade, as the final reflection of daylight silhouetted the figures by the pool. He could see them interacting, Frank taking Bruce's cock in his mouth, sucking him off right there in the open, neither one of them concerned, although they had almost been exposed by that reporter, that asshole Frank had wanted someone to take care of.

Now they'd moved, and the doctor was on his knees in front of Frank. Hugo's hand moved faster, his body bending forward as the thrilling sensation possessed him. His balls pulled tight against the underside of his cock; his heart raced in a whispered harshness in his chest. He could see the motions of Bruce's throat as the shrink took his lover's load, followed by the spurting of his own jism as his fingers flayed the length of his smaller, circumcised cock. Hugo's head tilted backward, and he struggled to suppress a roar of relief as his own fluid spurted into the shadowy area before him, soaking into the ground. And with the discharge of his pent-up juices, the frantic passions drained away as well. He still loved Frank, no disputing that, but his other feelings were not as clearly defined. Instead of being a potential object of sexual desire, Hugo's perception of Bruce assumed a more mundane aura. He was an obstacle, actually, a barrier that stood between Hugo and the object of his desire.

If Bruce weren't there, then what? Might Frank turn to Hugo, to the big, beautiful body that lusted for him? And if Bruce remained as he was, how much of a threat did he pose to Hugo? Of the three men living next door, he was the most likely to figure out where Hugo was coming from, and where he had disappeared to when Paul had run out after him.

The guys had gone inside, probably to get dressed to meet the kid. Hugo slunk back to the house. He still had at least an hour before the patrol came back, time to get something to eat, although the cupboard was getting pretty bare. He'd eaten all the canned food and packaged goods, and the stuff in the freezer was mostly too difficult for him to cook. He didn't know how to use many of the kitchen appliances, and almost all the frozen meat was in great big pieces. And now he didn't have any money left. Dennie owed him a week's pay, but he was afraid to go over and collect it. And even if he did get the money, he was afraid to use the bike for his trip to the liquor store. They'd be sure to see him.

It's all because of that fuckin' Paul! If he hadn't seen me, I wouldn't be in this mess. And Frank would help me. I heard him say he would. But Bruce! As long as he's in the picture I'm fucked! I'm fucked, and I'm hungry, and I gotta do something soon, but I don't know what. And there's nobody I can ask. Not even Momma. She'd just scream and cry if I asked her anything. And anyway, she's gone back to Texas, again. Frank's the one. If I can get him alone, sometime. I know he'd help me, maybe get my money from Dennie for me, if nothing else. Frank ... Frank. He kissed the air in front of him, closing his eyes and trying to imagine that the handsome Latin features were within his grasp.

■ ■ ■

Bruce and Frank had slipped back into their shorts, and Frank had gotten into a short-sleeved terrycloth jacket. He was just zipping it up when Dennie came outside to join them. Although he was dressed in well-washed jeans and a t-shirt, he was obviously freshly showered and had prepared himself for Jeff's impending arrival.

"Bruce, you've got to help me. with this," he said solemnly. "I don't know how to tell Jeff about his friend." He began to empty some charcoal briquettes into the hibachi, atop the ashes of Monroe's photos.

"I don't think it's going to be all that big a surprise," Frank told him. "I'm sure he's half expecting it."

"That's not necessarily going to make it any easier on him when he's confronted with the actuality," Bruce cautioned. "He's young, still at an age when he can believe in his own immortality — his and any friends in his age group. Death's a distant concept."

"So, how do we tell him?" Frank asked, at which point the front-door chime sounded.

Dennie started toward the house. "I'll leave it for you to take the lead," he said to Bruce.

But all of them had failed to anticipate the young man's own quick perception. He had hardly joined them on the patio and

127

cracked open a can of beer, when he looked at his three companions and responded to their inordinately restrained behavior. He took a chair next to Bruce, finally. "Alfie?" he said simply.

"Yeah," the psychiatrist told him. "Our friend Pete Jackson — the police lieutenant — just left. He stopped by to bring us something and we got the call from Abe — about Alfie — while he was here. Then Pete called in and confirmed it."

"Then he really is ... I mean, they didn't find him in a hospital or something?" Although he was ashen-faced and obviously shaken, Jeff was still dry-eyed, holding back his feelings.

"No, he's been dead for at least a week," Bruce told him.

The tears were glistening in the young man's eyes, and he swallowed hard, drew a labored, rattling breath. "Where did they find...?"

"In Griffith Park," Bruce told him. Jeff's face was buried in his hands now, and Bruce motioned Dennie over. The big man pulled Jeff gently to his feet, enveloped him in his massive grip, and guided him slowly into the house. "We'll be back in a few minutes," he whispered.

Bruce nodded, and when they were out of earshot, he spoke softly to Frank. "When I saw Pete Jackson out," he said, "I told him Jeff would be here tomorrow morning. He said he'd stop by and interview him around ten."

"And I bet he didn't bat an eye, as to why and how he'd be here," Frank replied.

"No, but after our little hairpin-dropping session a few minutes before, there wasn't much left to hide," Bruce reminded him. "You sound a little miffed. Did it upset you to be this open with him?"

Frank shook his head. "Not really," he said. "God, those pictures! They didn't leave much to the imagination. It's just this whole situation, I guess. The murders down the hill, then Haven Monroe, now Alfie. They've all got to tie into each other, Bruce. But how, and why? And ... well, who's next? And what about Huey — or Hugo? Is he somehow involved in all of it?"

"I can't answer any of this," Bruce admitted. "It's too bad that Paul Orsini had to spook Huey like that, though. I'd sure like to ask him a few questions."

"So would the cops," Frank reminded him.

"Somehow, I don't think they'd get the full story out of him."

"You think you could?" Frank asked.

Bruce shrugged. "I think he'd rather talk to you," he replied, reaching across and giving Frank's thigh a squeeze, then letting his fingers travel a little higher. "He'd probably like a little'a that, too."

The final glow of sunset had faded from the sky by this time, and the yard was in deep shadow, except where the underwater pool lights cast a muted glow through the area. The inside of the pool was painted a dark blue-green, however, and this lessened the overall illumination. Bruce got up to check on the coals in the barbecue, and Frank followed him.

"Where do you suppose Huey, or Hugo — I guess we oughta start calling him that. I wonder where he got off to?" Frank remarked.

"I haven't a clue," Bruce told him. "He moves pretty fast for a guy his size, but he's not exactly the kind to fade into the background. He's big and he's good-looking. People are bound to notice him."

"You don't suppose he's got some secret hiding place on the Orsini grounds, do you?" Frank suggested. "I mean, he apparently worked there since he was a junior in high school, and he's ... what? Twenty, twenty-one? That's enough time to really explore the place from top to bottom. And you know, I've always felt that was the kind of haunted house that ought to have sliding panels and secret passageways in the walls."

Bruce gave him a snorting laugh. "And maybe a ghost or two?" he suggested.

"Okay, laugh at my idea," Frank replied. "But ... hey, don't you have a date with that other kid?"

"Rupert? Yeah, he's coming tomorrow afternoon. But I don't expect much from him. I think he's only doing it to keep Halloran off his back. And I don't know what I'm supposed to do with him," Bruce added. "I feel out of my depth talking to either of them, because I don't have any clear goals."

"Aren't you just supposed to assuage their guilt?" asked Frank.

"What guilt? They aren't supposed to have done anything, remember?"

"Do you really believe that?"

"I don't think Paul's involved," Bruce assured him. "Rupert? I don't know; I haven't talked to him yet. But you can bet your boots Halloran wouldn't be giving me easy access to his clients if he thought there was the faintest chance of my turning up something adverse."

"So he believes they're innocent," said Frank.

"Yeah, I think so. Either that, or he figures them to be skilled enough not to give anything away."

"Have you ever met him?" Frank asked. "Halloran, I mean."

"Once, at a seminar I did on criminal profiling. He sat in the front row, I remember, and he only asked a couple of questions. But he's a tough cookie; I can tell you that. We had a drink afterwards, and he's not the lawyer I'd want on the other side if I went on trial for something."

"So, then, he does more or less know you, and he must be hoping you'll contribute something to the defense, when and if," Frank concluded.

"Yeah, although the need for a defense — as far as the two boys are concerned — appears to be more remote all the time ... Ah, Dennie's back." He watched his friend come out, onto the patio. "How's Jeff doing?" Bruce asked.

"He's okay. He'll be with us in a minute," Dennie told them.

TEN

"Jeff, didn't we save the leftover hamburgers last night?" Dennie stood in front of the refrigerator, one hand resting on the open door.

"I thought so," Jeff said, coming up behind him and joining in his perusal of the crowded interior. "You said Rudy could have them for breakfast." And at the sound of his name, the big Lab was there immediately, his nose poking into the lower shelves.

"Well, they sure as hell aren't here, now. Maybe Bruce and Frank came in for a midnight snack." Dennie closed the door and patted Rudy on the head. "Guess you'll have to do it with dog biscuits," he told the wriggling body.

The timer sounded on the coffee maker, and Dennie poured them each a mugful. It was barely eight o'clock, but Jeff had been restless, unable to sleep in for the extra hour they might have enjoyed together. Dennie watched him as he spooned sugar into the ceramic mug, responding again to the physical perfection of this slender youth who was so willingly giving himself into the big man's keeping. What Dennie was feeling was love — passion, lust, all the usual emotions that one experiences at the height of an affair; but there was an additional element that the older man had not sensed for a long time.

I'm pushing forty, and the kid's not even twenty. Twice his age. Jesus. Frank keeps teasing me about being a dirty old man, and he's right. Except I feel something more than just sex coming back from Jeff, too. Never said in so many words ... maybe just on the rebound, losing Alfie and all, but...

131

"Dennie, how well do you know this cop who's coming to interview me?" asked Jeff, breaking into the big man's reverie.

"Oh, fairly well. He's done a lot of work with Bruce, of course, not with me, so my contacts have been somewhat ... er, peripheral. I've never really had any meaningful talks with him, if that's what you mean — never had a one-on-one relationship."

"What do you think I ought to tell him, about Alfie and me, I mean?"

Dennie drew a deep breath. "Well, for openers, I wouldn't try to play any games with him. He's been around, and he knows the streets. He's sharp enough to trip you up if you try to lie to him, and then he's not going to give you any leeway."

Jeff nodded his understanding. "Yeah, I know if he wasn't a friend of Bruce's, I'd probably have been hauled downtown for interrogation. But, you know..." He made a sound halfway between a sigh and a groan, an expression of desperate uncertainty. "...I just can't figure out what happened. There wasn't any reason for Alfie's being killed like that! And, you know, it must have happened right after he left the apartment, 'cause he was going to take the truck, but didn't."

"Unless he met someone in the parking lot, and went off with him, and the guy killed him later that evening or the next day. They still haven't figured out exactly when he died. I'd almost—" Dennie broke off, as he saw Jeff's eyes begin to glisten, again.

"Well," the younger man managed, forcing the lump to recede in his throat, but speaking with a thickened tone, "I'm sure not going to be able to kid him about being queer, or about my relationship with Alfie. What I don't want to get into is the situation with Madam. I don't know if I could handle it, telling a cop that I've been working as a call boy."

"I suspect he already knows it," Dennie replied. "In fact, I have a feeling he'll only skim over that, unless he thinks it might have been one of your — or Alfie's — er, clients, who did it."

"It couldn't have been," Jeff told him decisively. "We were very careful about that. None of the johns ever knew where we lived. Madam knew, of course, because he owned the building. But he was so afraid we'd make a date on our own and cheat him out of his commission, he wouldn't even give our phone number to anyone."

"Alfie could have run into someone by accident," Dennie suggested.

Jeff shook his head. "It's so unlikely," he insisted. "The parking lot was in the rear of the building, and we always used the back door. There's just no way to 'run into' anyone. If Alfie met up with somebody, it had to have been deliberate, on their part or his."

Bruce came into the kitchen a few minutes later, wearing a lightweight, paisley robe. He poured two mugs of coffee, and went to the frig for milk. "We'll be in to join you shortly," he told them. "We've got a full day ahead of us." He tousled Jeff's uncombed hair as he squeezed past him to reach the sugar bowl. "And I wouldn't worry too much about Pete Jackson," he added. "He knows the score — straight, himself, but he's not looking for any problems. And, after all, your aunt is married to a police commissioner. Just tell him the truth, and don't hold anything back. Do that, and you shouldn't have any problems." He picked up the two mugs of coffee and moved off down the hall.

"Easy to say," Jeff muttered. "But it's *my* best friend who got killed, and ... hey, what about the stash we found in the storage locker?"

"Tell the truth," Dennie urged. "Bruce and Frank were there. They know you flushed it. A shame, too. All that good grass."

■ ■ ■

"Lieutenant Jackson, I don't understand why you keep harping on people I had contact with. Most of these guys never even knew Alfie existed." Jeff was already uncomfortable and needlessly defensive, realizing how much the policeman knew — or suspected — regarding his work for the escort agency. His questions seemed to imply his having a thorough knowledge, just as Dennie had said he would.

Jeff and Pete Jackson were sitting in the gazebo, on the upper edge of Bruce's property, their privacy assured by their distance from the main house. They could hear the grounds-keepers moving about the yard next door, and carpenters hammering in the framework on the new house going up across

133

the street. Dennie had sent the two of them out with a tray of soft drinks and some small, carefully trimmed sandwiches. Jackson toyed idly with one of the dainty wedges, which appeared white and somehow fragile in his large, thick fingers.

"Jeff, there's no obvious logic to this killing," he admitted. "It's the same M.O. as several others, as I assume Bruce has told you. So, whoever killed your friend did it for one of two reasons. At least, this is my theory. For the moment," he added. "He had to believe that Alfie knew something that he shouldn't have known. Or..." And here the detective allowed a significant pause to emphasize the importance of his second theoretical possibility. "...he had to believe that *you* knew something *you* shouldn't have known, and the person who killed Alfie got the wrong guy. After all, he was probably getting into your truck when—"

"You mean, you think somebody's after *me?*" Jeff stared at him in open horror, not knowing whether to credit the idea, or not. "Why should anyone want to kill me?"

"Why should anyone want to kill your friend?" returned the lieutenant.

"I don't see any reason at all, why anyone would want to kill either one of us. If it hadn't been for this stuff about the garrote, and you guys being so sure it ties everything in to the Orsini killings ... you know if it wasn't for that, I'd say someone killed him ... like, in one of those sex things you read about."

"Maybe," Jackson replied dubiously, "but he didn't take the truck. That means whoever killed him has to have intercepted him in the parking lot. That means he was lying in wait, deliberately sought him out."

"You know Alfie was dealing dope ... or wanted to," Jeff countered.

"Yeah, you explained that. But, again, I can't see any motive to kill him, unless he was witness to something. After all, he appears to have bought a small stash, and even if he'd bought it on credit — highly unlikely — but even if this were the case, they shouldn't have been after him for payment that fast. It did occur to me that he might have bought the dope for some ... uh, client he was planning to see later, but even if that were the case I can't see how it could have gotten him killed. I still think it must have been to keep him — or you

134

— from telling about something you've seen, or heard ... or somehow discovered."

"But I don't know what I could possibly have seen, or know, that anybody'd care about," Jeff insisted.

"Let's go step by step through everything you've done since you got here," Jackson suggested.

Jeff's face burned a bright red. "There are ... I mean, I've done some things that I..."

"I know what you've done ... generally," the lieutenant told him. "I know you've hustled, and I know you worked for a call-boy service. No, it's all right," he said, holding up a restraining hand. "Bruce confirmed my own suspicions, and ... well, I really don't care about all of that, except as it might bear in this killing. Kids like you come into Hollywood every day, and if they've got anything going for them — in the looks department — there's a good chance they get into selling their bodies, because it's all they've got to sell. I've heard all this before, and I assure you I'm not the least bit shocked by it. And I'm not going to blab to your aunt — or the commissioner. But you've got to tell me the truth. I've got problems every way I turn with this case, so all I can do is keep plugging at it until something falls into place."

"I have the feeling you're being more communicative with me than you normally are," Jeff suggested.

"I am," Jackson told him. "First, I think you're telling me the truth, as much as you think you can tell me. You're related to people I know and like, and trust, and ... well, I don't know exactly what's going on with you and Bruce and Company, but I know you've been staying here, so I assume—"

"I'm with Dennie," Jeff replied simply.

The black officer's face registered the slightest trace of surprise, but he continued as if he had fully expected the answer he got. "Regardless, you're part of the family, so to speak, and Bruce is going to know what's going on, probably end up knowing more than any of us." This last was said with a trace of bitterness, Jeff thought, but Bruce obviously enjoyed a unique position with the police department and its representatives.

The lieutenant now proceeded to take Jeff through an embarrassingly thorough account of his adventures since arriving in Los Angeles, starting with the first night in the dungeon of mannequins. At one point during his recitation, Jeff thought he saw a question forming on Jackson's lips, but the policeman never interrupted him, and Jeff continued without a break, after which the lieutenant did ask the questions he had been holding back.

Finally, after nearly two hours, Jackson seemed ready to terminate the interview, but just as Jeff was about to stand up, the policeman asked the most telling question. "So, exactly how would you characterize your relationship with the deceased?" he said. "Were you lovers? Just friends? How did each of you feel about the other one turning tricks?" The policeman watched his subject's handsome features as Jeff struggled to put his thoughts into words, but all the while in the back of his mind he kept thinking about the mannequins. Jeff had mentioned them just in passing, but that meant he'd been with the younger Orsini kid. Even so, was there any significance to the connection? Jackson couldn't see what it might be, but it was the only possible link between the Orsini murders and Alfie's. He wrenched his concentration back to focus on the present, forcing himself to tune into Jeff's reply to his question.

"...don't think there was any problem as far as either of us was concerned about what we were doing. And, I can only guess about Alfie's feelings for me, but I think they were pretty much like mine for him. I loved him like he was family, and we had really good sex together. I wasn't *in* love with him, but I'm not sure that he ... that he didn't think he was ... you know, in love with me."

Jackson nodded thoughtfully. "Well," he said, "that's about all we can do at the moment. Will you be here, if I need to talk to you again?"

"Yes. Dennie's asked me to move in, for the time being, at least. Ah, am I ... am I a suspect?" he added plaintively.

"Not in my mind, at least not if everything you've told me checks out," Jackson assured him.

■ ■ ■

"Come in, Mr. Orsini. Let's sit over here by the table. Dennie's just made us a fresh pot of coffee." Bruce guided his client into the office, as Dennie closed the door, giving the psychiatrist a jaundiced look over Rupert Orsini's shoulder.

"Look, Doctor, you don't have to give me all this bullshit. I'm here because my lawyer wanted me to come. So ask whatever questions you want, and I'll try to answer them. The sooner we can get it over with, the better."

It was a pattern Bruce had heard before, but it still rankled him. He would have liked to tell the guy to leave, but he knew that this was exactly what Rupert wanted. In a sense, to have Bruce do that would constitute a moral victory. For that reason, if no other, the psychiatrist simply smiled and sat down on the leather chair facing the hostile young man.

"The fact that your attorney wanted you to come here must indicate that he's looking for something good to come of it," Bruce suggested. "And the benefit will hopefully accrue to you, not mc."

"You're getting the fat check," replied the other sullenly.

"We all get paid what we're worth," Bruce shot back, and this seemed to strike the proper chord. Rupert's pasty face crinkled into a smile, and he accepted the cup of coffee Bruce offered him. The strain he had been under since the murder of his parents seemed to have left a deeper impression on Rupert than on his brother, at least outwardly. He was obviously very much on guard with Bruce — starting at any unexpected sound — and despite his tender years, there were creases around his eyes, heavy bags beneath them. He was pale, as if he seldom exposed himself to the sun, and — Bruce realized — this tended to make him seem less attractive than he really was.

"Look, Doctor MacLeod, I don't mean to appear uncooperative, but I don't know what's going to be gained by my coming here. I don't think the D.A. seriously considers me a suspect any more, and I'm really not having any emotional problems."

"You're not sleeping well," said Bruce evenly, "and you're jumpy. At a guess, I'd say you were afraid of something."

Rupert regarded him in silence for a full minute before responding. "What makes you think I'm afraid?" he asked finally.

"I think you may have good cause to be fearful," Bruce suggested. "You've certainly been through enough to throw the fear of God into anyone." His genuine tone of sympathy further softened Rupert's resistance, but his patient's natural tendency to withdraw made it difficult for him to relate, even with a professional who was probing for some common ground.

"I'm afraid of my brother," he said at length. "If he got the chance ... I don't know. He hates me; that's for sure. And he'd like to see me out of the way."

"You don't *really* believe he'd harm you, do you?" Bruce asked. In all honesty, Rupert's assertion had caught Bruce off guard. The very concept was so illogical, it was hard to believe the young man had seriously proposed it.

"If he got the chance, I think he'd kill me, just like he did our folks," Rupert continued. "He's a sick pervert, who gets his kicks by torturing other guys, or getting them to torture him."

In spite of himself, Bruce was momentarily stunned by the vehemence of this older brother's condemnation of his sibling. It had been apparent during his interview with Paul that the two were estranged, but he had also expected to encounter another young man of superior intellect. Clearly, Rupert was not as gifted as Bruce had been led to expect by Paul's comments. Still, under the circumstances, and in the face of all the evidence to the contrary, it was difficult to believe that Rupert could really suspect his brother.

"What makes you think he's the murderer?"

"Because he's a devious little bastard. He's always pretending to be the dutiful son, but behind Dad's back he was out doing things that make you sick to think about. Dad found out, 'cause he was takin' advantage of that poor dummy who worked for us, and he told Paul to straighten himself out, or else."

"Or else?"

"Dad was going to throw him out," Rupert replied smugly.

"With the things that go on in Hollywood all the time, I'm surprised a man as sophisticated as your father would react that way." *Shades of Dan Donovan,* Bruce thought.

"Dad was a man of old-fashioned virtues," Rupert insisted. His tone was clipped, now — his manner almost smug.

"And your mother? How did she feel about all this?"

"She didn't know. Dad couldn't bring himself to tell her." There was a suggestion of an emotional shift in Rupert's demeanor at the mention of his mother. For the moment, Bruce could only make mental note: something to explore later?

"How can you be so sure about all this?" Bruce asked, his every instinct telling him that the kid was feeding him a preposterous jumble of ... what? Deliberate lies? Misguided beliefs? Half-truths?

"Dad told me," replied Rupert. "We were very close."

■ ■ ■

"The kid's lying through his teeth," said Abe Javits. "Rupert seemed to have the inside track with his old man, but I'm sure Felix Orsini didn't know about Paul's sexual exploits. Rupert was holding that over his brother's head to keep him in line. This all comes out strongly in Pete Jackson's report of his interviews with a variety of observers." The commissioner shrugged and waved his hands as if in disgust at his own vehemence. He had stopped by on his way home to let Bruce know that Dan Donovan had returned to Los Angeles, and was now proceeding with his original mission.

"I'd better warn Dennie," Bruce said, laughing. "The old man's going to be after his ass for seducing his innocent young son."

"I think Dan's mellowed a bit," Abe answered. "You guys knocked some of the arrogance out of him on the last trip. He's in a panic, though, because of Alfie's getting killed. He's sure someone has to be after Jeff."

Bruce paused thoughtfully before responding. "And he might be right. By the way, did you know that Jeff suspects his old man might have been playing footsie with the drug mutts?"

Now it was Abe's turn to engage in some mental churning before he replied. "Jesus," he sighed. "That's hard to believe, but ... how ... why does the kid think this?"

"He suspects Dan is renting out his unoccupied buildings for storage, or transshipment points."

Abe shook his head. "I hope not, for Alice's sake ... for a lot of people's sake, including my own. I can see the tabloids now: *Police Commissioner's Brother-in-law Indicted for Dope Smuggling.*"

"Shit, Abe. He's doing it — if he's doing it — in Iowa. That's not going to affect you."

"Who knows?" Abe replied. "Just one more thing to worry about. But back to the Orsini brothers. If either one claims to have been on best father-son terms with Felix, he's lying through his teeth."

"I suspected as much," Bruce agreed, "but enlighten me. I haven't seen Jackson's report — didn't want to see it, and have it bias my own reactions. You obviously know some things I haven't gotten from the boys."

"Neither one of the kids got along with the old man, because neither of them was developing into Daddy's conception of the proper Orsini macho superhero," Abe replied. "The older one's a sneaky little bookworm; the other one's openly gay, although — as I said — I'm sure his SM interests weren't known to his father. Both kids acted like beaten curs when the old man came down on them for something. At least, that's how we put it together from various comments by friends and neighbors ... and from the live-in maid."

"That would be Hugo's mother? The mother of the kid everyone's trying to find?"

"You got it. She wasn't much help, of course; she'd been home with her family — in El Paso, I think, for about a week before the murders. She came back as soon as she heard, mostly because she was worried about Hugo. Then, when he turned up missing, she got hysterical — had to be put in the hospital for a couple of days."

"Where is she now? Any chance Hugo's hiding out with her?"

"Not likely. Rupert canned her, and she went back to her family in Texas. The investigators' best guess is that Hugo wasn't getting along too well with her recently, so ... who knows? All we can be sure about is that he was here, working for you, a couple of days ago."

"Did Pete pick up anything on how he got along with the Orsini sons?" Bruce asked.

Abe shrugged. "Hard to tell. Nothing written in the report, but reading between the lines, I got the feeling there may have been some hanky-panky with one or both, but nothing for sure. Each one — Hugo, plus both brothers, I mean ... each is a strange case in his own right."

Bruce let this go for the moment, keeping Paul's account to himself, but decided to tell Abe about the vacant lot. "Did you know the younger one used to spy on us — up on the hill?"

Bruce pointed to the same spot where Haven Monroe had taken his pictures.

Abe clucked his tongue and shook his head in dismay. "You'd better fence the inner side," he said. "Bad enough if *they* get on to you, but I'd hate to see Frank's naked butt smeared across the front of the *Yellow Star*, or one of the other supermarket journals." He made no reference to Pete Jackson's having prevented exactly that catastrophe, and Bruce thought it best not to bring it up. Abe probably knew — or suspected — but it was possible he'd prefer not to be officially aware of all the facts. If he wanted to do so, he would admit his knowledge at the appropriate time.

"Yeah, we're putting in a new fence on the upper lot — street side, and maybe something up above the pool. Dennie's working out details with the contractor now," Bruce replied. "We've been putting on shows for too many eager eyes. But what about Dan's sudden return? Didn't Alice know he was coming?"

"No, he just called to tell her he was back at the Hilton, and wanted to know where he could get hold of Jeff. She gave him the phone number at their apartment, then called to tell me I'd better warn you the old man's out here."

"Hmm, I wonder how long it's going to take him to figure out where Jeff is staying, and whom he's sleeping with."

"Not long," Abe said. "And he ain't gonna like it."

"You know," Bruce remarked, "there are some interesting similarities between Felix Orsini and Dan Donovan."

"Yeah," Abe drawled, with a wolfish grin. "Each one's got a potential link to the drug cartel, only nobody knows for sure. One's dead, and no one — not me, anyway — dares to ask the other, because he's afraid what answer he might get."

"I was thinking more in terms of each one having a sexually precocious son, and not knowing how to handle him. And now we've got the live one coming back here gunning for his son's potential adversary. Did he seem to share Pete Jackson's theory — that whoever got Alfie might be after Jeff, next?"

"Oh, I'm sure," Abe said firmly. "He didn't explain very much when he talked to Alice, and he'd caught her so off guard she didn't think to press him on why he'd come back. But you know that has to be it. I just thought I'd better make sure you knew he was in town, before he reappears on your doorstep."

141

"So, it's too bad if he doesn't like what's happened. We've got a lot more serious problems than one Bible Belt father to worry about. Pete Jackson is apparently very serious, thinking Jeff may be in some danger, from exactly whom — or what — I don't know. As I said, he did suggest the possibility that whoever killed Alfie may actually have been looking to get Jeff."

"Did he offer any more of a theory than that?"

"No, he didn't. I don't understand his logic. Maybe it's just policeman's intuition. Or maybe he's being overly cautious in order to stave off any outside risk to Jeff. He did make a remark in passing — about Jeff's being safer here than at the dump in Hollywood, because no one would know where to find him."

Abe nodded absently, silently agreeing with Bruce's account, then sat thinking for another minute, his lower lip contorted as he worked his tongue across his teeth in concentration. He sighed, finally, waving his right hand distractedly. "I know it's all a lot of bullshit," he said softly, "but Jackson's not senior man on this case. We're involved with a lot of departmental politics that are too complicated and asinine to go into now. But the long and the short of it is that the chief put Pete's boss — Captain Fullbright — in charge. Do you know Fullbright?"

"I only met him once, rather briefly," Bruce admitted. "I've talked to him on the phone a couple of times."

"Well, the guy's a political animal," explained the commissioner. "A real senatorial demeanor, as you may remember — white hair and black eyebrows, well-tanned face. He's a skillful manipulator, and a fundamentalist Christian. I don't trust the man, but Jackson's absolutely devoted to him, because the captain's done him a lot of favors." He stopped again, as if collecting his thoughts.

"Anyway," Javits continued, "we know each other in a sort of wary, circling-fighter kind of stance. He'd like to see Jeff arrested for Alfie's murder," he added abruptly.

"I can't believe that!" Bruce returned — surprised, and sitting forward in his chair.

"Believe it," Abe assured him. "If Jackson weren't so sure the kid was innocent, he'd be down in County Jail right this minute. And, just a further morsel for thought, remember that nothing would please Fullbright more than to see me off the

Police Commission. I'm far too liberal for him, and he's made several remarks that convince me he's concerned I might make an issue of his religion sometime."

"I don't understand," Bruce admitted, genuinely confused by Abe's somewhat disjointed account. "You've been appointed by the mayor, confirmed by the city council. He can't bounce you off—"

"I'm sorry to appear obtuse," the commissioner continued, "but when I mentioned politics I didn't necessarily mean the process you see up front and in the media. The real politics go on behind closed doors, and in the proverbial 'smoke-filled rooms.' As for Fullbright — he's been criticized for allowing his religious views to color some of his command decisions, and also to determine his recommendations for promotion. Some of this has gotten into the press, at least on the editorial page."

"Where does that leave Pete Jackson? If Fullbright's the redneck you make him out to be, how come he's taken a black guy under his wing?"

"Pete's on the sidelines, in some ways. He's a good family man — probably goes to church. I couldn't swear to that, but I'd be surprised if it weren't the case. But he's in a unique position. To some extent he's the 'show black' — the guy the captain can point to when they accuse him of right-wing bias, and say: 'Hey, how can you call me a redneck when my right-hand man's black?' On the flip side, Pete's not privy to a lot of the inner political mechanizations of the Department. Fullbright relies on him to do the bulk of the real police work — and rewards him for his successes. But beyond that, there's a good-old-boy insiders club that Pete will never penetrate."

"So, when it comes to the inner sanctum, it's born-again white Christians only. Yeah, I know the name of that game. Except, you can usually add 'heterosexual' to the list of qualifications."

"Yeah. Unfortunately, in this instance it has some more-serious ramifications," Abe added glumly. "If Jackson — or someone — doesn't come up with an alternative suspect, Fullbright's told him to take Jeff into custody. He's given him a week."

"But, why?" Bruce was dumbfounded. Jeff was so obviously not the guilty party.

143

"There's a lot of pressure on the captain," Abe explained, "and making an arrest — even one the D.A.'s probably going to refuse to prosecute — is going to make it easier for him."

"That's a shitty excuse for tossing an innocent kid into the can," Bruce replied bitterly.

"Not from the standpoint of a born-again asshole," Abe reminded him. "All queers deserve to be punished, remember? Besides, Jeff's my wife's nephew. Arresting him could embarrass me — *would* embarrass me. And one more potential problem," added the commissioner, "Pete's apparently told the captain everything he's done — and everything he's thought — on the case, even stuff that isn't in the written reports. Fullbright knows about the Monroe pictures, although he never saw them. He also knows that the three of you flushed Alfie's stash. He's a little pissed at you for that."

■ ■ ■

Hugo scrunched down in the bushes, feeling moisture from the ground soaking into his cutoffs. But he had heard Bruce and Frank come outside, and he wanted to know what they were talking about. He had not been able to hear much that had been said between that black policeman and Jeff, because the gardeners had been there for most of the time the two were together. But when the workmen had finally left, Hugo had crept out of his hiding place in the storage shed, and had caught the last of Jackson's conversation with the kid.

He also knew that the guy in the Rolls Royce was some kind of a cop, too, and he had been inside with Bruce for a long time. Frank had come home just before the Rolls pulled out, so it was a safe assumption that the two lovers were going to discuss a lot of the things Hugo had been unable to overhear. Besides, he really enjoyed being able to watch Frank, without the other knowing he was there. He only wished ... really longed for the chance to strip off his own clothes along with the others, to jump into the pool, occasionally allowing his body to rub against Frank's, to imagine how it would be to possess that lean, yet powerful body ... to hold it, force it to his will.

He watched as Bruce came outside, after having returned to the house for a tray of food and drinks. Hugo swallowed hard, feeling the hunger pangs in his gut, the emptiness in his

144

stomach reflecting the void in his loins. He wished Bruce would go away, leave Frank out there alone for him, like a maiden left to appease the dragon. The idea pleased him, and Hugo grinned in the darkness, knowing he would think of Bruce again tonight as he had on several other occasions lately ... planning how he could cope with him, the tortures he might force him to endure in punishment for taking the place that was rightfully Hugo's, in bed beside Frank.

"I can't believe they'd really arrest Jeff," said Frank. "He's so obviously innocent."

"From what Abe said, it's more a matter of keeping the powers-that-be off of Fullbright's back," Bruce told him. "What really concerns me is that once they actually make an arrest, it then becomes in the interest of the Department to seek a conviction — exoneration for having committed themselves in the first place — that, and the age-old assumption that a person wouldn't be arrested if he weren't guilty. It takes away the incentive to keep looking for an alternative suspect."

"And he's making noises about me, too?" Frank asked.

This last brought Hugo almost to his feet, as he leaned forward to hear better.

Bruce laughed bitterly. "Only as a long shot," he replied. "The fact that Pete brought you the pics and you burned them places Fullbright in the peculiar situation of being unable to do anything about you. Pete Jackson, after all, is *his* man — his most dependable minion — a man who's been promoted and given choice assignments, all on the captain's recommendation. Now, if he turns around and gets on Jackson for compromising evidence, it reflects right back on the captain."

"You know, this whole case is a fucking mess!" Frank said vehemently. "First the Orsinis get strangled. Then Alfie gets killed the same way, although his body isn't found until after that Monroe asshole gets it — also via garrote. And the cops have to assume all four were killed by the same guy — or guys — because of identical M.O.s. But they can't find one suspect to fit all three instances. It's crazy. Isn't it possible they had a copycat on the subsequent killings, or ... shit — just coincidence?"

"I don't know. Of course, neither does anyone else. I talked to Pete Jackson for a few minutes before he left, after his session with Jeff. He says they're going to mount a major manhunt to find Hugo. They figure he must know something — and also want to put him in a lineup. It seems a couple of witnesses place him, or someone who looks like him, in the vicinity of Monroe's hotel the night he got it."

"That's interesting," Frank mused. "He was with us, in the pool, I think, wasn't he? That was the night we were talking about Monroe, because he'd been up on the hill. It all happened so fast, but ... yeah, I'm sure Hugo was there. Hard to remember for sure."

Bruce sat quietly for a moment, trying to remember the details of that particular night, finally nodding agreement. "Yeah, I think you're right."

"You don't think Hugo...?" Frank's voice trailed off. "No, he couldn't," he scoffed. "He didn't even know where Monroe was staying."

"Oh, I think we mentioned that," Bruce replied thoughtfully. "And Hugo was here all afternoon. So he may have heard a lot more than just the things we said outside by the pool. Interesting. And I remember, now. He *was* in the pool with us. He even asked me who Monroe was. And when he left here he was wearing just his cutoffs and a tank top. The description of one hotel guest was, 'a half-naked giant, with a body like Conan the Barbarian.' That certainly sounds like our Hugo."

"Well, I hope they find him without having to shoot him," Frank said. "I don't see how he could really be guilty of anything."

"We won't know for sure till they find him and interrogate him," Bruce replied. "Hey, why don't we take a quick dip and then go inside?" He stood up and shucked his shorts, standing within easy arm's reach of Frank's chair.

His friend reached out and seized the tempting mass of genitals, using them to guide Bruce an extra step closer, near enough that Frank could lean into him, his tongue working against the pliant flesh. "I think it's time to worry about ourselves for a while," he whispered. "All this horror story going on around us is tough on the glands."

Bruce gently disengaged himself and was just about to dive into the pool, when the phone rang inside the house. "Shit! Who could that be at this hour?" he grumbled, starting toward the door to his office.

146

"Why don't you let the service get it?" Frank asked, disappointment obvious in his tone.

"No, I'd better answer it myself," Bruce sighed. "I've got one suicidal patient, and this might just be an emergency."

"I'll keep it warm for you," Frank called after him, standing up in his turn and stretching, then pulling down on his foreskin as Bruce glanced back over his shoulder. Rudy had followed Bruce inside, and wandered off to his water bowl in the kitchen as Bruce picked up the receiver. The digital clock on his desk made it just a bit after 10:30.

"Sorry to call so late," said Abe's voice, "but I thought you'd want to know. Fullbright had Jackson arrest Paul Orsini again. They found what appears to be the same kind of silk thong used in the killings in the kid's workshop."

"I thought they'd already searched that."

"They had, but that was right after the Orsini murders before Monroe and Alfie got it. Seems someone put a bug in their ears, and they went back to check again, and found the stuff. It's a woven silken rope, with a distinctive pattern and fiber."

"You know, it sounds like a frame, all the way around," said Bruce. "If it were really Mafia, they'd be using a wire garrote. And the drug nuts ... why a silken cord? Why not hemp, or clothesline?" He was standing in the dimly illuminated room, naked, idly stroking himself. He looked over his shoulder toward the pool, but couldn't see Frank. *Coward must be slipping in at the shallow end. Can't stand to jump into the cold water,* he thought, grinning, not allowing his impatience to reflect itself in his tone, but eager to return to his lover.

"It's a distinctive kind of material, all right," Abe agreed. "It's more like the stuff they use in Taiwan for decorative macrame ... weaving. Tough fibers, but extremely flexible. In fact, Fullbright says it's like the material used by the *Phansigars,* the noose killers in nineteenth-century India. He's had a team of explorer cadets researching the whole history of the garrote, so he's become quite an authority on the subject."

"He surely doesn't think someone's imported some Thugee cult of Kali?" Bruce laughed.

"No, even our most imaginative romantics couldn't push it that far, but there *is* a possibility that someone else researched it beforehand, and planned the killings to be done in some ancient tradition, for whatever reason, God only knows."

"And the killer," Bruce added.

"Yeah, and the killer ... or killers."

"Oh, are they finally willing to admit that it might be more than one killer?"

"Well, they've always thought it was more than one," Abe told him. "It had to be at least two for the Orsinis."

"No, no. I meant different perps in either Monroe's or Alfie's killing from the original Orsini—"

"I'm with you," Abe assured him. "But to answer your question — yes, it does look like the multiple-perp theorists are winning for the moment — mostly because they can't make it work out any other way. For instance, Paul Orsini was in jail when Monroe got it, so he's only a suspect in his parents' murders."

"And Rupert?"

"He's still loose — there's nothing to tie him in. In fact, the two kids are so hostile toward each other, it's a good bet that if one of them's guilty, the other probably isn't. Anyway, I'm not going to keep you any longer. Just thought you'd want to know about Paul. Talk to you tomorrow."

Bruce hung up the receiver, and turned thoughtfully toward the outside door. He was momentarily distracted from his earlier lustful fantasies, but the thought of Frank began to rekindle his arousal. He was already half-hard when he stepped out into the slight chill of the backyard. Everything was quiet, with no motion except for a gentle ripple on the pool, the soft underwater light casting a dull glow from the dark plaster walls.

In the first moments, Bruce assumed that Frank must have gone inside to use the bathroom, or to get something in the kitchen. He sat for a moment on the edge of a chair, then decided to slip into the water. When Frank had still not appeared after several minutes, Bruce climbed out of the pool and dried himself enough to go inside. There was no sign of Frank in either of the bathrooms in the main part of the house, nor in the one off Bruce's bedroom. Finally, almost panic-stricken, he made a quick tour of the entire property with Rudy padding along behind. Frank was nowhere to be found.

He was still standing in the front hall, naked, the towel hanging like Pavarotti's handkerchief from his left hand, when a key grated in the front door, and Dennie entered with Jeff.

"Jesus, what a greeting!" said the big man. "You scared the hell out of me!"

"What's the matter?" asked Jeff, who sensed the anxiety immediately.

"Frank's disappeared," replied Bruce helplessly. "I went to answer the phone, left him by the pool. When I came back he was gone."

ELEVEN

"Should we call the police?" Jeff asked.

"No, not just yet," Bruce replied. They had moved into the den, and Bruce had gotten back into his cutoffs and shirt.

"Well, Frank's car's still in the garage," Dennie remarked. "Unless he decided to take a walk, he has to be ... Hey! Bruce, did you guys raid the refrigerator last night?"

"No. What's that got...?"

Jeff also regarded the big man with a quizzical expression. Then the same thought occurred to him, and he nodded. "Yeah! The leftover hamburgers you promised Rudy."

"What are you guys talking about?"

"We've been missing food from the kitchen, several times," Dennie explained. "I thought I must be losing my mind, but don't you see? If you guys weren't raiding the frig at night, it had to be Hugo. Remember how fast he disappeared when Paul recognized him?"

"Of course," Bruce agreed. "I'll bet he's holed up right here in the neighborhood — next door, do you think? The house has been empty for weeks!"

"Sounds like a good bet to me," Dennie agreed. "Should we go for a little breaking and entering?"

"No need for that," Bruce told them. "I've got a key. Old Man Rush gave it to me over a year ago, just in case of emergency. He's got one for this house, too. Hang on a minute. I'll go get it."

On his way to the bedroom, Bruce kept trying to recall everything he and Frank had said, wondering how much Hugo might have overheard if he'd been listening by the fence. *This house is getting to be a regular goldfish bowl. First, they're watching us from the hillside; now, we've got a maniac hiding out next door. Christ, I hope Frank's okay. I know Big Stoop was in love with him ... just hope we didn't say anything to make him change his mind. Must have forced Frank to leave, though. Not a good sign.* "Ugh, where're those fucking keys?" he muttered. Then he found them, tucked into a corner of his jewelry box. Fear was seizing control of his senses, and he felt a frantic need to hurry. But he paused long enough to slip his feet into a pair of sneakers, then hesitated again. There was a 9mm Baretta hidden under a pile of sweatshirts on the shelf above his suits. Abe had given it to him when he first bought the house and he'd hardly seen it since, didn't like the idea of owning it, but ... Quickly, he reached under the pile of soft fabric and found the weapon, which he fumbled into his left hip pocket, remembering Abe's telling him that it would be exactly the right fit.

Jeff and Dennie were waiting for him in the front drive, and the three of them took off on the run for the Rushes' heavy wrought-iron gates, with Rudy yelping in frustration at being left behind in the backyard. Bruce worked a key into the unit that activated the electric locking mechanism. As the gate swung slowly inward, the trio of would-be rescuers were inside before it was a quarter of the way open. They raced up the drive, then stood quietly before the high double doors, listening for some telltale sound. Rudy, much to everyone's surprise, was suddenly beside them, wagging his tail and jumping about in excitement.

"Well," said Bruce, bitterly, "we know there has to be a hole in the fence, too. I think it's time we started charging for the tourist trips. And you, you useless chow hound, go find your buddy!" he added to the prancing Lab.

"Where do you think he'd be?" Dennie whispered.

"I'd guess the kitchen area, or maybe the servants' quarters," Bruce replied. They all started as the gate automatically clicked shut, some twenty-five feet behind them. "We'll have to go in the front way, regardless," Bruce continued. "I don't think this key fits any other doors." He slipped the second key into an ornately outlined lock. The massive portals swung open, revealing a wide, marble-floored atrium, with a double circular staircase ascending on either side. As his companions entered, Bruce barred Rudy's way and left him outside when he closed the door behind them.

"The kitchen's this way," Bruce said, leading them off to the left, "and there's at least one maid's room behind it."

"There's some kind of a room over the garage, too," Dennie suggested.

"Yeah, and I think there's a stairway going up to it from a back hall," Bruce said softly, suppressing the urge to whisper.

They had reached the butler's pantry which separated the dining room from the kitchen. Up to this point, there had been enough light seeping in from the many high windows, that they had no trouble seeing their way. Now they had to pass through an area of almost total darkness. "Wish I'd thought to bring a flashlight," Dennie muttered.

Bruce cautioned them to keep quiet, and led the way into the kitchen, where it was still quite dark because of the many tall trees in the Rushes' backyard. But the shadows could not conceal the distinctive cooking odors that assailed their senses.

"Someone's been burning the pork chops," Dennie whispered.

Bruce's foot skidded out from under him as he stepped in a patch of grease, and Dennie grabbed him just in time to keep him from falling. "Yeah, someone's been using the kitchen," he rasped, "and not doing much of a cleanup, afterwards. Here, this way," Bruce added, guiding them toward a door on the far side of the room. He eased it open and slipped through into the darkened corridor beyond.

Edging his way along the wall, Bruce was several paces ahead of the others as he reached the end of the passageway. The door to a small bedroom stood ajar, and he froze in place as he thought he heard a sound again, something scraping. He was within the room, now, and there was just enough light for him to see an outside door in the far wall. There was definitely a shadowy figure just beyond the glass panel, apparently trying to work the doorknob.

Bruce slipped across the small space, having to skirt the bed, as the others moved in behind him. He pressed himself against the wall beside the portal, where the shadow of a man was clearly silhouetted by the night glow of sky. As he felt the comforting reassurance of Dennie's bulk behind him, he took a deep breath and yanked the door open.

The figure hurled itself backward, and Bruce bolted through after him, realizing only after his arms had made contact that the man was too small to be Hugo.

"Bruce! What the fuck? How did you get inside?" Frank stared up at him from the ground. He was naked except for a pair of walking shorts and tennies.

Bruce had to laugh in spite of himself. "I had a key," he said simply. "What's your excuse?"

"Hugo," replied the smaller man as he tried to get up, finally holding out his hand to Bruce. "I think you broke my back," he groaned. "Help me up!"

"What about Hugo?" Bruce demanded. "Is he here?"

"Yeah. After you went to answer the phone, I remembered that we'd left some glasses and stuff in the gazebo. I slipped back into my shorts and went up to get them, and I caught Hugo in the act of scrounging the leftovers. He took one look at me, and hightailed it over here. I didn't take time to think about it; I just chased him. He went through a hole in the fence, hidden by the bushes down below the gazebo. Anyway, it took me a minute to find the opening after he ducked through, so I wasn't right behind him, and I'm not a hundred percent sure where he went — I thought maybe that door, but ... well, I guess not."

"It's probably a good thing you didn't catch him," Dennie growled from the background. "The asshole might have pulverized you."

"He wouldn't have done any worse than you guys," Frank groaned, rubbing his left arm. "Anyway, he's around here someplace."

"Yeah, and he's probably watching us right now," said Bruce, speaking at a slightly elevated volume. "If he'd let me talk to him, I'm sure I could save him a lot of problems."

Frank picked up on his friend's tactic and called out. "Hugo, where are you? Come on, we only want to talk with you."

"And if you're hungry, we'll give you something to eat," Dennie added.

The four of them were standing in a small herb garden behind the kitchen. There was a gravel walkway, surrounded

153

by several beds of plants. The tall pine trees along the rear of the Rush property cast a deep shadow over the back portion of the yard. Although there was enough light for the interlopers to see clearly about their immediate vicinity, they could not discern anything in the darker portions beyond the garden area. Rudy was yelping from the front of the house, but was barred from joining them by the latched gate — required by law in California for any yard that had a pool.

The giant, hulking form of their quarry was less than ten yards away, in the shadow of the garage. He could hear them distinctly, and was tempted to respond, would have done so if there hadn't been so many of them. In truth, he was afraid of Dennie, because the big man had always been so stern with him. He also found Bruce intimidating, and increasingly an object of dislike because of his relationship with Frank. Still, he might have answered them, except at that moment the beam of a flashlight pierced the darkness. The harsh challenge of the private patrol rang out, and Rudy came charging past the rent-a-cops to join his friends.

It took Bruce several minutes to convince the patrolmen that he was, indeed, the next-door neighbor, with a key to the premises. Then, because he had to make up some excuse for their being on the property at this time of night, he told the guards that they had chased a prowler into the Rushes' yard. This resulted in the men entering the house through the open maid's-room door.

"This is all going very badly," Bruce muttered, as the four of them waited outside, watching the guardsmen's flashlights travel about the interior. "They're going to know someone's been living in there."

"So what?" asked Jeff. "It's no skin off our ass, is it?"

"I was hoping for a chance to talk with Hugo," Bruce replied, again speaking loudly enough that anyone in the enclosure could hear him. "If he'd talk to me, I know I could help him, that Frank would help him. Wouldn't you, Frank?"

"Sure, he's a nice kid," Frank replied. "I don't want to see him get into any more trouble than he's already in."

"Well, I guess he must have gotten away by now," Bruce added, "but if he were to come around later..."

But Hugo had already beaten a hasty retreat, and was well beyond the sound of their voices. Even Rudy's ranging of the property's perimeter turned up no sign of his erstwhile playmate.

"Hey, this place's a mess!" shouted the senior patrolman. "Looks like some homeless bum's been holed up in here!"

■ ■ ■

Everything escalated for the next hour. The patrol called in a burglary report, and within minutes another car from their office arrived, then two police cars, and moments later a helicopter. There was certainly no question of sleep for anyone. Using the few moments before the police arrived at his front door seeking a statement, Bruce had called Abe Javits — woke him up, and told him what had transpired since their conversation a couple of hours before.

"I'll call Pete Jackson," concluded the commissioner. "Think you guys can stay up long enough to talk with him?"

"Not much chance of getting any sleep right now," Bruce had told him. "It sounds like the Inchon landing out there, and you know the cops are going to want a statement before..." He returned Jeff's pantomime, announcing the arrival of the police patrol at the front door. "They're here now," Bruce told him. "I'm going to stick to my story, that it was an unknown prowler, until we've had a chance to talk to Jackson," he added. "Better make sure Pete does call me tonight. I want to pass it on to him right away — that it was definitely Hugo — so I don't get accused of withholding information."

"Good idea," Abe agreed. "But you've already told me. I'll tell him before he calls you. That'll put you in the clear."

The young policeman who took Bruce's statement was polite to the point of being solicitous, especially when he realized that the psychiatrist had written one of the monographs he had studied at the academy. He also seemed a bit awed to recognize Frank. Although meeting TV and screen personalities was not a rarity in Beverly Hills, they were not all young, male, and attractive, which seemed to color the policeman's response. Sensing this, and hoping to play on the young man's sense of community, Bruce emphasized that the four men were gath-

155

ered for a regularly scheduled card game. The policeman gave him a slightly protracted look, but he dutifully recorded the explanation in his notebook. Although Haven Monroe was gone, his breed of yellow journalism abounded. No need to give them pause to wonder why Frank DeSilva had been interviewed at an all-male gathering on Saturday night.

Despite his apparent desire not to offend or intrude, the policeman finally did press on a couple of points. "You had no idea someone was camped out next door?" he asked. "The guy had to have been there a while. The place is a real mess: the contents of all the cupboards and half the freezer have been decimated."

Bruce shook his head. "No, but with all this construction going on, there are strangers in the neighborhood all the time. It wouldn't be hard for one more to go unrecognized." He hated being evasive, and glanced at his watch, wishing Pete Jackson would call.

Mistaking the gesture, the policeman remarked that "he wouldn't be much longer," at which point the phone rang.

"Yes, I'm in my office, and there's a policeman with me right now," said Bruce.

"Why not let me talk to him," said Jackson, and Bruce gratefully relinquished the receiver.

After a few minutes' conversation, the young officer handed the phone back to Bruce and excused himself, going back outside without further comment.

"Bruce, I told them that you've been working on a case with us, and that the prowler might have been snooping around because of that. But I don't think they bought it, because that clown's been hiding out next door. I think you're right, though; Hugo's not going to show up if he thinks there're cops around — unless they nail him, of course."

"If they don't catch him, I think he'll eventually show up here."

"That could be good or bad, Bruce," the lieutenant told him guardedly. "I'd like you to have a chance to interview him without our interference, but ... You know, he might be the one who killed Monroe, might even have been involved in the Orsini murders."

"You don't really believe that, do you?" asked Bruce.

"The Orsinis — no, not really. He's a long way down on the list of suspects. But the Monroe murder, he's right at the top. Whatever you do, Bruce, don't let him get you alone, without someone in easy calling distance."

"I know the routine," Bruce assured him. "There are times when it's best if the therapist not sit between the client and the door."

■ ■ ■

When the police finally left, without finding Hugo, the four men had gone to bed — well after two-thirty. Bruce had half expected the fugitive to appear from some unsuspected hiding place, once the last police car had departed. He even spent an extra few minutes sitting beside the pool with Frank, discussing the advantages that would accrue should the young giant contact them before the police found him — as they inevitably must. Still no Hugo, so they had eventually gone to bed.

It was Sunday morning, and by mutual agreement it was close to noon before the two couples emerged from their respective ends of the house, converging on the dining room almost simultaneously. Dennie kept a sourdough starter going — had for several years — and Bruce's one great concession to their normally fat-restricted diet was Sunday pancakes with sausage patties — preceded by a couple of Dennie's spicy Bloody Marys. It was a ritual to which they all looked forward — even Jeff, who had only shared one other "naughty meal," as Dennie liked to call them, and who thus far seemed content with his Master's "almost-virgin Marys." In fact, he accepted the whole idea with good-humored amusement, the fact that Dennie was treating him in every way as an adult, except when it came to alcohol. Somehow, the big guy seemed to balk at serving booze to a minor. *Okay by me*, he thought. *I don't much care about it, anyway. Just as long as he doesn't decide I'm too young and innocent to be tied up and abused. Certainly didn't seem to think so last night.*

A second bit of ritual involved the Sunday funnies, with a four-way sharing of both "Doonesbury" and "Outland." So popular an event had this become, in fact, that the pancake syrup was kept and served in an "Opus the Penguin" pitcher. It was thus in the middle of this bit of light banter that Jeff

157

suddenly emitted a shout of surprise: "Hey, that's the guy —
the guy with all the dummies in his dungeon!"

He was pointing at the front-page news picture of Paul
Orsini, which headed a two-column account of his being
rearrested, along with an overview of the entire case to date.

"You mean, that's the guy you had sex with that first night
you were in town?" asked Dennie. "April ... what? Sixteenth?"

Jeff was nodding. "Yeah, and that's the guy; I'm sure of it."

"If it really was Paul Orsini you got it on with that night, it
means you were the one who was with him when his parents
were killed. Do you realize you're his alibi? And come to think
of it, he *did* tell me about—" The psychiatrist shook his head
in dismay. "I did halfway connect it," he grumbled. "But the
date — just didn't click!"

"Jesus," Jeff muttered. He sat silently for a couple of minutes, as the full implications of all this sank in. "You mean,"
he continued finally, "I'm going to have to get up in court and
tell a square judge and jury that I tied a guy up, whipped his
ass, and fucked him? Oh, God! I mean, I'll do it; I'll have to do
it, but it's so embarrassing!" His expression was of total distress, and he looked helplessly back and forth between Bruce
and Dennie.

"It won't go that far," Bruce assured him. "I'll give Pete
Jackson a call, and once you give them a statement..."

"Hey, Bruce," Dennie interrupted. "Look here, further down
in the story. It says that 'veteran attorney Mickey Halloran has
announced his withdrawal from the defense of Paul Orsini,
citing a possible conflict of interest. Mr. Halloran will continue
to represent the other Orsini brother, Rupert.' What do you
suppose that's all about?"

"Interesting," Bruce replied thoughtfully. "I'd say it means
friend Halloran thinks he can defend Rupert successfully, but
plans to throw Paul to the hounds. I wonder what he'll say when
he finds out Paul really does have an alibi?"

"Why don't you give him a call?" Frank suggested. "You have
his home phone, don't you?"

"Yeah, I have it," Bruce replied slowly, still considering the
options. Then he grinned mischievously and reached for the
instrument. "Dennie, read his number off to me. It's in the
book there in the niche. We'll give this arrogant bastard some-

thing to think about — and maybe start the ball rolling to get Paul Orsini out of jail a little quicker." Despite his display of levity, Bruce's real concern was Paul, remembering how emotionally devastating his last stint in jail had been, hoping to spare his patient at least a modicum of the discomfort this time.

Despite his higher motivation, however, Bruce's apparent good humor had been infectious — probably due to its contrast with the serious nature of the previous several hours — or maybe Dennie's extra-potent Bloody Marys. At any rate, Bruce was actually laughing as the lawyer's voice came through the receiver. "Mickey!" Bruce greeted him enthusiastically. "Bruce MacLeod here."

There was a moment of silence on the other end of the line, Halloran obviously having been caught by surprise. Then he replied, forcing a joviality to match his caller's. "Well, top of the morning, Bruce. What can I do for you?"

"Ask rather what I can do for you."

"Okay, I'll bite. What can you do for me?"

"I've found the kid who was with Paul Orsini the night the parents were murdered," Bruce said bluntly, winking at Jeff across the table. "I thought you might like to start the ball rolling to get your client out of jail."

Again, the famed attorney was silent for several seconds, and Bruce looked at the eagerly awaiting group around him, making an openhanded gesture in emulation of the lawyer's presumed puzzlement. Finally, Halloran seemed to regain his voice.

"That's very interesting," he said calmly. "And who is this person, and more important, *where* is he?"

"His name is Jeffrey Donovan," said Bruce, "and at the moment he's sitting three feet away from me at the breakfast table."

"Paul mentioned this kid to me early on," Halloran returned. "Said he came from Indiana ... Iowa, some such place. Drove a red pickup truck."

"That's the guy," Bruce told him.

"But, but I thought..." Consternation was obvious in the attorney's voice. "...I thought he got killed ... murdered ... some sex thing. Body found up in Griffith Park."

"The kid who got killed was his friend Alfie, Alfred Stimson," Bruce explained, speaking almost absently now, as his mind began to branch off on a different tangent.

"Well, that's all very interesting," Halloran repeated, suddenly back to his more strident manner. "If it's all as you say it is, and provable, it will make quite a difference. Does the kid seem ... er, credible to you?"

"Extremely so."

"And when can I speak to the lad?"

"Whenever. He's staying at my house for the moment."

"Let me get back to you," said Halloran, and he clicked off.

As soon as he replaced the receiver, Bruce lapsed into a state of thoughtful silence, concern etched on his features. "That may have been a mistake," he said at length.

"How so?" asked Frank, when his friend again lapsed into silence.

"I don't know," Bruce mused. "I just don't get a good feeling with that man, and I can't tell you why."

"Did he say anything about not being Paul's lawyer any more?" Dennie asked.

Bruce shook his head. "No. Well," he said, brightening, "let's finish up here and I'll go in the office and call Abe. Probably should have done that in the first place." But he remained silent for the rest of the meal, his mind churning. *In the first place, Halloran's a lot sharper than that. He knew Alfie's name, and he knows the cops have tied his murder into the Orsini case, because of the M.O., the garrote. He knows it wasn't "a sex thing," either. The asshole! Why's he playing dumb? Lawyer's gimmick? Sent his clients to me for interviews, but never followed up, never requested a report, and Dennie hasn't gotten Rupert's off to him, yet. And why'd he dump Paul? And why didn't he mention that to me? 'Course, he might have had a couple of Bloodys this morning, too.*

■ ■ ■

"Yeah, that's just it, Abe. I'm sorry now I called him, but what's done's done. Where do we go from here?"

"I'll give Jackson a call — or you can. I don't know that there's any real urgency to it. They can't set the machinery in

160

motion to let Paul out until tomorrow, anyway. And even then, it may take a couple of days."

"Couldn't Fullbright get him out on his own, like right now?"

"He wouldn't, even if he could. The political crap is just getting more sticky all the time. At the moment, you for sure can't count on Fullbright's help, and Pete's going to be treading lightly while his boss is on the griddle. If you read the 'Opinion' section of the paper today you'll see what I mean. They're really going after his whole little clique, charging religious bigotry, among other things."

"You're not involved, are you?" asked Bruce.

"Hell, no! I'm staying as far away from all this controversy as possible. The damned commission's taking up too much of my time as it is. It's getting to a point where I'd have trouble making a living if I didn't have some top-notch office help."

"So, anyway, will you call Pete Jackson, or should I?"

"I'll take care of it," Abe assured him. "But don't be surprised if he waits until tomorrow to take a statement from Jeff. Oh — one more thing. Dan Donovan's probably going to get on you very shortly. Alice had to tell him Jeff was staying with you."

"I'm glad Dennie's bigger'n he is," Bruce replied lightly.

"Yeah, well, she didn't tell him anything about Dennie. I think he got the impression the kid was sleeping on the sofa. If you want to keep it that way..."

"We'll play it by ear," Bruce told him.

■ ■ ■

Jeff's affair with Dennie had been going on just long enough that there had ceased to be any reticence on Jeff's part, or in fact on the part of any other household member, regarding their lack of attire in the pool. However, with the possibility of Dan Donovan's imminent arrival, Bruce made sure that the front door, as well as both side gates to the yard were locked. Each of them brought a swimsuit outside with him, too. Beyond that, it was Sunday in the sun, as usual. Also, the new fence had been installed on the upper lot the previous afternoon, which renewed the old sense of privacy.

Jeff positioned himself on the chaise next to Bruce, and his anxiety over his father's anticipated arrival was obvious. "How should I handle him?" he asked. "Dennie says I can tell him whatever I want, as far as he's concerned. Trouble is, I'm not sure what *I* want to tell him."

"It's a hard call to make," Bruce replied. "He already knows you're gay. He doesn't know anything about the SM aspects, except that he found all your sketches back in Iowa. It's too bad he never gave you a chance to explain that they were pure JO fantasies. My guess is, he'll assume you're playing bondage games, even if you don't tell him."

"Where's that going to put Dennie? And you, for that matter?"

Bruce shrugged, lying back on his chaise and putting on a pair of dark sunglasses. "It doesn't matter about either Dennie or me," he said simply. "Even a year ago I might have been hesitant to be so uninhibited, but now I just don't give a fuck. Both Dennie and I are such openly gay men, neither of us cares what your dad knows or doesn't know. You're technically underage as far as drinking and signing certain contracts are concerned, but otherwise you're an adult ... very much a man," he added, patting the solid flesh of the youngster's thigh.

"Hey, watch that!" Frank called from the pool.

"Yeah, keep your hands off my baby," Dennie chimed in from Jeff's other side.

"Better look out, kid," Frank added. "Next thing, he'll want to play doctor."

And on that note of levity the front doorbell sounded.

Dan Donovan was conducted onto the patio by Dennie, where he was greeted by the others — all properly attired in swim trunks, although Frank's Speedo left very little to the imagination.

"Well, Dan!" said Bruce, pushing himself up from the chaise. "Alice just called to say you were in town." He extended his hand and motioned the newcomer to a seat next to Jeff, who responded with a simple: "Hi, Dad."

The elder Donovan had a healthy glow about him, his well-tanned face and arms showing from his short-sleeved yellow sports shirt. He was also wearing a pair of light blue Dockers and canvas deck shoes. If anything, he seemed slimmer — somehow in better shape than during his earlier visit, except that his face was more deeply lined.

162

There now followed an awkward silence, during which Frank and Dennie slipped into the pool, while Bruce tried to think of something appropriate to say. Jeff was sitting astride his chaise, his toes making idle patterns on the flagstone decking, and his face averted to watch the steepling, alternate twisting of his fingers. His father perched on the side of his chair, watching his son with an indefinable expression.

Finally, Bruce stood up and moved to join his two friends in the water. "Look, I'll leave you two alone," he said. "Feel free to go inside if you like."

Jeff looked up sharply, with an almost pleading expression in his eyes, as if beseeching the psychiatrist not to leave him alone with his father. Bruce looked back at him with a slight shake of his head. *You've got to face it sooner or later, kid. Might as well get on with it. The sooner you start, the sooner it's settled.*

"Yeah, Jeff, we do have a lot to discuss," said Dan Donovan in a husky tone. The younger man was nodding agreement as Bruce slipped under the water, out of hearing. He then made a point of joining the others at the far side of the pool until Dan stood up and guided his son back to the gazebo.

"Wonder how long before he discovers our guilty secret," Dennie muttered.

"I don't think that's going to be a problem," Frank specu-. lated. "If Jeff doesn't tell him, I doubt the old man's going to ask."

The father-son conversation lasted for close to half an hour, before the others could hear Jeff's angry response: "There's no way I'm going back there, Dad, and that's final!"

By this time Bruce, Frank, and Dennie had all come out of the pool, and were lying in the warm afternoon sun. At the sound of the heated conversation, Bruce looked across at his two companions. "Maybe it's time to offer Dan a drink," he suggested. "I don't want to interfere, but..."

"Bruce, could you come up here for a second?" Jeff called, and as Bruce drew near he added: "Would you explain to Dad that I'm perfectly all right? He's bound and determined I should go home before someone gets me like they did Alfie."

"You know, as I've told both of you, this isn't a decision anyone else can make for you. I don't think you're in any great danger; of course, I can't make any guarantees. If you want to stay in L.A., you certainly have as much or more going for you than most guys your age. You're welcome here with us as long as you like, and your aunt..."

"And what about staying here?" Dan suddenly demanded. "How's he paying his keep?" He regarded Bruce with a surly sneer, the kind of facial challenge that frequently precipitated a poke in the nose.

"Jeff's been taking care of the grounds," Bruce answered evenly, "and doing some of Dennie's errands for him. We're also looking into an illustrator's job..."

"Drawing naked men with oversized genitals?" asked Donovan mockingly.

"You know, Dan," Bruce countered, sitting down to face him, "back when I was trying to help you find Jeff, you assured me you weren't going to be such an asshole when you found him. Remember?" Even as he said it, Bruce regretted his lack of reticence — not out of any fear of Dan Donovan, but because it annoyed him to lose his temper.

However, Donovan did not share in such squeamishness. In less than a second he was out of his seat, throwing himself at Bruce. But he was not quite fast enough. The psychiatrist twisted out of the wrought-iron chair, hit the ground in a roll, and came up on his feet just in time to counter the first wild punch with his left arm. Donovan never had a chance to throw a second. Bruce landed a single, solid uppercut to the jaw, and the bigger man went down. Before he could clear his head and stagger to his feet, the others were there, separating the antagonists.

The elder Donovan was now the very picture of poorly contained fury. There was still the same vital desperation in his insistence that Jeff come home, which had puzzled Bruce back in the spring when they had been searching the dregs of Hollywood for the two young men. Now, as he watched his guest trying to regain a modicum of composure, he wondered again at the man's real motivation. Then, without giving it further thought, he asked: "Why do you really want Jeff to go back to Iowa, Dan? You've been trying to bullshit me for the better part of four months. Why don't you try the truth for a change?"

Dan Donovan was on his feet now, steady enough to shake loose from Dennie's restraining grip. "It's none of your fucking—" He stopped abruptly, glaring at the circle of men. "You're all a bunch of sick fucking faggots!" he growled. "My own son just as sick as all the rest of you. But he *is* my son. I want him back." There was no mistaking the tears which glistened in his eyes as he staggered away, toward the house ... to the front drive and his rented Mustang. The last thing he said before slamming the door closed on the circle of onlookers was the most revealing of all: "If he stays here, he's going to die!" whined the father. "He's going to die just like Alfie." Then he yanked the little car into gear and roared out of the circular drive.

■ ■ ■

"I'm sorry, Alice, but I thought I'd better call and tell you," said Bruce. "I didn't mean to pop him, but he made me so goddamn mad! Jesus, I'm still shaking," he added.

"I know, dear. I lost my temper with him, too. In fact, he's so angry with me, I doubt he's going to call back. But ... well, maybe I shouldn't tell you this, but please, Bruce, just between you and me; I haven't even told Abe. You see, I called Betty — my sister-in-law, you know. Well, I called her, and she let something slip, and then when I threw it up to Dan, that's when he really blew up. But he admitted it, so ... he ... he's involved, somehow ... I'm not sure — I don't think Betty was either, but ... Oh, Bruce, he's involved in something to do with illegal aliens, letting them stay in some of his empty buildings. I don't think it's very profitable, and it sounds all too altruistic for my brother, but there it is. Betty thinks the INS is ready to come down on him. And, I don't think he's so much afraid of getting caught and facing the legal consequences, as he is of ... well, of having to admit he's been doing such a humanitarian thing — especially in Iowa, where people aren't going to understand ... will probably call him a 'card-carrying liberal,' or some such. I don't think he could stand that! But if he gets convicted and sent to jail, he's just obsessed with the idea that Jeff has to be there to take care of his mother."

"Jesus Christ!" Bruce sat staring at the wall before he could say any more. "You're sure?" he asked at length. "He wasn't playing footsie with the local drug dealers?"

"Oh no, I'm sure," said Alice Javits. "His whole thing with Jeff is that he wants him home, and he's desperately afraid the boy is going to get into trouble. I really believe him, Bruce. He was so afraid, and felt so guilty when Jeff first ran away, he went through all that business on his first trip. But he did know Alfie was dealing drugs back in Iowa. He's been afraid Jeff was involved in that, and I couldn't convince him otherwise. Then, when he heard about Alfie getting killed, Betty says he simply went to pieces. That's why he's out here again, and that's the other reason why he's so frantic to get Jeff to come home. He's just sure the same people are after him. And he doesn't believe that Jeff isn't dealing drugs, or using them."

"And I had to pop the guy in the mouth," said Bruce unhappily. "I feel like a real shit!"

"Don't waste time on self-recriminations," Alice replied, encouragingly. "Put that big brain to work and figure out who's been out there killing people with a silken cord."

TWELVE

o understand exactly what happened next, it would be best to have a good mental picture of the front of Bruce MacLeod's house. The arched drive up from the street was paved in black cobblestone, recently added atop the original asphalt. The house itself was a good thirty feet from the roadway, and the area between the drive and the street surface was heavily planted in tropical ferns and ornamental shrubs, making it impossible to see the house except by looking up from either end of the drive. There was a high *porte cochère* at the front door, which extended out the full width of the drive. Because the house was built in a "lazy U," the walls tended to cant back slightly from the front portal — Bruce's suite being on the far left, and Dennie's wing on the right, where the ground sloped away at a steeper angle. For this reason, a three-car garage had been built directly under his bedroom. But due to the sharp falloff, there was only a slight downgrade into the garage areas. The gazebo was in the yard, off Dennie's side of the house, and beyond this the Rush property — situated on the end of the cul-de-sac.

On this particular Monday morning, three cars were parked behind the closed, electrically controlled garage doors: Bruce's two-seater Mercedes, Dennie's four-door Buick, and Frank's yellow Nissan convertible. On the lower edge of the drive, facing outward past the *porte cochère* and directly opposite the garages, was Jeff's red pickup with its Iowa license plates.

Across the street was the construction project that had been such an annoyance to Bruce — to everyone in the house, in fact. As was their custom, the workmen had arrived early, and began their noisy labors at precisely eight o'clock — the first moment the law would allow. The new house was now far enough along that much of the building material had been removed from the street, but a large pile of cinder blocks still remained, as well as a battered, graffiti-decorated chemical toilet and a disreputable old house trailer. The contractor had apparently used the latter as an office at one point, but for the moment it was padlocked and scarred, with soil compacted in several lower recesses, as if it had been stored at the base of an unstable hillside.

Because of all the activity over the weekend, none of the occupants of Bruce's house was quite ready for the normal chaos this Monday morning; but it started as usual at — in Bruce's words — "the crack of dawn." Roofers were at work, hammering in the rails for a Spanish tile roof, and the inevitable cement mixer was grinding away in the street. A babble of voices rent the air, each man seemingly out to prove that by shouting whatever he wished to say in his own language — at a high enough volume — it would somehow make it more intelligible to the others. The builder was a Frenchman; the electricians were Korean; and the carpenters were Latinos. None of them spoke English with total fluency, but it was their only common language. The resulting racket, however, was more than jangling to Bruce's nerves. As he did his sit-ups that morning, he looked up at Frank, who was just emerging from the shower, his slim, hard body aglow from the vigorous toweling.

"I'm really not a violent man," Bruce said, "but I'd bet even Dr. Schweitzer could find some excuse to eliminate those assholes. In fact, I wouldn't mind having that contractor on the rack for an hour or two."

Frank laughed, rubbing his butt, where the previous night's nonviolent exchange had left him a little sore. "Remember, SM is based completely on consent," he quipped.

■ ■ ■

The only patient Bruce had scheduled for this entire day was Rupert Orsini, due to come at one in the afternoon. However, at his boss's request, Dennie had tried several times to reach

168

him and cancel the appointment. By ten o'clock he had still been unable to locate him. In the meantime, Pete Jackson had arrived to talk with Jeff. In order to be away from everyone else, they opted to sit in the gazebo.

"You know, if this weren't such a pleasant locale," the lieutenant told his witness, once they were settled, "we'd be down in the dungeons of Parker Center."

"That's an interesting suggestion," Jeff replied. "We must both have dungeons on the brain. Does it bother you to deal with a guy who plays these games?" Jeff was walking a narrow line, he knew, trying to make light of his SM interests — probably to delay the moment when he would have to repeat his story to this heterosexual black policeman — although their last session had left the youngster feeling relatively comfortable with him. Still, Jeff had previously glossed over some of the finer details of his initial sexual encounter in Los Angeles. Now, he knew, he would have to describe the exchange in painfully exacting detail.

"I deal with all kinds of people, all the time," Jackson replied, "and I've heard so many variations on the theme, it really doesn't bother me any more. Everybody has his own sexual secrets — the doc'll tell you — even if they're just fantasies."

"It sounds like Bruce gave you a quick course," Jeff laughed. But his tone was forced, and Jackson was perceptive enough to sense it. His interrogation was nonthreatening, brief but thorough. When he finished, there remained no doubt in his mind that Jeff was telling the truth, and that Paul Orsini was innocent of his parents' murder. His problem, now, was going to be persuading Captain Fullbright to take the word of a self-admitted sadomasochist hustler. *Because, regardless of any other attributes the kid may have, that's how the captain's going to think of him. A year ago, that's how I'd have thought of him.* But Pete Jackson never made it to his office that morning to confer with his superior; the basic parameters of the case were about to take a dramatic change.

■ ■ ■

While Jeff was outside with Jackson, Dennie went into Bruce's office and closed the door, glancing about almost furtively as he did so.

169

"What's with the dramatic entrance?" asked the psychiatrist.

"I don't know if you want to tell Pete, but we're missing some food from the kitchen again."

Bruce looked up at him in surprise, then grinned. "You really think Hugo's still hanging around?"

"He has to be," Dennie told him. "Unless you or Frank ate half a chicken last night. And there's at least a quart of milk gone, plus some bread ... and, oh yeah, the rest of those fat-free, sugar-free, taste-free cookies Frank brought home. Whatever else that kid may be, if he ate those things he *is* a fool!"

"This is incredible!" Bruce couldn't help laughing. "The kid is barely able to plan his next bowel movement, but he's hiding out right under our noses — and the noses of the police — and none of us can figure out where the hell he is! Who's the fool in this situation?"

"It sure beats the shit out of me," Dennie admitted. "Oh, and speaking of fools, I haven't had any luck finding Rupert. You'd better gear up for a session."

"I'll have to worry about that when he shows up," said Bruce resignedly. "In the meantime, though, I think we'd better tell Pete Jackson about the missing food. Hugo's had ample time to come and talk to us; he's obviously not going to do it on his own. You know, we really should have had the sense to take turns sitting up to catch him last night."

Dennie shrugged. "Yeah, I guess," he agreed, "but ... well, I locked the door and set the alarm. How'd he get in?"

"He might have found the keys I left with Old Man Rush, or he could easily have seen one of us picking up the set we keep under the flowerpot."

"Or he could be an *idiot savant* who knows how to pick locks," Dennie suggested. "But I'll tell you, I'm not eager to try grabbing that moose and holding him, if he doesn't want to be held."

"So, we'll do it in shifts of two," Bruce conceded.

"Plus a stun gun," Dennie muttered.

It had been at this stage of their conversation that the detective had completed his questioning of Jeff, and had made an appointment for the youngster downtown, to give a formal statement. Bruce and Dennie saw the two men coming back from the gazebo. Jackson had paused by the pool to finish his cigarette before coming into the house. Jeff had gone through to his pickup.

Bruce went outside to join Jackson. "How'd it go?" he asked.

"Oh, fine," the detective assured him. "He's a nice kid, and I think he told me about everything. In fact, a little more than I really needed to know."

"Oh?"

"Well, I'd seen that setup Paul Orsini has in Echo Park, so I wasn't too surprised."

"Yeah, you know I'd picked up on the mannequins — suspected Jeff had gotten it on with Paul Orsini, but I didn't connect the date!"

The black detective nodded. "Me, too," he began, "it just didn't fall into place until—" Jackson's remarks ended in midsentence, as a violent explosion rocked the house, followed by several shouted oaths and the tinkle of breaking glass. Bruce's first thought was that some mishap on the building site had done it, but within a couple of seconds, Dennie staggered out from the den. "Bruce!" he shouted. "Out front ... Jeff ... his pickup..."

Both men raced through the house, where numerous items had been knocked from shelves and tables. Most of the front windows had been shattered, and as they passed through the open door, Bruce peripherally noted that one of the pillars on the *porte cochère* was cracked and canted at an angle. The red pickup was a blackened mass of rubble, still aflame, although two men from the construction site were already trying to douse it with fire extinguishers. Jeff lay facedown on the drive, not moving, his clothes all but torn from his body, which was mottled with patches of sooty black intermingled with raw, bleeding wounds.

A pair of Latino workmen were bending over him, talking helplessly, not sure what to do. They backed off in alarm as Rudy rushed toward them, barking, then standing as if on guard beside the battered youngster. Bruce motioned the workmen away, absently muttering a word of thanks. He felt for a pulse at Jeff's neck. "He's still alive," he told Jackson. "Better call for an ambulance."

"I already did," said Dennie, coming up behind them. The big man had the cordless phone in his left hand. "Do you think he's ... I mean, has he got a chance?"

"I'm all right," gasped Jeff, unexpectedly conscious. "I got away before it exploded. Note, in the dust on the door." All of this came in starts and stops, accompanied by a racking cough.

"Don't try to talk," Bruce cautioned. "Dennie, get a blanket, and take Rudy back into the house." The dog had been trying to lick at Jeff's wounds.

Dennie galloped off for the blanket, as Bruce began running his hands over Jeff's arms and legs, then down his spine, carefully probing around the neck. Jeff had started to shake, then, his whole body trembling as if suddenly seized by a terrible chill. "He's going into shock," Bruce said, "but I don't think he's hurt as badly as it looks." On his own, the victim had moved enough to indicate that he had sustained no major skeletal damage.

Dennie returned with a blanket, which Bruce threw over Jeff's shivering body, and tucked in gently all around him. As he did this, his face was close to Jeff's, who strained to whisper. "Note," he repeated, "a warning, in the dust, on the car door."

Bruce looked up at Pete Jackson, who had been hovering helplessly in the background, and repeated the youngster's remark. The detective moved to the truck, then, where the workman had extinguished the fire. The door on the driver's side had been blasted loose, and hung by just the upper hinge. Gingerly, using his handkerchief, Jackson pushed the battered metal back enough to see the remains of a crudely written message: DONT START MOTAR.

The wailing of sirens could now be heard down the hill, and within moments the emergency vehicles started to arrive. First were two fire trucks with paramedics, followed by a black-and-white police car, then an ambulance, and finally an assortment of other police vehicles. Bruce had taken the phone from Dennie and called a doctor friend at a small, local hospital. The man had fortunately been on duty, and Bruce made arrangements for him to take care of Jeff Donovan.

They had the youngster bundled onto a gurney and were about to roll him into the ambulance, when he called out to

Dennie. The big man was already at his side. "Come with me," he urged. "I don't want to go alone."

"Is it okay?" Dennie asked one of the drivers.

"You family?" countered the fireman.

"No, a friend," Dennie replied.

"Then you'll have to follow in your own car," the man told him.

Dennie looked at Bruce, who had already joined them. "I'm the victim's doctor," Bruce told them. "Mr. Delong is my assistant. I want him to accompany my patient." He then told the paramedics where he wanted them to take their passengers, which was closer than the regular emergency facility.

The fireman shrugged. "Okay," he agreed grudgingly. "We're wasting time."

Bruce had already moved to one side when the ambulance doors were closed behind Jeff and Dennie, his fingers starting to punch Abe's number into the cordless phone.

"I know you want to make some more calls," said Jackson as the ambulance began its wailing withdrawal, "but take a look at this first." He led the psychiatrist to the pickup, and showed him the note, scrawled in the dust of the door.

Bruce nodded knowingly. "Yeah, I think I can guess how that got there," he said. "Ironically, I had just come out to tell you..."

"I think you had better tell us, too, Doctor ... MacLeod, is it?" This from a tall, graying man in an untidy business suit with a detective's badge affixed to the breast pocket. "I'm Sergeant Davis, Beverly Hills P.D."

"Yes, I'm Bruce MacLeod, and this is Lieutenant Jackson of the L.A.P.D."

"And you own this property?" asked the detective, with a barely perceptible nod to acknowledge Jackson's introduction.

"Yes."

"And what was it you were going to tell the lieutenant?"

"We've had a prowler," Bruce replied evasively, very uncomfortable with this man, who he knew had every right to demand cooperation. Jackson was out of his jurisdiction, and Bruce did not have much of a relationship with the Beverly Hills Police. Yet he knew it had to have been Hugo who left the warning that very likely saved Jeff's life. He wanted desperately to talk with the kid, and was afraid of how a police chase could end. Hugo was big and hostile, and possibly armed — at least with a knife or some other object.

Jackson stepped in, however, and insisted on drawing the other detective aside. "Why don't you call the commissioner?" he said over his shoulder to Bruce, making a slight head motion to indicate that this was the time to move away. To his fellow officer he began to make a half-whispered explanation: "The victim is Commissioner Javits's nephew..." This much Bruce heard before moving out of earshot.

The Beverly Hills detective had thus far made no objection, so Bruce took advantage of the moment. He went all the way in to his office and used the desk phone to place his call to Abe Javits. It was only as he was punching the button on his automatic dialer that it struck him. *Pete asked me to call Abe, and I'm doing this before he's had a chance to report in to Fullbright. Interesting.*

Bruce had called on Abe's private line, at his Century City office. His friend answered on the second ring, and Bruce explained what had happened.

"All right," Abe told him. "Just hang tough, and try not to sic them on that poor dumb kid. I've got some friends upstairs in Beverly Hills. Let's see what I can do. In the meantime, would you mind calling Alice and telling her what happened?"

"What about Dan?"

"He had a flight to Des Moines at eight o'clock this morning," Abe told him.

■ ■ ■

"Short of setting a bear trap in the kitchen, I don't know how we're going to get him," said Bruce, "or more to the point, how we're going to hold him, if we do catch him."

He was standing in the bedroom with Frank, surveying the bomb damage. Mostly, it was broken glass from the windows, but the shards were everywhere. "I'm glad I'd already made the bed," Frank remarked absently, poking at the scraps of glass on the heavy spread.

"Who could have planted that bomb?" Bruce wondered aloud. He could see the special investigations team still working on the pickup, while a police tow truck stood by, ready to haul it away as evidence. Pete Jackson had stayed with them, but he now turned and headed for the front door. On the street, beyond the yellow police barrier tape, a pair of media vans had arrived, and several TV cameras were trained on the scene of destruction. Bruce went to let Jackson in.

"I think it might be a good idea to open the garage," said the detective. "Let the bomb squad take a look at your cars, just to be on the safe side."

Up to this point, Bruce had been outwardly calm. Although a lump of fear had formed in his gut, it didn't show on his face or in his overt behavior. But Pete Jackson's suggestion momentarily unnerved him. "Jesus, Pete, do you really...?"

"Open the garage, Bruce, and we'll see."

They had been standing on the front steps, and Pete made a slight gesture with his hand to remind Bruce that they were in range of the TV cameras. "Unless you want to be on the evening news—," muttered the detective. They moved inside and Bruce depressed a small plastic panel beside the doorway. Both garage doors hummed and started to lift.

"I don't see how anyone could have gotten in there," said Bruce. "Not only does it lock when it's closed, but it's hooked into the alarm system. Of course, a pro—"

Jackson squeezed Bruce's arm, and went down the steps to join the other officers, who now clustered at the far side of the drive as the bomb squad members, in their white space suits, entered the garage. Bruce stood just inside the doorway, wondering if he should try to shield himself from an explosion. Frank came up to join him, but Bruce moved to stand between his friend and the open door. "TV cameras," he cautioned. Frank nodded, and stepped back into the darker part of the hall, where he could see out but remain beyond camera range.

After about ten minutes, the leader of the bomb squad emerged from the garage. He was holding a small gray box in his hand. "You the owner?" he called to Bruce.

"Yeah. Did you find anything?"

"No bombs." The officer came up the steps to Bruce. "But this was on the Mercedes." He held up the gray object, and before Bruce could question him he added: "It's a beeper — not the kind used by any police department that I know of."

"What's it for?" Bruce asked.

"It sends out an electronic signal," explained the policeman. "This one ought to be good for about two miles. If someone wants to tail you, it makes it easier. The guy doesn't have to stay in sight of you, and he can find the car again if he should lose you."

"Christ, I wonder how long I've been driving around with that thing on my car."

"Not very long," the officer assured him. "There's no road dust to speak of. I'd say a day or two at the most, but probably planted last night by the same guy who did the bomb."

Pete Jackson had come close enough to hear most of the exchange, and he looked at Bruce with a worried expression. The tall gray detective had come up behind him. "Doctor MacLeod, I think we'd better have a few words."

Bruce, Frank, and the two detectives walked through the house, and went outside onto the rear patio. The portion of flagstone pavement nearest the house was in shade, and had remained comfortably cool. The Beverly Hills detective had just taken out his notepad, preparatory to questioning Bruce, when the phone rang. Frank went to pick it up, then called to the policeman. "Are you Sergeant Davis?" he asked. He had picked up on the cordless phone, which he now gave to Davis.

With an unhappy expression, the officer took the instrument, and after a few moments' conversation he glanced at his companions and moved a few feet away from them, turning his back as he spoke.

"Abe was going to call someone he knew..." Bruce's voice trailed off as the detective turned back and handed the phone to Frank.

"Okay," he said. "They want you to lead the way," he continued, inclining his head toward Pete Jackson, "but I'm supposed to stay with you." His normally hangdog expression seemed to deepen even further.

Jackson shrugged. "I don't have the answer," he said honestly. "I'm about ninety percent sure it ties in, somehow, with the Orsini murders, and even more likely with the killing of Alfred Stimson."

"And Haven Monroe," Bruce added.

Jackson shrugged his shoulders again. "Maybe," he conceded.

Bruce wanted to push his ideas further, but he was inhibited by Sergeant Davis. He also wanted not to appear to be usurping Pete Jackson's leadership. But both detectives surprised him.

"Say whatever you feel like, Bruce," said Jackson. "We need all the help we can get."

"I've been liaison on the Orsini case since the beginning," Davis added, "and I agree with the lieutenant. If you have any ideas, tell us. And ... um, I know you wanted to say something earlier, something about the note on the door of the truck."

"The key to your whole case is Hugo," Bruce told them. "I wasn't so sure before, but I'm convinced now that he has to know what really happened."

"If he didn't do it himself," said Davis dryly. "You *are* talking about the big dummy from the Orsini place," he added for clarity.

"I don't think he did anything," said Bruce, glancing about uncomfortably, as if uncertain whether Hugo could be lurking behind some bush. "He's mentally — or at least emotionally — handicapped, as I'm sure you know, and there's too great a degree of sophistication in all of this for him to have been responsible for it. But if he weren't afraid of something more than the police, he wouldn't be so hard to find."

"Unless he was an accomplice — actually helped the killer," Davis suggested.

"That's also unlikely," Bruce replied. "From everything I've observed about Hugo, he's an isolate. He dislikes most people on sight. He doesn't trust anyone. Paul Orsini was the only person who seemed to have any rapport with him, and Paul was in jail, is still in jail," he added, with an accusatory glance at Pete Jackson.

"What about the Monroe killing?" Jackson countered, ignoring Bruce's jibe. "He's as much as been identified as being on the hotel grounds by at least two witnesses."

"If I were a betting man," Bruce told him, "I'd lay odds that, even if Hugo was there, he didn't kill anyone."

"How can you be so sure?" asked Davis.

"From the various conversations I've had with him, and heard him have with other people, I think he tends to sublimate the greater part of his aggression. By that, I mean he engages in elaborate fantasies about how he's going to avenge himself, for example, or even how he's going to have sex with someone. But he won't actually do it."

"Not even the sex?" asked Frank.

Bruce rubbed his chin in thought. "I think it would be very difficult for him to initiate a sexual exchange. He's too fearful, too insecure. He'd go along with it if someone else got him started. In my opinion he's incapable of committing an act of overt aggression, let alone violence."

"You seemed to think, at one point, that he was hostile toward both Orsini brothers," Jackson reminded him. "Are you saying he'd be incapable of hurting either of them?"

"I don't think he'd hurt them physically," Bruce replied. "And even to harm them by lying — I don't think he could do that, either. Of course, his feelings toward one are very different from his feelings for the other. He's angry with Paul, because he feels betrayed." And at a quizzical look from Davis, he added, "They had been lovers, of sorts. And..." He paused, as his own thoughts began to coalesce. "That's why he's so determined not to be caught by the cops!"

"What, because he had a sexual affair with Paul Orsini?" asked Sergeant Davis in a dubious tone.

"Oh, no. I'm sorry, Sergeant. I guess I just had a sudden brainstorm and didn't communicate very well." He turned back to Jackson, and continued enthusiastically. "He knows, Pete. I'm more convinced by the minute. He knows who killed whom, and I wouldn't be surprised if he were an actual eyewitness ... to the Orsini murders, I mean, and maybe Haven Monroe's, as well. We've got to find him, and you've got to make sure someone doesn't get trigger-happy and shoot him."

"Do you really think he's nonviolent, then?" asked the Beverly Hills detective doubtfully.

Bruce spread his fingers, and pursed his lips. "No, I didn't say that, exactly. If you corner him, or frighten him badly enough, he could very well fight back. The best of all worlds would be if Frank or I could get him to come and talk to us of his own free will."

"Well, I'll tell you, Doc," said Davis. "I'm just about at the end of my rope on the Orsini thing — and so are the higher-ups, both in my department and in Jackson's." He looked at his fellow detective for support, and received a nod of agreement. "If you really think you can get this fool to come in and talk to you, I'd almost be willing to go along with you — except ... How do I know he isn't going to kill you? I mean, you *could* be wrong. Everything you've told us is simply deduction, supposition. Right?"

Before Bruce could answer, Pete Jackson did it for him. "I've trusted his intuition before," he said. "Right now, it's the best thing we've got going, the only thing we've got going."

Davis nodded agreement. "The fact that you seem to think he's the one who scrawled that warning on the truck door," he said to Bruce, "...that's what tips the scales. Would you care to speculate as to why the bomber — or whoever — would want to be able to trail you, badly enough to plant a beeper?"

"My guess would be that he — they — think I know where Hugo is, and want to follow me to him," Bruce replied.

"And do you know?" asked the detective sharply.

"No," said Bruce simply.

"But don't forget," added Pete Jackson. "Whoever planted that bomb — and the beeper device — he must be badly frightened, unnerved to a point where he isn't thinking clearly. I'm sure they went after Jeff because he was Paul Orsini's alibi. If the big stoop saw who it was, he's in a lot of trouble."

"I think the kid's been in a lot of trouble for long time," said Bruce. "My guess is that someone got his signals crossed and killed Alfie, thinking he was Jeff ... and if you stop to analyze that one, you get an interesting set of probabilities. It was a week before the police found Alfie's body, but once they did it was only a day or so before they identified him and published his name."

"But it took all this time for someone to come after Jeff!" Jackson interrupted, suddenly enthusiastic as his own deductive processes clicked on. "That means that the killer — killers — didn't know who he was, not by name."

"Just that he was a kid in a red pickup, with Iowa plates," Bruce finished for him. "Now, who knew what and when?"

"I guess it's got to be our first order of business to figure that out," said Davis. "Maybe if Lieutenant Jackson and I compare notes..."

"Your first order of business is to get Paul Orsini out of jail," Bruce told them. "Hugo may be the biggest key, but Paul has also got some answers. Once someone assures him he isn't ever going to be a suspect again, he might just decide to open up all the way. He came closer to it with me, but I'm sure he could tell us more about his father's associates." *Maybe about his brother, too,* Bruce thought, but this he kept to himself.

■ ■ ■

Promptly at one o'clock, Rupert Orsini appeared on Bruce's doorstep. Because Dennie had not returned from the hospital, Frank answered the bell.

"Hey, what's happened?" asked the visitor. "Looks like someone set a bonfire in the driveway, and the TV clowns were out there taking my picture."

The police had departed almost an hour before, taking the remains of Jeff's pickup with them. At Davis's instructions, they had removed the yellow "Crime Scene — Keep Out" tape. Thus, the only evidence remaining outside Bruce's house was the blackened patch in the drive and adjoining bushes, as well as the broken windows — except, of course, for the media hounds, who were still milling about in the street. Bruce had called his own security service, and they had sent a man to keep the newsies off the property.

"We had a little trouble here," Frank told him. "We tried to call and cancel your appointment, but couldn't reach you."

"Oh, I was out shopping," he said offhandedly. "I didn't even go home, just had lunch in town and came directly by."

"Well, you might as well come in, since you're here," Frank said, rather ungraciously. He stood back, allowing Rupert space to enter.

The visitor was hardly inside when he stopped and looked about in evident surprise. The usually neat, well-maintained interior was still in disarray, although Frank had been doing his best to put it into some degree of order. Even as they stood in the entryway, a glass company truck drove in. This motivated Frank to guide Rupert quickly into Bruce's keeping, while he went back to handle the glaziers, waiting until they had mounted the steps to the front door. Then, he stepped back to let them enter — as he had done with Rupert — never allowing the newsies to get a clear video shot of him. Up to this point, as best he could tell, no one had recognized him.

"Rupert, I don't know that I'm in very good shape to talk with you today," Bruce said, as he came around the desk to receive his client.

"Yeah, I can see. What happened?"

"We had a bombing," Bruce told him.

"Was anyone hurt?"

"No one was *killed*. But yes, one person was injured."

"Who?" asked Rupert eagerly.

"No one you'd know," Bruce told him, wary now, wondering.

"Oh." His client suddenly seemed chagrined, as a child who had been chided for some breach of manners. "I just wondered," he bumbled. "Didn't mean to pry."

"No harm done, but as I told you, I'm really not in very good shape today."

"That's okay, Doctor MacLeod, I can make it some other time."

"Why don't you give Dennie a call tomorrow, and he'll set up an appointment for you. Oh, and by the way, did Mickey Halloran do anything about getting your brother out of jail?"

Rupert gave him a jaundiced look. "I dunno," he replied. "Shithead can stay there, for all I care."

"You know he's innocent," Bruce suggested.

Rupert shrugged. "No, I don't know that. I do know he'd like to kill me, if I gave him the chance."

So would a lot of people, I'd bet, Bruce thought. "Let's go into this at your next session," he replied dryly.

"If I'm still alive," said Rupert.

■ ■ ■

Dennie arrived by cab late in the afternoon. "Jeff's going to be okay," said the big man. "He's got a moderate concussion, a broken eardrum that's probably going to heal itself, and lots of abrasions."

"Was he able to tell you anything?" asked Bruce.

"Yeah, a little; but the cops came in to question him, and they threw me out. He was able to say that he saw the note on the truck door, and didn't know whether it was somebody's idea of a joke. But he had a camera and a couple of other things on the floor behind the seats. He decided to get them out, just in case. He opened the door, and heard something click. That was enough, and he tried to run — got as far as he was when we found him before it blew."

"That goddamn Hugo," Bruce muttered, shaking his head in disbelief. "He must have been around last night to scrounge the food, and saw whoever tampered with the pickup. They also found a beeper thing on the Mercedes," he added.

Frank joined them at that point, and helped Bruce bring Dennie up to date on the details of all that had happened since his departure. The big man was as amazed as the others at Hugo's seeming uncanny ability to evade detection. "Where do you suppose he is?" he asked at length.

"That has to be our first order of business," Bruce told them. "We have to either find him, or get him to find us before the police mount a major manhunt. I just have a bad feeling that, if he's cornered, the kid will do exactly the wrong thing and get himself killed." He pulled a pad of lined yellow paper from a desk drawer. "Okay, let's make a list. Where, oh where, has our little giant gone?"

"The lot above the house?" Frank suggested.

"Could he have snuck back onto the Orsini property?" asked Dennie.

"Or back to the Rush house, next door," Bruce speculated. "He has to be hiding right under our noses. I was wondering if he might have gotten into that trailer by the construction site."

"That's padlocked," Dennie reminded him.

"But when I took Rudy out last night, I noticed the window in the overhang is broken out," said Frank.

"That's barely a foot high," Dennie observed. "I'm sure I couldn't squeeze through it, and Hugo's every bit as chesty as I am."

"We could take turns staying up and watching the kitchen, like Bruce was talking about," Frank suggested. "He seems to be making regular trips in there for food."

"That's too iffy," Bruce replied. "All this commotion may very well scare him off, and I think it's essential we find him as soon as possible."

The phone rang and Dennie answered it, covering the receiver with one massive palm. "It's Paul Orsini."

"Yes, Paul," said the psychiatrist. "Are you out of jail?"

"They're going to release me in an hour or so. But I'm afraid to go home. Can I come by your house? I just called Mr. Halloran, and he thought it was a good idea."

"Sure," Bruce told him, inwardly pleased that getting hold of the younger brother was going to be so easy. "Just take a cab out, and if you don't have enough cash on you, we'll see..."

"I think I've got enough money, Bruce. Thanks," Paul replied. "I'll be there as soon as I can."

"How did that happen?" asked Frank.

"Either Abe pulled some strings, or..." Bruce suddenly went silent, pulling at his lower lip in thought. Then he stood up, a half grin on his features as he glanced at his watch. "I've got a group session at the Center," he announced. "It'll only take a couple of hours. I should be back before dark."

"Can't you beg off for one night?" Frank asked.

"I'd rather not," Bruce replied. "It's no big thing. Paul won't be here for at least two or three hours." With that, he was out the door, leaving his two companions to look at one another in puzzlement.

■ ■ ■

Bruce had been back for less than two minutes when, just at dusk, Paul Orsini rang the front doorbell. He was hollow-eyed and seemed almost dazed. "I didn't sleep very well," he explained.

"Well, I think you've seen the last of the county jail," Bruce said. "Even your most serious detractors now seem to agree you're innocent."

"Grudgingly," Paul said grimly.

"You were an easy target," Dennie told him. "I guess it took some pressure off when they were actually able to put someone in jail."

"It's a fucked-up system," Frank remarked. "I don't think they have any more idea who the real killers are now than they did the day it happened."

"But I do," said Paul, unexpectedly.

All three of his companions looked at him in anticipation. "If you give me a drink, I'll tell you," continued the young man, forcing a grin.

Dennie got up to oblige, and Bruce suggested they might be more comfortable on the patio. In a few minutes they were all settled in the plastic chairs, back several feet on the flagstone decking that surrounded the pool. "Okay," Bruce continued, "you've got your drink. Now tell us who the killer is."

"It's my brother," said the younger Orsini. "I suspected it from the start, but now I'm sure. See, he was getting involved with Dad's business right near the end, and ... well, I'm not sure exactly what the problem was, but they had a lot of arguments, because Dad wouldn't do whatever it was Rupert wanted. Now he's doing things he won't explain to me, spending a lot of money, and he's after me to sign some papers so he can use my share of the estate, too."

"Have you signed them?" Dennie asked.

"No, and I'm not going to. That's why he wants to kill me," Paul insisted.

Listening to all of this, Bruce withdrew into his own thoughts, wondering how much of Paul's diatribe against his brother was possible, or even logical. *Sibling rivalry ... first thought that comes to mind. Each brother accusing the other. Still...*

"How about Halloran?" Frank asked. "Does he think you should sign the papers for Rupert?"

"He's the one who drew them up," Paul replied.

"Interesting," Bruce said, thoughtful again, silent for a protracted moment.

"Have you been able to find Hugo?" Paul asked, bringing Bruce back to the present.

"No," the psychiatrist told him. "Do you have any idea where he might be?"

Paul shrugged. "He liked to play frontiersman, or Indian tracker," he said. "Big as he was, he could move without making much noise, and he knows his way all around this neighborhood."

"Including that area above our pool," Frank added dryly.

Paul gave him a sheepish glance. "Well, that's really my fault," he admitted. "I discovered your vacant lot back when I was a kid and had a secret hut up there. Then later, when I took a walk one night, I went to see if it was still there and heard noises from the pool. It was one of those times after they did a lot of tree-trimming on the upper street."

"Probably the time they knocked our fence down," Dennie added.

"Right. I hardly had to climb, just the toppled chain link and onto the lot, and I looked down into the pool area," Paul explained. "Then, once I'd discovered you, I used to go back from time to time ... climb the fence when you had it replaced. And I took Hugo with me once. I guess he kept coming back on his own. I'm not sure, because that was shortly before I broke it off with him."

"Why did you break it off?" Frank asked.

Paul paused, looking uncomfortable, not knowing how to reply until Bruce reassured him. "All of us share your interests. You haven't done anything we wouldn't do," he added in a lighter tone, which seemed to unlock some of the tension.

Paul still seemed intimidated for another few seconds, then shrugged and continued. After all, he'd already told most of this to Bruce. "I had him playing Top," he said slowly, "but he didn't know when to stop. I was afraid he'd really hurt me."

"But you play a dangerous game, anyway," Dennie remarked, and at a questioning look from Paul, he continued. "Like picking up Jeff that night. How did you know he wouldn't kill you?"

Paul grinned. "I wasn't worried about him," he said. "He was a big dumpling right off the turnip truck. If I'm doubtful about a hustler type, though, I lock a chain around his neck ... a long one, bolted to a ceiling ring. It leaves him free to move around the dungeon, anywhere he wants to go. But the key is hidden outside, so he can't get loose until I go get it."

"From what Jeff told me, you used some drugs that night," said Bruce quietly. "Do you do that all the time?"

Paul leaned forward in his chair, clasping his hands, his head bowed over them. He nodded. "Yeah, coke mostly, more often than I should, I guess. But if you can promise a hustler a few snorts, he's more willing to go along with whatever you want."

"And Jeff? Did he seem ... er, experienced in the use of cocaine?" Bruce asked.

"Oh no, I don't think he'd ever used it before. At least, I had to show him how to line it up and how to use the straw. I only gave him a little — good thing, too. Just that much almost knocked him on his ass."

As they had been talking, the final streaks of sunset had faded from the sky, and the backyard was now dark. The only light came from the neon panel over the stove, glowing dimly through the glass upper half of the kitchen door. The light breeze which had helped to cool the patio when they first came outside had now receded, and it was almost uncomfortably warm.

"Why don't we all take a dip?" Dennie suggested.

"Good idea," Frank agreed. He had gotten up and started to remove his shirt, but stopped when he saw that Bruce wasn't moving.

"Uh, why don't we wait a few minutes?" he suggested.

"Why?" Dennie demanded.

"Yeah, I've been wanting to skinny-dip in your pool ever since I first discovered it," Paul chimed in.

"All right, go ahead," Bruce told them. "But ... uh, Frank ... stay here for a minute, will you?"

Puzzled, the slender actor sat down next to Bruce, as Dennie stripped and headed for the pool, followed by Paul. Rudy, who had been lying beside Frank's chair, got up to follow them, then suddenly stood stock-still, just as Dennie disappeared over the side of the pool. Paul was standing on the edge, apparently uncertain whether to jump in, or sit on the rim and slide under the surface. Then Rudy bristled, the hair standing up on his shoulders. For the first time in living memory, the big Lab actually growled! Bruce called him, and after a moment Rudy grudgingly obeyed. The psychiatrist got his hand on the dog's choke chain just as Paul dropped into the water. Then, startling everyone, the big Lab went into a paroxysm of barking.

"What's going on?" Frank asked.

Bruce put his free hand on his friend's arm, pulling him back into his chair, just as a bright beam of light arched across the patio. This came from the direction of the side gate on Bruce's wing of the house. "Just stay put," Bruce whispered, "and play the game; just remember it *is* a game." And that was all he had time to say.

A dark figure had now emerged from the shadows, holding a large flashlight in his left hand, and a nasty-looking, square-barreled weapon in the other. There was just enough sky glow to make out the gunman as dark-skinned, wearing a red ski mask, and speaking in heavily accented English. "Hold your dog, or I shoot him," he said to Bruce, then he gestured at Frank. "You," he snarled, "you come here."

Bruce, sitting between his lover and the big dog, who was now straining to get away from his grasp, could only whisper, "Go. It's okay. Play the game."

Puzzled, Frank got up and moved slowly toward the gunman, who now gestured menacingly with his weapon. "We go," he said, nodding toward the gate on the far side of the yard.

Frank, still uncertain whether to be frightened or amused by the obviously phony accent, and the strange behaviors of the intruder and of Bruce, did as his friend had indicated he should. He stepped slowly in the direction of the gate. In the meantime, Paul and Dennie had emerged from the pool, standing in dripping nakedness on the decking. Bruce motioned them to stay put. Frank had just gotten to the gate and reached out to open it, when a large figure emerged from the bushes behind the gunman.

In less than a second, the great dark shadow had wrapped his arms around the intruder, who emitted an almost feminine shriek as his six-foot-four frame was sent crashing to the ground. The gun fell off to one side, striking the flagstones with a strangely plastic sound. Bruce was on his feet, still holding Rudy, who was struggling to escape and attack to defend his master. "Dennie," he shouted, "Frank! Forget about the gunman! Hang on to Hugo!"

T H I R T E E N

The wild melee continued for several more minutes, the pile of mostly naked men scrambling for purchase, Frank and Dennie trying to follow Bruce's shouted demands that they hold on to Hugo. Then Bruce was with them, still struggling to keep Rudy from launching an attack. But the confusion seemed to have pacified the big Lab, who had now become more interested in playing than in trying to bite anyone. Bruce took a chance and released him, freeing up his own hands so that he could reach into his back pocket and extract a length of rope. As Rudy pranced, barking, around the perimeter of the human ménage, Bruce hit the wall switch, activating the overhead floodlights, then plowed into the fray.

Dennie saw immediately what his friend was attempting to do, and helped him by clamping his own legs around Hugo's in a scissors, long enough for Bruce to hog-tie the ankles. "Okay, let go of him," Bruce shouted. "He's not going to run off."

"Mercy! Yo'all didn't tell me they was gonna try 'n' kill me!" The tall, hooded figure was struggling to pull the ski mask off his head, sitting on the ground with his long legs spread wide apart.

"Henry ... Henry van Porter!" Dennie called out, laughing. "You dizzy old spadequeen; what are you doing here?"

"I think I'm everybody's punching bag," he moaned. "Oh, mercy! I'll have bruises for a month. Hope they didn't mess up my face!"

"Let's get Hugo onto the patio, and we can start sorting all of this out," Bruce told them. Paul had come up behind him, having been the only one to hold back during the wrestling match. "What's going on?" he asked.

"I think Bruce has pulled another of his coups," Frank told him dryly. "Why didn't you warn me?" he added directly to his lover. "You might have gotten me killed!"

"I didn't have a chance," Bruce said. "I was afraid Hugo would overhear me. Besides, he wouldn't have hurt you — not any more than he'd hurt any of us right now," Bruce added, looking their bedraggled captive in the eye. "Would you, Hugo?" To which the dark-haired giant shook his head, looking down at his feet. "That's why we don't need to tie your hands, right?"

Hugo shook his head again, still not looking up.

They were now back on the patio, Dennie and Frank supporting the nearly naked giant, whose feet were effectively hobbled by Bruce's ropework. They placed him on one of the recliners, and at Bruce's direction, tilted it back. This unbalanced the big body enough that Hugo couldn't reach his feet to untie himself. However, he seemed to accept his capture, perhaps relieved to finally have it over with.

"Okay. Let's all relax, now, and see if we can add ourselves up," Bruce began.

"Poor ol' Henry needs a drink," said Henry van Porter, settling himself onto a chair beside Bruce. He was the only one of them who was fully dressed. Dennie and Paul were still naked from being in the pool. Frank and Bruce wore only cutoffs — Hugo, too, although his powerful body was caked in grime.

"Yes, let's all have a drink," Frank suggested. "Then Bruce can explain this great dramatic production to us." His tone was still acid, expressing his annoyance at having been left out of the secret until the last moment — then used as bait.

■ ■ ■

They were settled comfortably on the patio. Dennie had turned off the heavy spotlights, so that the backyard was now illuminated only by the glow from the pool. The tension level was greatly reduced; even Frank seemed placated.

"I knew Hugo was watching us," Bruce explained. "But there wasn't any way to get him out in the open unless he wanted to be in the open. When I was at the Center tonight, I got the idea when I saw that toy plastic Uzi on Henry's desk."

189

"That's when he talked me into being the Latino gunman," Henry added, all trace of his Stepin Fetchit accent gone for the moment. "That toy gun was in with a bunch of stuff somebody left as a donation, and the Center people didn't want to send it on to the thrift shop. When Bruce offered ten bucks for it, we were glad to accept the donation."

"We were getting desperate to nail Hugo before the cops got after him," Bruce continued, directing his comments toward their prisoner, "or the killers," he added. "This seemed the quickest way — make him think Frank was in danger. I figured that would flush him out, if anything would."

"You're gonna get me killed!" grumbled the giant, taking a swig from the can of beer Dennie had given him. "Everybody's looking to hunt me down. You'll get me killed for sure!" he repeated.

"No, I won't," Bruce assured him. "I'm gonna keep you from getting killed, and together we're going to solve this whole tangled nightmare."

"How ya gonna do that?" Hugo demanded.

"First," Bruce said, "you're going to tell us everything you know, and once you've done that there won't be any reason for anyone to want to kill you, any more — because you won't be the only one who knows. Do you understand what I'm telling you?" he demanded.

"You mean, if other people know ... Yeah!" A smile spread across the handsome features. "They won't need to kill me, 'cause everybody'll know!"

"What *do* you know?" asked Paul, moving into the group and perching on the edge of Hugo's chaise. His hand rested idly on the big captive's thigh.

"I know who killed your dad and your mom," he said simply.

"Well, who?" Paul demanded.

"It was that Spanish guy," said Hugo, "Paco. The one that Rupert liked so much. And Rupert, he was there, too."

"Who's Paco?" Bruce asked Paul.

"He's one of the South American reps that Dad hired a couple of years ago. You know, the company — Dad's distribution company, not the production company — they bought two big film libraries ... not for domestic rentals, but for outside the country. Paco's office was in Venezuela, Maracay, I think, near Caracas."

"Okay," said Bruce, holding up his hand to Paul Orsini. "Now, Hugo, tell us exactly what happened that night."

"Well, I was having a treasure hunt," he said. "I mean ... I know it's dumb, but ... see, there're some sliding panels in the house that not everybody knows about. Rupert, he don't like for me to play with them, but I do, sometimes, 'cause Paul and me ... we used to pretend there was treasure back there." He paused, and Paul nodded agreement, saying, "We used to play lots of games."

"Yeah, he used to like to suck me off back inside the wall when his dad was having a business meeting right out in the room," Hugo continued with relish, watching Paul squirm in discomfort.

"Okay," said Bruce, interrupting the reminiscence that was obviously embarrassing Paul. "Tell us what happened."

"Well, I'm not sure why they got started arguing. They'd done it before — something about money ... 'moving money.' I didn't really understand. But, anyway, I was there in the secret place behind the bookshelves in Mr. Orsini's office, and the three of them came in, so I couldn't get out. Rupert and Mr. Orsini, they were really mad at each other, much worse than I ever saw before. And they're screaming about this money thing, and Rupert's saying as how they could make so much on it. Then Mr. Orsini hits him and knocks him down, and Rupert, he's real mad, then, and he's screaming at that Paco guy. 'Kill 'im!' he says. 'Kill 'im like we talked about!'"

Hugo paused to take another swig of his beer. "Frank, I won't run away if you untie me," he begged plaintively.

"You promise?"

"Yeah, I promise."

Frank looked questioningly at Bruce, who nodded to Paul, who reached down and undid the ropes.

"Now, tell us the rest of what happened," Bruce urged.

"Well, Paco, he got behind Mr. Orsini, and he grabbed this rope off Mr. Orsini's desk. It was a sample of some kind, I think, 'cause it had cardboard tags on it. Anyway, he wrapped it around his neck. But Mr. Orsini started to struggle, so Rupert got up and he had to hold his dad while the Spanish guy strangled him. I just stood there where I was. There was a little peephole, so I could see most of it, and I thought maybe I oughta come out and do something, but I knew that Paco guy had a gun on him sometimes, and besides, Mr. Orsini, he was already dead. And Rupert, he says to Paco: 'We gotta get outa here,' and he runs to the door. And when he does that, I can't see him any more, 'cause he's too far over to the side. I think he went all the way outside, but I'm not sure.

"Then Mrs. Orsini, she comes running into the room, and she's screaming and really carrying on when she sees Mr. Orsini on the floor. And that's when Paco takes that rope, and he strangles her, too. Well, I liked Mrs. Orsini. She was a nice lady; so I got back to the panel, and I came out in the room, and I hit Paco to make him let go of her. Rupert's standing in the doorway, then; but I don't know how long he's been there. Anyway, Paco, he runs away. Then Rupert, he goes and looks at his mom, and he says she's dead, and he starts to cry. I'm really scared, then, so I take off as fast as I can go, and Rupert's yellin' at me to come back, but I don't stop. And Paco, he's by the front door — just outside, and he tries to grab me, but I smash him in the gut and I keep going and he's yelling after me in that Spanish accent — choking-like, because I knocked the wind out of him: 'I going to keel you; I going to keel you!'"

"And that's when you moved into the empty house next door to us?" asked Frank.

Hugo nodded. "It was easy to get in. I know how to open locks."

"And where have you been staying since the night we came over looking for you?" Frank interjected.

"Everywhere. One night I'm at the place next door, one night in Paul's little house over at the Orsinis'. One night, the night all the cops was lookin' for me, I got into that trailer across the street." And in response to quizzical looks from Bruce and Dennie, he added: "I picked the paddle-lock on the door, and went inside and unlocked the window. Then I went back outside and locked the paddle-lock again, and climbed back in the window, and locked it from inside. I stayed there and laughed at all them cops. But later, I was afraid to keep sleeping there, so I just kept moving around, and as long as I did that nobody could find me."

"All right," Bruce urged, glancing at Paul, who was sitting with his head bowed, saying nothing. "Let's go on to the night when Haven Monroe got killed. What happened then?"

"Well, I was gonna kill him," Hugo declared defensively, looking directly at Frank. "I really was! I wasn't gonna let that mutherfuck ruin Frank's life. But nothin' worked right. See, first the rent-a-cops arrived, so I had to wait for them to go before I could leave the house. Then I rode the bike down to that hotel you'd talked about, but when I got there ... well, see, I guess I hadn't thought about it so good, 'cause I only had on a pair of shorts and a tank top — and my tennies. And I was too cruddy to go into that fancy lobby and ask what room the guy was in. I didn't know just what to do, so I was standing outside under the trees where it was dark, watching the place. I coulda just stood there and waited for the guy to come in or go out, but I didn't know what he looked like.

"Then, all of a sudden I seen Paco! Now, I know that fucker wants to kill me, and I wouldn't't'a been afraid of him, if I didn't know he packed a gun. Anyway, I followed him when he went inside — he used one of the back doors — and I saw him go up the stairs. I thought maybe I could jump him and get his gun, and maybe kill him before he could kill me. And then I heard other people coming, so I tried to duck out of sight. By that time Paco was gone. Then the lady saw me ... one of the ladies in the group. I think there was five or six people. Anyway, the lady saw me and she yelled. She didn't exactly scream, but I knew I'd better get out. So I ran back to the bike, and I came home."

"So you've never actually killed anybody, have you?" Bruce demanded softly.

Hugo looked down dejectedly, as if ashamed to admit his lack of homicidal experience. He shook his head without looking up.

Bruce now turned his attention to Paul. "It sounds like this Paco is a professional killer," the psychiatrist said.

"Yeah." The younger Orsini brother was now very restrained, refusing eye contact with any of the men around him.

"Paul," Bruce urged gently, "you've got to fill in some of the blanks, now. Tell us what else you know about this Paco character."

"I always thought he was a hood," came the strained voice. "I didn't know him very well, mostly because I didn't like him and I tried to stay out of the way when he was around. I know

he was with my brother a lot of the time before ... the folks ...
you know." He took a moment to compose himself, then looked
up at Bruce. "He's been hanging around all the time since
then," he continued. "It's like he and Rupert are joined at the
hip. I don't know if it's a sex thing with them, or not. And I'm
not sure how he originally got onto the payroll, but I think Dad
met him through Mr. Halloran."

"Halloran?" Bruce almost shouted the name. "Of course,
Halloran!"

"What's the big deal with Mickey the Great?" Frank asked.

"Yeah, I thought he was just the defense lawyer, brought in
after the murders," Dennie added.

"That's just it," said Bruce. "He was around *before* the
murders. And," the psychiatrist added, "he was the only person, outside of our own immediate group ... including us, Pete
Jackson, Abe, and Alice ... other than us, Halloran was the only
one who knew Jeff was staying here."

"You mean, you think he sent someone to plant the bomb?
Paco?" Dennie began.

"Yeah, it was Paco. I seen him do it," Hugo told them. "That's
why I wrote on the truck door. I didn't know what else ta do.
I'm sorry that nice boy got hurt," he added. "Is he going to be
all right?"

■ ■ ■

"I don't think it was Halloran who gave the order," Bruce said.
He was standing on the edge of the pool with Dennie and Frank.
The others were in the water.

"But you said he was the only one who knew," Frank
protested.

"Yeah, except I'd bet he passed the word on to Rupert, and
I think it was Rupert who put Paco up to it — probably without
Halloran's realizing he was going to do it."

"Why?" asked Frank. "I'm not following you."

"I think this whole mess is of Rupert's making. I think he
killed his father on an impulse, although he probably discussed
it with Halloran beforehand. But whatever plan he might have
formulated with the lawyer was forgotten in his moment of
anger. It wasn't done very cleverly. And whatever else Halloran
is, he ain't stupid."

"He's just greedy," Dennie added bitterly. "What a rotten son of a bitch."

"I suspect he was egging Rupert on — before the murders — trying to get him to persuade Daddy to do a little money laundering. That international film distribution setup would have been a perfect cover. But Daddy wouldn't go for it, so Halloran and Rupert discuss removing him. Only, before Halloran can work out a foolproof plan, Rupert loses his cool and pulls the plug — using Halloran's hit man to do the job."

"And the mother gets killed by accident, because she walked in at the wrong time," Frank suggested. "So Rupert didn't order his mother killed, got upset about it, but..." He shook his head in disbelief. "He sure didn't act very guilty, did he? He must really be a sick-sick-sicky!"

Bruce nodded without saying anything for a moment, thinking back on his conversations with the elder Orsini brother. "Certainly a nihilistic response," agreed the psychiatrist.

"What you'd call a sociopath," Dennie suggested.

"Well, sort of," Bruce replied hesitantly. "But for the moment, we don't need to psychoanalyze him. From what Hugo told us," Bruce continued, "Rupert was, at least, the prime motivator in his father's murder. How the law will look at his involvement in his mother's killing is, again, something that doesn't concern us at the moment. Getting back to the night it all happened, though, I think things really began to get more than a little out of hand ... at least from Halloran's standpoint. Rupert must have decided he could frame his brother for the murders — kill two birds with one stone, so to speak: eliminate himself as a suspect, and end up with the whole estate when Paul got convicted. Except, he wasn't smart enough to pull it off."

"But he got Paco to murder Alfie, because he thought he was Paul's alibi?" Frank looked back and forth between Bruce and Dennie. "What a shitty thing to do, kill an innocent kid."

Bruce was nodding agreement. "Except that Halloran had to have been in on that somehow, because Rupert wouldn't have known where to find the kids. He had to have tumbled to it when Alfie bought his stash. Some way, the drug underground connected and Halloran got the address, maybe through some one of his other clients, maybe had the word out all along — he's got a huge criminal law practice, after all. And then, when he realized he'd killed the wrong guy, Rupert didn't have the sense to back off. Instead, when he learned that Jeff was actually the witness, and that he was here with us, he sent Paco after him — and I'd lay money that Halloran didn't know it was going to happen, even though he had to have been the one who told Rupert that Jeff was here."

"And by Rupert's stupid logic, he also figured to tail you and get Hugo, too? Jesus, Bruce, that's really incredible! It's hard to believe he could be so inept." Frank shook his head in disbelief.

"I still think that's how it went," Bruce told them. "And because it was so bungled — and illogical — no one, including the police, has been able to figure it out. But, if I'm right, we've got two things left to worry about."

"Jeff!" said Dennie sharply.

"Right. Rupert might very well go after him in the hospital, because he may still think he can kill his brother's alibi," Bruce replied.

"And the second problem is Hugo?" Frank suggested.

Bruce looked down at the splashing figures in the pool — Hugo wrestling playfully with Henry. "No," he returned. "No one knows Hugo's here. I'm thinking that Halloran must be about at the end of his rope with Rupert. The kid's made too many mistakes, and by doing this he's become a serious liability — Paco, too, for that matter. This compulsive need to eliminate his brother's alibi — first Alfie, whom he mistook for Jeff, then Jeff himself — it's asinine, not something Halloran would do, or condone."

"But Halloran hasn't actually committed a crime, then, has he?" asked Frank. "If all the killings were Rupert's doing, and he gets rid of Rupert, he could come out smelling like a rose."

"I'm not so sure about Haven Monroe," Bruce told him. "Halloran had to have had a hand in that. But even if he wasn't the one who ordered the Orsini murders, he was certainly involved in a conspiracy with Rupert, to convert the Orsini international business into a money-laundering operation. I'd say he might find that sort of exposure embarrassing, to say the least. I'm sure that's what's motivating all this subsequent involvement. Of course, eliminating both Rupert *and* Paco..."

"So the killer's on the hit list, himself," said Frank. "Serves him right!"

"Maybe, but do we just sit by and let it happen?" Bruce asked.

"Why not?" asked Frank.

"Because he's my brother." All three looked down, to where Paul Orsini was hanging on the edge of the pool, listening to them. "I know he's been a real shit, killed Dad, responsible for Mom — tried to frame me. But ... well, he's all that's left. If someone killed him, and I knew about it and didn't do anything, I ... that would be hard to live with."

"I guess it's time for Pete Jackson, again," Bruce told them, and he started toward the house. Frank watched in silent appreciation as his lover's solid, naked form was outlined by the soft glow through his office window. Bruce slid back the glass panel, allowing Rudy to bound through ahead of him, then stepped onto the thick royal blue carpet.

"A boy and his dog," Dennie quipped, watching the interplay.

"It's a man and his bodyguard," Frank returned. "And don't you forget it!"

■ ■ ■

Frank and Dennie had slipped into the water, waiting for Bruce to finish in the house.

"I'll be glad to see this thing wrapped up," Frank remarked. "It's been a real strain on all of us, especially on Bruce."

"Well, we can leave it all in the hands of the police from here on..."

"Dennie! Frank!" Bruce called. "We've gotta get over to the hospital!"

"What's the matter?" Dennie asked, as both men piled out of the water, followed by Hugo and Paul.

"I can't get Jackson. He's out of touch for the moment. And I got Abe's answering machine. I remember, now — Alice said something about a concert tonight. Anyway, I can't get either of them, so I called the watch commander at Sergeant Davis's division, and he as much as told me to write him a letter. We've got to get someone over there to watch Jeff."

"What about my brother?" Paul asked.

Bruce hesitated. "You're right," he agreed. "Dennie, why don't you and Frank go to the hospital. I'll go with Paul and Hugo, over to the Orsini property, and try to keep an eye on Rupert until we can get some cops on the job."

"Unless Rupert's already at the hospital, trying to murder Jeff," Frank suggested grimly. "I don't know why you're..." Seeing Paul's anxious expression, he left off his diatribe on Rupert.

"It's still a human life," Bruce replied softly.

"Now all you folks, you jes' wait a hot minute," called Henry van Porter. The tall, slender black man stood in dark nakedness at the shallow end of the pool. "You ain't goin' off and leavin' po' ol' Henry all by hisself, all alone wif dat big dawg."

"Knock off the corn pone," said Dennie, laughing in spite of himself. "You can come to the hospital with us."

"No, better if you stay here," said Bruce thoughtfully. "I left a message on Abe's answering machine, and also with the switchboard at Jackson's division. If either of them calls, I'd like someone here to tell them what we're doing."

There was a quick flurry of motion, trips into the house, then back outside, as everyone got dressed in jeans or slacks, shirts, and proper footwear. Henry had slipped on a pair of shorts and sat on a plastic chair, watching the others, idly stroking Rudy's head. "I guess it's just you and me, honey," he muttered.

Then they were all heading for the front of the house. "Help yourself to whatever you want in the kitchen," Dennie called back to Henry. "Use the TV in the den, if you like."

As the garage doors were lifting, Bruce handed his keys to Dennie. "Why don't you take the Mercedes," he suggested. "Let me have the Buick ... better for three people."

■ ■ ■

Once inside the grounds of the Orsini estate, the three men made their way on foot toward the main house. The car had been left on the street, and they had entered through a smaller pedestrian gate a few feet distant from the huge wrought-iron barriers. Opening the main entrance would have set off a warning light in the house, Paul had explained. The small gate wasn't wired.

There were no lights showing in any of the windows; the whole mansion seemed dark and deserted. "I guess you don't have any secret way in, do you?" asked Bruce.

"Oh, no," Paul Orsini replied. "There really aren't any secret passages, either. Hugo and I just used to play at it. That little hidden space off Dad's office was an accident when the folks redecorated the house. They were always going to put a big walk-in safe back there, but never got around to it."

"And that's the only place like that?" Bruce asked.

"As far as I know," Paul told him. "Do you know of any others?" he asked, glancing back at Hugo, who was a few feet behind them.

"There's the place behind the kitchen," he replied. "Mom said it used to be a root cellar, whatever that is."

They had now reached the front door, which Paul unlocked. The house was pitch black and totally silent, except for the ticking of a grandfather clock on the stair landing above them. Paul tried the light switch, but it didn't work. Bruce cast the beam of his powerful flashlight around the interior. The huge entryway was all in gleaming hardwood, with a few scattered Persian carpets — large by any normal standards, but dwarfed by the enormous vault. There was a wide trestle table in the center of the space, and a long bank of wooden seats along the far wall. The staircase, which was easily twenty feet wide at the base, curved gracefully upward, covered in thick, burgundy carpeting.

Paul led them across to the left, opening the door to his father's — now his brother's — office. Again, the light switch failed to work. This room was also empty, but there was the faint trace of cigarette smoke in the air. Bruce walked across to a side table, where there was an ashtray with several crushed butts in it. He felt them tentatively. "Cold," he said. "At least we didn't chase anyone out, but somebody's been smoking in here within the last half hour or so."

"Probably Rupert," said Paul, offhandedly, then stiffened, sniffing the air. "No," he said. "That's not cigarette smoke, Bruce; it's that cheroot smell, the things Paco smokes!"

"There're only cigarette butts in the ashtray," observed the psychiatrist.

"Shit!" Paul was already heading toward the door, motioning for Bruce to accompany him. Hugo trailed along behind. They raced quickly across the wide entryway, checking out the formal living room on the far side, then the dining hall. Both Bruce and Paul had flashlights, and the twin beams explored well enough to assure them that no one was hiding on the ground floor — at least not in the front section of the house. Bruce suggested they try Rupert's room, and Paul led them upstairs.

The door to Rupert's suite stood wide open. The whole place was in chaos: furniture overturned, broken knickknacks scattered all over the floor, a large oil painting ripped from the wall, its frame smashed to kindling wood.

Paul ran through this front area, into the bedroom beyond. It had also been the scene of a ferocious struggle, and in the bath there were traces of blood on the tiles, beside the sunken tub. The three men stood in perplexed silence, uncertain of exactly what had happened. But of Rupert Orsini there was no sign, and their collective thoughts were to determine where he might have gone, or been taken.

■ ■ ■

At the same moment that Bruce and his companions were trying to ascertain Rupert's fate, Dennie and Frank stood facing almost as blank an obstacle. Ms. Louise Turner, R.N., chief of Night Nursing, stood in the center of the corridor, her substantial body effectively blocking their entry. "It is after visiting hours," she repeated, "and unless you are a blood relative, coming to see a patient who is on the critical list, *with your doctor's permission,* you can not come in!"

"Miss Turner," Frank tried.

"It is *Mizz* Turner, and you can't visit Mr. Donovan," she replied sternly. "If you don't leave, I'm going to call Security."

"Call them," said Dennie. "Maybe they'll make more sense than you do."

"They will do precisely as I tell them," she retorted.

"Look, Ms. Turner," Frank cajoled, "you know how Jeff Donovan got injured, don't you?"

"No, I don't believe I do," she told him. "Industrial accident, wasn't it?"

"No, someone planted a bomb in his car," Dennie told her. "He was almost killed. Now, we have reason to believe that—"

"Then call the police," she told them. "You still can't come in."

Finally, after a good fifteen minutes of futile argument, Ms. Turner did summon the night security supervisor, who agreed to "keep an eye on Mr. Donovan's room." That was as close as they were going to get, and under the watchful eye of Nurse Turner, they retreated via the front door.

Standing outside on the walkway, Dennie looked up at the imposing hospital facade. "So what do we do now, climb the ivy to the kid's balcony?" he asked sardonically.

"I'd say we gamble on the killer not already being inside, and watch the entrance to make sure he doesn't go in. We know what he looks like: tall, rangy Latino with a bushy mustache and arms like an ape."

"I wonder if the back doors are locked. The place is small, as hospitals go, but I'd bet there're more possible entrances than the two of us can watch," Dennie replied.

"Well, if the killer's going to make it inside, why can't we?" Frank asked.

"Probably because he'd be willing to kill that Turner bitch, and we aren't," Dennie replied.

"I am," Frank said grimly. "Let's walk around the back and see if we can spot a way to get in, past the human barricade."

■ ■ ■

"He's not in the house, Bruce. But that blood in his bathroom ... Where the hell could he be?" Paul Orsini stood in the center of the huge front hall, rubbing one hand across his lips.

"That's his car in the drive, isn't it?" Bruce asked.

The younger Orsini brother nodded.

"So he should be here, unless, of course, he's gone off with someone else — logical explanation."

"I don't think so," Paul mused. "He never goes in a car with anyone else driving, if he can possibly help it, not since Dad ... Let's go back to the kitchen; maybe I can find the master light switch." He started toward the rear of the great hall. "Where the hell could he be?" he repeated.

"He's in the dollhouse," said Hugo.

The other two men regarded him in surprise. It was the first time the big guy had spoken since they entered the mansion.

"What makes you think he'd go to my old workshop?" Paul asked.

"It's the only place left," replied Hugo simply. "It's where I'd go if I wanted to hide."

Bruce and Paul looked at each other questioningly, then both shrugged and Paul led the way through the rear portions of the house, onto the wide expanse of lawn, past the enormous swimming pool with its complex of reflection ponds and fountains. At the base of the slope was the large flower garden, where Ruth Orsini had raised blooms to be cut and used in the dining room. Beyond this was the wooden outbuilding where Paul had started manufacturing his mannequins. Although a half moon had come up while the three men were in the house, the yard was still in semidarkness. And through the dim illumination Bruce could see that the door to the small building stood ominously ajar.

■ ■ ■

Frank gazed up at the rear wall of the hospital. "Can you tell which windows are Jeff's room?" he asked.

"It's on the corner, third floor," Dennie told him. "Must be there," he added, pointing to a firmly sealed expanse of glass, completely covered on the inside with a heavy, off-white drapery. "Can't tell if he's got a light on or not. They've got those blackout curtains," he said. "The kind that keeps the light from waking you up in the morning."

"A lot of good that does someone in a hospital," Frank quipped. "They're usually in before first light with a specimen bottle or an enema bag, anyway."

"Oh, stop that; you're turning me on!" Dennie sucked in a slithering lungful of air. "Can't you imagine the thrill of having Nurse Turner flip you over at five a.m. and stick an enema tube up your ass?"

"You're too much," muttered Frank. "How the fuck are we going to get up there without that old harridan catching us?"

"More to the point, how would someone intent on killing a patient get in?" Dennie countered.

Frank sighed. "Of course he wouldn't care about anything but getting in, doing his thing, and getting right back out again. We want to go and baby-sit." He strode around the corner, still

202

trying to decide. "What about the emergency entrance, the one over on the side, there?"

"Worth a try, but I bet it's locked," Dennie said, joining his companion in a quick trot across the concrete platform. A ramp of the same material led up from the drive. A blue light glowed above the door, spelling out "EMERGENCY" in large neon letters. Below, to the right of the steel door, was a small, illuminated red button, with the legend "Ring for admittance."

Dennie tried the door, which indeed was locked. He looked at Frank in desperation. "We've got to get in there," he said. "Christ, that Paco asshole could be inside right now."

"How would he get past Nurse Turner?" asked Frank.

"Look, give me a minute to get back to the front door," said Dennie. "Then start ringing that bell like there's no tomorrow. Make as big a commotion as you can. I'll bet you the old bitch'll show up in person, and maybe I can sneak in while she goes after you."

"It's worth a try," Frank agreed.

■ ■ ■

Bruce was the first to reach the doorway. He paused only a moment in front of the intimidating blackness, then bolted inside — wishing, for once, that he'd thought to bring the gun. He stopped abruptly, the hair seeming to stand upright on his neck as he found himself face-to-face with a mob of distorted human figures. A plastic arm seemed about to grab him, as a headless torso leaned forward, partially blocking him.

Paul slipped past and threaded his way through the confusion of his own creativity. "Back here," he called. "If anyone's around he should be ... Oh, oh God!" His final words ended in a high-pitched squeal.

It was now Bruce's turn to brush past Paul. "Get a light on," he said, kneeling down next to the narrow mattress and box spring that lay directly on the floor. A long, gangly figure lay sprawled across the disheveled coverings. Paul fumbled for the switch, which produced only a bright red glow. "It's the only light I've got," he muttered, "'cept for the strobe."

"It's enough," Bruce replied softly. "I'm afraid ... no, wait a second. This isn't your brother," he said. "Do you know...?"

"Jesus!" Paul whispered. "That's Paco!"

"Well, he's deader'n a mackerel," Bruce told him. "He's been shot several times, but the body's still warm. Do you have a phone in here?" Paul pointed to the instrument. "Dial nine-one-one. No, wait! If we call the police, they'll hang us up here for God knows how long. This guy's dead. No one can do anything for him. I'm going to call the hospital and see if everything's okay with Jeff. Whoever did this may have gone there next." It was on the tip of his tongue to say "Rupert" instead of "whoever," but he sought to spare Paul the additional discomfort.

"This is Louise Turner, night-shift supervisor."

"Nurse, this is Dr. Bruce MacLeod. You have one of my patients there, a Mr. Jeffrey Donovan. Two of my friends should be with—"

"Your two ... er, friends have been trying to violate hospital protocol all evening," she replied coldly. "In fact, they just attempted to break in by the back door."

"You mean to tell me they haven't been allowed inside?" Bruce demanded.

"That is precisely what I'm telling you, Doctor."

"Now you listen to me," said Bruce sternly. "I am presently at the scene of an apparent homicide. As soon as I call the police, I'm coming down there to look after my patient; and if you haven't allowed my friends inside by then, I am personally going to—" He checked himself before anger got the better of his judgment. "Nurse, let those men in! Get your security people to go with them. I want as big a contingent of personnel as we can get outside Jeffrey Donovan's room."

"That is a job for the police," she replied coldly, but Bruce could tell that her resolve was weakening.

"If anything happens to that boy because of your officious obstructionism, madam, I will see to it that you never work in any hospital in this state again. Do you understand me? I'll be there just as fast as I can, *with* the police."

"Yes, Doctor," she replied smartly.

■ ■ ■

Henry van Porter lay back luxuriously on the oversized leather sofa. He had a can of beer in one hand, and the remote control for the TV in the other. He was watching an MCA music video on one of the cable channels, whooping along with the singers.

Despite his six-foot-four physique, Henry was anything but the model of macho charisma. He was twenty-eight years old, and in plain street parlance, he was a queen.

And he enjoyed being a queen. People seemed to like him that way — at any rate, they seemed to enjoy him. Now that he no longer had to live in the slums of Philadelphia, where his effeminacy had made him a target for all the neighborhood hoodlums, he was able to expand his repertoire. He would have loved to be an actor, but that didn't seem to be in the cards. Instead, he had become everyone's homegrown comedian. He loved being the center of attention in a group of guys, even if it meant resorting to some rather dreadful racial impersonations — in addition to his comedy drag act. He often laughed at the really butch ones, made fun of them, knowing they wouldn't do anything about it. After all, a *really* butch man wasn't going to strike a lady.

Rudy was lying on the floor beside Henry's chair, watching for the occasional fall of popcorn, whenever the funny-acting man reached for the bowl on the coffee table. The big Labrador had never met anyone quite like this before, and his little doggie brain wasn't fully attuned. But he liked the man, as he tended to like almost anyone, and he was content to be with him. He had tagged along behind both times Henry had gotten up to answer the telephone. And now it was time to get up again. His normal hour for a walk was definitely past, and nature was calling.

Rudy stood, lay his head in Henry's lap, his dark brown eyes assuming their most plaintive stare. At first, the visitor thought he wanted another piece of popcorn; and while this was gratefully accepted, it didn't solve Rudy's problem. Instead, the Lab began to nudge his visitor, and in the end Henry got the picture. "Now, which way do you go, dawg?" he asked. "I bet they don' like you takin' a dump out in that nice clean backyard. Come on, we'll go out front."

■ ■ ■

Bruce arrived at the hospital at the same time as Abe and Alice, only a few moments ahead of Pete Jackson. Paul Orsini had stayed at the house to greet the police — this at Abe's suggestion, after the psychiatrist had finally connected with him at his Century City apartment. Hugo, however, had decided to walk up the street to Bruce's house before the cops arrived.

A very subdued Nurse Turner sat at the desk as the visitors entered, making no effort to keep them out. The whole assemblage gathered in Jeff's room, where the youngster — now much recovered from his ordeal — seemed delighted to sit up in bed and receive them. But no intruder had made any attempt to enter his room, and after a half hour everyone departed, leaving a pair of policemen on guard outside his door.

On the front walkway, Bruce paused to confer with Abe and Pete, while the others stood a few feet away — Frank and Dennie accompanying Alice while she had a cigarette. "I'd like to know who actually killed Paco," Bruce said anxiously, "and more to the point, where he went afterward."

"Why?" asked Abe. "If it was Rupert who killed him, he's probably halfway to Mexico by now, and if Halloran's behind this, as you seem to think he is, there's no reason for him to send anyone after Jeff. But we've got him protected, anyway. He might like to get his hands on Hugo, though," he added thoughtfully. "By the way, where is the silver-eyed monster?"

"He walked up to my house, after we left the Orsinis'," Bruce told him. "I didn't see any point in having him stay there and have to fend for himself with the cops. He should be okay. The only one who'd want to hurt him would be Halloran, and he doesn't know where he is—" He saw the look of consternation on Pete Jackson's face. "What is it?" he asked.

"Captain Fullbright," said the detective. "I'm under strict orders to keep him informed of every move I make on this case — regardless of the time of day or night. I called him on the car radio on my way over here, and he was on the phone with Halloran, put him on hold to talk to me."

"So?" asked Abe.

"Well, the kid who answered the phone at your house ... a guy, I guess, right?" And at a nod from Bruce, he continued. "Well, he told me what had happened, catching Hugo and all, and I told Fullbright."

"And Fullbright almost had to have told Halloran!" Bruce finished for him. "Christ, we've been guarding the wrong guy!"

"Now, now wait. Not necessarily," Abe told them, raising a restraining hand, as Bruce's exclamation had brought the others to join their conversation. "If Fullbright told Halloran anything while Pete was on the way here, there's no way that Halloran could communicate the information to whoever he's using as paid assassin these days — not if the guy was already out..."

"That doesn't fly, Abe," Bruce insisted, starting toward the parking lot. "Paco had to have been killed either by Rupert or by some other hired gun sent by Halloran. If it was Rupert, he could have gone straight up the hill to my house. Or — if it was another hired gun — the killer may have gone directly back to Halloran after he killed Paco. In that case, he'd have been on hand when Fullbright gave him the news. Or, Halloran might have access to more than one hired gun."

"Who might have a phone in *his* car! Let's go!" said Pete Jackson.

Fifteen minutes later, the little caravan pulled into Bruce MacLeod's circular drive. Pete Jackson had been in the lead, and he had to brake sharply to avoid crashing into the rear of a black-and-white police cruiser, parked at the psychiatrist's front door. Everyone piled out of their respective vehicles, just as two uniformed Beverly Hills cops emerged from the front bushes, holding either arm of a very combative, handcuffed Mickey Halloran. "There's an L.A.P.D. police commissioner," shouted the lawyer, as he spotted his audience. "He'll identify me!"

"What's going on?" asked Abe.

"You the commissioner?" asked one of the policemen.

"Yeah." Abe Javits fumbled in his breast pocket and produced an I.D. card.

"The ... er, houseman caught this guy outside when he went out to walk the dog," explained the cop. "The suspect had a gun in his hand, and the dog attacked ... took the weapon away from him. Then the ... ah ... houseman slugged him, and sat on him until we got here."

"Who the hell's the 'houseman'?" asked Abe, looking back at Bruce.

"Me, Boss," called Henry, waving at them from the door. "Me 'n' Rudy, we done coch'ed ourselves a burglar. 'Course, Hugo, he come along jest in time to help."

"That's Henry," Bruce explained. "He was our bogus intruder to help flush Hugo. And, Henry ... where *is* Hugo?"

"He done go after the other one," Henry replied.

"What other one?" asked Abe.

"Are you going to identify me for these cops, or not?" Halloran demanded. "I forgot my wallet, and they won't believe who I am. MacLeod, tell 'em I'm your guest."

"I never saw him before in my life," said Bruce. "He looks like a high-priced cat burglar to me."

"I don't know him, either," Abe echoed, turning away to hide his smile. "What the fuck's he doing here?" he whispered to Bruce.

"I'd bet he decided to take care of Rupert and Paco in person," Bruce rasped in return. "Let's let the Beverly Hills cops haul him in. Pete can go along and try to sort it out with them."

And at that moment, Hugo emerged from the far end of the drive, half carrying, half dragging the struggling form of Rupert Orsini. He had hold of him by the scruff of his neck, and by the back of his belt. He grinned when he saw Bruce. "This is the guy you been lookin' for," he beamed. "The other one was tryin' to kill him, when Rudy came out an' jumped him."

"My God, that attack training took," Frank remarked, truly amazed at the whole account, but most especially at Rudy's part in it. He knelt down and hugged the big Lab, who licked his face with joy at having so pleased his master.

Within minutes another black-and-white arrived, and nearly an hour later both cars departed, taking Halloran and Rupert to the Beverly Hills lockup.

As the police roared out of sight, Abe looked around the group and laughed. "Halloran will finally get to feel what it's like to be where his clients have been so many times," he said. "I wonder if he's going to defend himself when it goes to trial."

"I dunno," Bruce returned, "but we're all going to sleep better with that pair locked up."

"Right," Abe agreed. "I've always said Halloran was arrogant, but I never thought he'd make such a stupid blunder. Of course, I have to admit, I didn't suspect him of being the actual killer, either."

"He must have been desperate to get rid of both Rupert and Paco," Bruce mused, "...probably decided to take care of it himself so there wouldn't be yet another potential witness. Thought he could get away with it, behind those ten-foot walls

— no one else to see him, figured to take his victims by surprise. Only somehow, Rupert — or Paco — got suspicious at the last minute and managed to hit the main light switch and get away from him. Then, in a real panic, Halloran chased him, and Rupert came here — probably the only place he could think to go. Unfortunately for Halloran, Rudy came out the door at just the wrong moment."

"Halloran must have taken Fullbright's call on his cellular phone, on his way up here from the Orsinis' — Jesus, talking calm as hell to a police captain while he's on the way to commit a double homicide! Knew he'd get a crack at both Rupert and Hugo," Abe thought aloud. "I bet he was happy as a hunter on the trail of some big game! Except he probably wasn't so concerned about Hugo. Once he got Rupert out of the way, he'd have broken the chain that tied him in to all the nonsense the kid had been up to. Hugo, after all, didn't actually see him do anything."

"Only, the Terror of Beverly Hills got to him first," Bruce laughed.

"And you guys keep making fun of my little dog," said Frank, squatting down to give Rudy another hug, at which the big Lab sat down and pressed hard against his human. "He really saved the day. Caught the bad guys just in the nick of time."

Everyone was still clustered about the front door, each in the throes of an adrenaline high.

"I think we all need a nightcap," said Bruce. "We've certainly earned it."

EPILOGUE

It was a month after the night of Halloran's arrest, and Bruce was giving a little party. Besides himself, Frank, and Dennie, the Saturday night gathering included Abe and Alice Javits, Pete Jackson and his wife Jeannie, Hugo, Paul Orsini, Henry van Porter, Jeff Donovan, and Rufus Wolfe — Frank's corpulent agent. Bruce had been a bit apprehensive about asking the Jacksons, but he had made the composition of his guest list plain to Pete, and the lieutenant had seemed almost eager to accept the invitation.

There had been a grand jury session earlier in the week, which had resulted in Mickey Halloran being indicted for conspiracy and the attempted murder of Rupert Orsini. Rupert was awaiting trial for the murder of his parents, but his new attorney was seeking a bargain — no more than a life sentence if he testified against his former lawyer, who was about to be indicted in the Monroe murder, as well as the murder of Paco. As yet, the D.A. had not made up his mind whether he wanted to prosecute Halloran in the Orsini slayings, as well. But regardless of how all the legal chips might fall, the case was closed, and Bruce's little group was ready to celebrate.

Well into the evening, when everyone was mellowed out, Pete Jackson cornered Bruce outside by the pool. His wife and Alice Javits were sitting just on the other side of the glass panel, gossiping together like two old friends. "You know," said Pete, "you're getting to be the best detective on our unofficial roster."

"Oh, I don't know, Pete. I almost blew this one," Bruce replied. "It was just dumb luck that Henry took Rudy out when he did. Otherwise Halloran might have killed both Rupert and Hugo — and gotten away with it."

"Yeah, we can thank Brother Henry for catching the son of a bitch," Jackson agreed. "But you were the first to figure it out."

"There was still a lot of luck involved," Bruce insisted. "And the way Hugo ran us ragged for the better part of a week — I'd give him two gold stars for every one of mine."

"Be that as it may, it's a relief to get it solved and settled!" Jackson concluded, speaking a bit absently. His attention had been drawn to the pool, where Hugo stood with a can of beer in his hand, and Henry hovered by his side, as he had been doing all evening.

"That kid's such a lady, it's hard to believe he wrestled Halloran down," Pete remarked softly.

"He comes from a pretty tough section of Philadelphia," Bruce reminded him. "He probably learned to fight before he learned to mince."

Pete chuckled, and the voices drifted over to them from poolside: "Honey, why don't you and me get it on tonight?" Henry cooed.

Hugo shifted uncomfortably. In truth, he wasn't at all bothered by the other man's color — especially after having seen his endowment in the pool the night of Halloran's capture. He simply was turned off by the unmasculine behavior.

"Come on," urged Henry. "Why not try it?"

"Because ... because I don't like black guys," he said, finally, unable to admit his true reasoning.

"Oh, honey, I know what you mean," Henry gushed. "I can't stand 'em either. That's why I wanta get it on with a big handsome white boy, like you." He stood back and seemed almost to be batting his eyelashes, when some unspoken communication passed between the two of them. "If you want me to be a man, I can do that, too," he added in a rolling baritone, his natural range.

"Yeah," said Hugo, grinning. "Like you were that night you beat up the lawyer."

211

"That's me," said Henry. "B.B.B. — big, butch, and black. Wanna talk about it?"

Hugo nodded. "Yeah, let's go sit down." And the two of them strolled into the shadows around the side of the house, toward the gazebo.

"You know, Frank deliberately invited Henry tonight, because he wanted his agent to meet him," Bruce remarked. "The kid's such a natural comedian, he thought Rufus might tumble to him."

"Did he?"

"Yeah, I think so. I don't know if anything'll come of it, but you can't say we didn't try."

"Well, the two of *them* seem to be content for the moment," said Jackson. "How's it going with you and Frank?"

"In what way?" Bruce countered. The question seemed somehow out of context.

"I mean, we were able to head off that Monroe clown on this one; or rather, Halloran was. But next time around, Frank might not be so lucky."

"We've decided to let the chips fall where they may," Bruce told him. "We'll do our best to keep Frank's private life private, but if the facts come out, he'll survive. We'll be okay. But," he paused, brow wrinkled in concern. "One thing I've been meaning to ask you ... haven't been completely sure about. I know Halloran contrived to have Paco do in Monroe, but why did he take the risk? It's always seemed like overkill to me. Pardon the pun."

Jackson laughed. "I finally got one up on you," he said lightly. "Monroe did himself in. He not only came around spying on you; he went by the alley in back of the Orsini place a couple of times, and he scooped up all their trash. Then he went through it, piece by piece. Rupert wasn't all that careful what he wrote down, and that put Monroe onto Halloran. He apparently tried to force an interview with the great barrister by hinting at some of the material he'd uncovered. Probably scared Halloran more than he intended."

"Which put Paco onto Monroe. It all fits, then," Bruce told his friend. "A really tangled web."

"Wait till it all gets into court," Jackson laughed. "That's the only chance Halloran's got. Confuse the jury. But then, I got a question for you. How about the silk rope they used? How ... why?"

"You know, after all our trying to figure out the historical angle, the ethnic angle, the gang angle, it all turned out to be happenstance. Felix Orsini had a sample of silk cord on his desk, because it was supposed to be for a theater — you know, how they rope off an aisle or a doorway? Well, once Paco used it, he must have decided to confuse the issue by using it again. Then Rupert hid it in his brother's workshop for the police to find, when they did a second search after the Monroe killing."

"That was another place where we missed the boat," Jackson sighed.

"It was Fullbright's fault," Bruce replied. "He was all too willing to see the kid in jail, when everyone else was convinced he had to be innocent."

"The captain's coming out poorly all around on this one," Jackson admitted. "He was really embarrassed by the fact that he was on the phone with a killer, while the guy was in the middle of trying to commit a double homicide."

"Why was he calling Halloran in the first place?" Bruce asked.

"Well, you know the captain's one of the 'good old boys' in the Department," Jackson replied in a confidential tone. "He and some of his clique were trying to get one of their own appointed to the Police Commission. Halloran was involved, probably putting up some of the money. Anyway, that's the excuse for their talking to each other. It was just bad timing that the captain returned Halloran's call right at that particular moment. When Fullbright had to put him on hold to talk to me, it must have simply been a natural for him to repeat what was said ... just innocent gossip, from his standpoint."

"Yeah, it must have been a real shock when he realized he was aiding and abetting a killer," Bruce agreed, caustically, "but you'll have to admit, Pete, he was a real prick throughout this whole investigation."

Jackson sighed again. "I know," he admitted. "The guy's been a good friend to me. I hate to see him going downhill like he is — in departmental politics, I mean. But he's gotten more involved in all this fundamentalist church stuff, and that's brought a lot of—"

"What are you guys up to out here?" asked Frank, stepping outside to join them.

"Planning the end of the world," said Jackson.

"More like the beginning," said Frank. "I think this is the most compatible group we've ever put together."

"Especially out in the side yard," Jackson told him.

"Oh?" Frank glanced around at the people inside and out, counting noses. "You don't mean Hugo and Henry?" he asked in disbelief.

"They're talking," Bruce told him.

"Well, good," said Frank. "Hugo needs a friend, whether it's a lover or just somebody to talk to."

"You planning to keep him around?" asked Jackson.

"He's already part of the family," Bruce told him. But whether his host was referring to Hugo or to Henry, Jackson wasn't quite sure, and he thought it best not to ask. His friends — and they really *were* his friends, he realized — they all seemed happy and back to normal. *Normal,* he thought. *Strange I should come up with that word; but it fits. They're about the most normal guys I know.*

Other books of interest from
ALYSON PUBLICATIONS

MASTERS' COUNTERPOINTS, by Larry Townsend, $10.00. A handsome actor is kidnapped, tortured, and raped by two men who keep him blindfolded throughout the ordeal. His therapist, Bruce MacLeod, soon discovers other men in town who have gone through the same experiences. MacLeod's investigation leads to adventure, love, S/M sex ... and a father-son partnership that's gone too far.

LEATHERFOLK, edited by Mark Thompson, $13.00. There's a new leather community in America today. It's politically aware and socially active. This ground-breaking anthology is the first nonfiction, co-gender work to focus on this large and often controversial subculture. The diverse contributors look at the history of the leather and S/M movement, how radical sex practice relates to their spirituality, and what S/M means to them personally.

THE GAY BOOK OF LISTS, by Leigh Rutledge, $9.00. Rutledge has compiled a fascinating and informative collection of lists. His subject matter ranges from history (6 gay popes) to politics (9 perfectly disgusting reactions to AIDS) to entertainment (12 examples of gays on network television) to humor (9 Victorian "cures" for masturbation). Learning about gay culture and history has never been so much fun.

I ONCE HAD A MASTER, by John Preston, $9.00. In these intensely erotic stories, John Preston outlines the story of one man's journey through the world of S/M sexuality, beginning as a novice, soon becoming a sought-after master.

THE LOVE OF A MASTER, by John Preston, $8.00. What could possibly follow the elegant S&M party in John Preston's last book, *Entertainment for a Master*? Certainly not the reclusive life his hero had been living in the mountains of New England. Now the Master surveys his world, wondering how he can feed his needs. There's always the city with its erotic underground, or the secretive Network with its willing sexual slaves. But it would be so much more ... *interesting* if he could discover the dark sexual dreams of one of the young men around him who might be looking for *The Love of a Master*.

ENTERTAINMENT FOR A MASTER, by John Preston, $9.00. In this second volume of the Master series, John Preston continues his exploration of S/M sexuality. This time, the Master hosts an elegant and exclusive S/M party. To prepare for the festivities, the Master recruits volunteer masochists who are to instruct and entertain the Master's three guests.

GOLDENBOY, by Michael Nava, $9.00. Jim Pears is guilty; even his lawyer, Henry Rios, believes that. The evidence is overwhelming that Pears killed the co-worker who threatened to expose his homosexuality. But as Rios investigates the case, he finds that the pieces don't always fit together the way they should. Too many people *want* Jim Pears. to be found guilty, regardless of the truth. And some of them are determined that Henry Rios isn't going to interfere with their plans.

THE LITTLE DEATH, by Michael Nava, $8.00. As a public defender, Henry Rios finds himself losing the idealism he had as a law student. Then a man he has befriended — and loved — dies under suspicious circumstances. As he investigates the murder, Rios finds the solution as subtle as the law itself.

MACHO SLUTS, by Pat Califia, $10.00. Pat Califia, the prolific lesbian author, has put together a stunning collection of her best erotic short fiction. She explores sexual fantasy and adventure in previously taboo territory — incest, sex with a thirteen-year-old girl, a lesbian's encounter with two cops, a gay man who loves to dominate dominant men, as well as various S/M and "vanilla" scenes.

DOC AND FLUFF, by Pat Califia, $9.00. The author of the popular *Macho Sluts* has written a futuristic lesbian S/M novel set in a California wracked by class, race, and drug wars. Doc is an "old Yankee peddler" who travels the deteriorating highways on her big bike. When she leaves a wild biker party with Fluff (a cute and kinky young girl) in tow, she doesn't know that Fluff is the property of the bike club's president. *Doc and Fluff* is a sexy adventure story but it also confronts serious issues like sobriety, addiction, and domestic violence.

THE ALYSON ALMANAC, by Alyson Publications, $9.00. How did your representatives in Congress vote on gay issues? What are the best gay and lesbian books, movies, and plays? When was the first gay and lesbian march on Washington? With what king did Julius Caesar have a sexual relationship? You'll find all this, and more, in this unique and entertaining reference work.

GAY SEX, by Jack Hart, $15.00. Today's gay man faces a very different world than his predecessor did. This lively, illustrated guide will appeal to all gay men, but especially to those just coming out. The entries cover everything from "Dating" to "Dildoes," from "Finding a Lover" to "Frottage," and all the steps in between.

THE ADVOCATE ADVISER, by Pat Califia, $9.00. The Miss Manners of gay culture tackles subjects ranging from the ethics of zoophilia to the etiquette of a holy union ceremony. Along the way she covers interracial relationships, in-law problems, and gay parenting. No other gay columnist so successfully combines useful advice, an unorthodox perspective, and a wicked sense of humor.

THE GAY FIRESIDE COMPANION, by Leigh Rutledge, $9.00. Leigh Rutledge, author of *The Gay Book of Lists* and *Unnatural Quotations,* has written fact-filled articles on scores of subjects: unusual gay historic sites in the U.S.; fascinating mothers of famous gay men; footnote gay people in history; public opinion polls on homosexuality over the last twenty years; a day-by-day, year-by-year history of the AIDS epidemic.

IN THE LIFE, edited by Joseph Beam, $9.00. When writer and activist Joseph Beam became frustrated that so little gay literature spoke to him as a black gay man, he did something about it: the result was *In the Life,* an anthology which takes its name from a black slang expression for "gay." Here, thirty-three writers and artists explore what it means to be doubly different — black and gay — in modern America. Their stories, essays, poetry, and artwork voice the concerns and aspirations of an often silent minority.

BROTHER TO BROTHER, edited by Essex Hemphill, $9.00. Black activist and poet Essex Hemphill has carried on in the footsteps of the late Joseph Beam (editor of *In the Life*) with this new anthology of fiction, essays, and poetry by black gay men. Contributors include Assoto Saint, Craig G. Harris, Melvin Dixon, Marlon Riggs, and many newer writers.

THE TROUBLE WITH HARRY HAY, by Stuart Timmons, $13.00. This complete biography of Harry Hay, known as the father of gay liberation, sweeps through forty years of the gay movement and nearly eighty years of a colorful and original American life. Hay went from a pampered childhood, through a Hollywood acting career and a stint in the Communist Party before starting his life's work in 1950 when he founded the Mattachine Society, the forerunner of today's gay movement.

BI ANY OTHER NAME, edited by Loraine Hutchins and Lani Kaahumanu, $12.00. Hear the voices of over seventy women and men from all walks of life describe their lives as bisexuals. They tell their stories — personal, political, spiritual, historical — in prose, poetry, art, and essays. These are individuals who have fought prejudice from both the gay and straight communities and who have begun only recently to share their experiences. This ground-breaking anthology is an important step in the process of forming a community of their own.

THE MEN WITH THE PINK TRIANGLE, by Heinz Heger, $8.00. For decades, history ignored the Nazi persecution of gay people. Only with the rise of the gay movement in the

1970s did historians finally recognize that gay people, like Jews and others deemed "undesirable," suffered enormously at the hands of the Nazi regime. Of the few who survived the concentration camps, only one ever came forward to tell his story. His true account of those nightmarish years provides an important introduction to a long-forgotten chapter of gay history.

VAMPIRES ANONYMOUS, by Jeffrey McMahan, $9.00. Andrew, the wry vampire, was introduced in *Somewhere in the Night,* which won the author a Lambda Literary Award. Now Andrew is back, as he confronts an organization that has already lured many of his kin from their favorite recreation, and is determined to deprive him of the nourishment he needs for survival.

B.B. AND THE DIVA, by Rupert Kinnard, $7.00. Meet the Brown Bomber — a young, African-American superhero-fairy — and his best friend, Diva Touché Flambé, a reincarnated, African-American, lesbonic, vegetarian, feminist educator, as they confront George Bush, the pope, Jesse Helms, and others with an ageless form of therapy known as "slapthology," in this lively antidote to the white world of the Sunday comics.

THE BUCCANEER, by M.S. Hunter, $10.00. The pirates of the seventeenth-century Caribbean created history's only predominantly gay society. In this well-researched novel, M.S. Hunter presents the exploits of Tommy the Cutlass and his shipload of randy buccaneers. Join them as they get involved with some of the past's most notorious individuals — and most exciting adventures. This is historical fiction at its swashbuckling best.

THE CARAVAGGIO SHAWL, by Samuel M. Steward, $9.00. Gertrude Stein and Alice B. Toklas step out of the literary haut monde and into the Parisian underworld to track down a murderer and art thief. While Gertrude and Alice dig for clues in literary salons and art exhibitions, Johnny McAndrews, a gay American writer, takes us on a wild and wicked romp through the decadent side of Parisian life.

FINALE, edited by Michael Nava, $9.00. Eight carefully crafted stories of mystery and suspense by both well-known authors and newfound talent: an anniversary party ends abruptly when a guest is found in the bathroom with his throat slashed; a frustrated writer plans the murder of a successful novelist; a young man's hauntingly familiar dreams lead him into a forgotten past.

SOMEWHERE IN THE NIGHT, by Jeffrey N. McMahan, $8.00. Here are eight eerie tales of suspense and the supernatural by a newfound talent. Jeffrey N. McMahan weaves horribly realistic stories that contain just the right mix of horror, humor, and eroticism: a gruesome Halloween party, a vampire whose conscience bothers him, and a suburbanite with a killer lawn.

SUPPORT YOUR LOCAL BOOKSTORE

Most of the books described above are available at your nearest gay or feminist bookstore, and many of them will be available at other bookstores. If you can't get these books locally, order by mail using this form.

Enclosed is $_____ for the following books. (Add $1.00 postage when ordering just one book. If you order two or more, we'll pay the postage.)

1._____

2._____

3._____

name: _____

address: _____

city: _____ state: _____ zip: _____

ALYSON PUBLICATIONS
Dept. I-9, 40 Plympton St., Boston, MA 02118

After June 30, 1994, please write for current catalog.